PRAISE FOR THE SILVER MYSTERY SERIES

Tarnished Silver is a fabulous debut novel! Abby Strickland is someone I can relate to, my kind of heroine. I admire the way she rises to the challenges thrown in her path. She's a brave and loyal person whom I would love to call a friend (if she were real, of course). Susan Reiss is a great storyteller, and I'm really looking forward to more stories in the Silver Mystery Series.

-- Kassandra Lamb,
Author of the Kate Huntington Mystery Series

Silver, art and murder lead to an exciting read!

-- S. Jennifer Sugarman, Artist

Susan Reiss captures the magic, mystery and charm of that quintessential Eastern Shore town – St. Michaels. Secrets lay hidden for generations among the stunningly beautiful estates along the Miles River. Can't wait for her next "silver" adventure.

-- Kathy Harig,
Proprietor of Mystery Loves Company Bookstore

Books in the

SILVER MYSTERY SERIES

Tarnished Silver

Sacred Silver

Painted Silver

By Susan Reiss

Published by Ink & Imagination Press
ISBN: 978-0-9893607-4-6

Cover Design by Gemma S. Boyer
Author Photo by Bob Bader

Website: www.SilverMystery.com
Facebook: Susan Reiss
Twitter: @Susan Reiss
Goodreads.com: Susan Reiss, Goodreads Author

To Jen, Bruce and Kristen,
Artists dedicated to the written word.

CHAPTER ONE

It is your responsibility to care for every piece of silver in the House, from the punch serving bowl to the small silver frame that holds a precious memento.

—"The Butler's Guide to Fine Silver" Mr. Hollister, 1898

The champagne was nicely chilled on that warm July evening. The catered dinner served on the lawn was delicious; the candlelight was an elegant touch. Everything was perfect until a woman screamed.

And screamed and screamed.

I flashed a look across the banquet table at my friend Lorraine. She was all right. So was I. As if on cue, we shot out of our chairs and joined the crowd surging out of the tent toward the back of the estate house.

When the screaming stopped, so did we – art lovers and artists, supporters and volunteers, all gathered to celebrate the opening of the tenth annual Plein Air-Easton Art Festival, now following a trail of terror.

At first, murmurs floated through the crowd: What's happened? Who screamed? Then, rumors and superstition raced around. It was a woman. Don't be silly, it was only a bird – a hawk or eagle catching its dinner. It's an omen - somebody's going to die.

It was supposed to be a night of art and elegance, not murder.

Much later, waiting for the police, I sat staring at the flat champagne in the abandoned glasses on the table, trying to make sense out of what happened.

Lorraine had insisted we attend this by-invitation-only dinner and art sale to open Plein Air Easton, the major art festival in Talbot County. I was the "and Guest" on her invitation. Since last fall, I'd lived and worked at Fair Winds, the estate farm owned by my friend and employer, Lorraine Andrews, a woman in her late fifties with enough energy for three people. She thought the special event would be a nice break from the work I was doing with her extensive sterling silverware collections.

It was mid-afternoon when we took our place in the line of traffic inching its way onto Bruff's Island, the location for the opening event. I said I was tempted to park the car and walk in. It would be faster than driving.

"It would have been faster if we'd come by boat," Lorraine said as she pointed to the open water on our left. "That's the Miles River out there. We could have motored across the river from Fair Winds and made a short run up the Wye River. That's the way it is here on the Shore – quick by boat, hours by car."

She was referring to the Maryland Eastern Shore of the Chesapeake Bay, a land out of time, where people can slow down. They savor life, instead of dashing past it. Baltimore and Washington are worlds away, even though you can get there in two hours or less.

Thinking about it, it was when we drove on to the

island that things started getting a little strange.

As we drove through the gated entrance, Lorraine asked me to slow down. "I want to keep an eye out for the lovely Helene on horseback." She scanned the broad lawns that ran to a line of trees.

"The lovely Helene? Is that a special friend who is invited to the party tonight?"

"Oh, the lovely Helene of the golden hair is invited to every party here. If we're lucky, she'll be riding her alabaster steed."

"Wait, what?" I was so confused.

Lorraine tore her eyes away from the countryside to explain. "Helene Schuyler and her husband owned this island more than a hundred years ago."

A hundred years ago. "That means she must be..."

"A ghost! That's right, Abby. People see her riding the property from time to time," Lorraine said, her blue eyes sparkling with excitement.

"In broad daylight?" I challenged. "I doubt it."

"You never know. Just keep your eyes open. There are so many ghost stories around the Shore that some of them have to be true. Helene first lived here as a young woman. They say this was her most favorite place in all the world and that's why she returns to ride again."

Her excitement was contagious and I found myself searching the shadows, too. We both jumped when the car behind us honked to get us moving faster.

"I'll look, you drive," she suggested. "I might even spy an artist or two at work. They started painting early this morning and the results will be on sale tonight."

I turned to her in disbelief. "We'll see finished

paintings started this morning?" The right tires growled as my car drifted off the edge of the road.

"You'd better keep your eyes on the road, while I..." Unconsciously, she rubbed her hands together and looked from side to side.

While I steered the car back to the center of the road, I wondered what she would do if she saw something. Then, my thoughts returned to reality. "I don't understand. How can an artist finish a painting in a few hours... and have it be any good?"

"That's part of what makes this competition unique. Tonight, the paintings on display will still be wet, but they'll be amazing. Oh, there's an artist." She pointed toward a line of trees.

I caught a glimpse of someone painting at a portable easel among the trees. Beyond the woods, along a skinny strip of beach with white sand, two more artists were working at their easels. The panoramic view of the water out to a small lighthouse would be perfect at sunset. Judging by the traffic and the huge white tents set up for dinner ahead, we'd be joined by two or three hundred of our closest friends. Bluff's Island had lots of places to explore, lots of places for artists to find inspiration, as well as lots of places where a ghost could spy on the present-day inhabitants.

As someone directed us to a parking place, I noticed another artist gazing at an interesting scene across the river. Two large sailboats were tied up to a long private dock close to a large barn with a bright red roof and a cupola on top. Official-looking staff pointed us toward the tents set up on the lawn near the main house. As we trudged up the drive along with other guests, the heat was starting to wear me down. Lorraine looked fresh in her floral print sundress. It was appropriate for a slim woman in her late fifties, but it made her seem younger and full of energy.

"I'm glad we came, Abby. It should be a fascinating evening."

"Yoo hoo, Mrs. Andrews?" We both cringed and turned slowly to face Harriet, the town busybody with curly white hair rushing toward us followed dutifully by her husband, Ben. "Good evening. Isn't it a lovely night?" She didn't pause for a response. "Abby, isn't it? I didn't know you were interested in art and that nice young man I met at the Christmas party isn't with you?"

Lorraine jumped in. "Abby is interested in many things and—"

"Lorraine!"

We turned toward the voice calling out and saw a tall, shapely woman in an apricot silk sheath coming to our rescue. She was stunning, with hair the color of fine silver, cut to frame her face. She came right over and gave Lorraine a hug and air kisses. "Oh, Lorraine, I'm so glad you're here."

Standing together, Lorraine explained that she and her friend, Janet had served together on several volunteer committees over the past few years. Harriet and Ben, not part of the conversation, wandered away. When I was introduced to the woman, she cried, "You're Abby! I should have guessed." She threw her arms around me and added an air kiss to each cheek. "I've heard so much about you, I feel like I know you." She grabbed Lorraine's hand and mine then led us up to the front door of the main house. "Now, you have to come inside. There's something you must see!"

Lorraine tried to slow her down. "Janet, we've just arrived and —"

"You have to see it before you get distracted by all the art festivities. Abby, I just know you'll find this absolutely fascinating."

Intrigued, we followed her into the entry hall and through to the dining room. She lined us up opposite the mantelpiece, then swung out her arm dramatically toward the painting above it. "Behold! The portrait of silversmith Thomas Bruff."

I didn't recognize the name from my research. The old oil painting in a heavy gold gilt frame didn't stir my interest. It was very dark, except for the man's face and the bright silver pieces on the table beside him. It was reminiscent of the stiff portraits of wealthy European patrons with a country house or favorite horse in the background and trusted dogs curled at their feet. This painting didn't have the refined look of those done in old Europe. I glanced at Janet, who was waiting eagerly for my response since Lorraine had already said, How interesting.

"Is it American?" I asked.

"Oh, yes. Isn't it magnificent?" Janet gushed.

I stammered. "It's very nice. I must admit I don't know very much about art —"

Janet put her hand to her chest and gasped. "Oh, Abby, I didn't mean the portrait of the man." Her little laugh tinkled like a tiny bell. "What's important is the silver. Lorraine, it proves it really did exist."

As Janet prattled on about the joy of finding the painting, I considered the silver pieces: a tankard, a bowl with a handle, and six teaspoons. A curious selection. It was difficult to see any real detail, but the graceful lines of the silver pieces were clear. "What time period are we talking about?"

Janet considered the painting. "Sometime in the late 1600's, I think. They identified the man in the painting only recently. Up until now, we had no proof that silver made in America by Thomas Bruff even existed."

Lorraine stepped closer. "Bruff silver with its simple lines is truly magnificent, the stuff of Maryland legend. Some people thought he stopped making silverware when he came to America. What a waste that would have been."

I held up my hand for them to stop. "Okay, you've lost me. Maybe you could start at the beginning?"

The two women looked at each other for a moment. When Lorraine nodded, Janet began the tale. "Thomas Bruff worked as a silversmith in London in the early- to mid- 17th century. He came to the New World and bought this island in 1655. That's why it's known as Bruff's Island. What I don't understand is why he would give up a lucrative trade in London to come to this wild place where people were scratching out a living. There wasn't much time or money for nice things like sterling silver."

"Maybe I can help you there. You said 1655, right?" Janet nodded. "There was religious persecution in England. It was a rough time for Catholics and anyone else who didn't fit in."

"The big question was, once he came to the Eastern Shore, did he work in silver or did he make his living some other way?" Lorraine said.

Janet gestured to the painting again. "There's your proof. Thomas Bruff and his silver."

That didn't sound right to me. I'd learned that a silversmith didn't always sell everything he made. "Um, if he worked in London, maybe he brought the pieces over with him."

Janet frowned. It wasn't what she wanted to hear.

I continued quickly. "Of course, that doesn't mean he didn't make them here." Her frown eased. "Where are the pieces?" I asked. "Someplace in Baltimore?"

Lorraine shook her head. "No, but they might still be here on the Shore. Remember, things were pretty raw back then, no bank vaults for personal valuables like there are today."

Janet said, "I guess people had to find ways to protect their valuables from thieves when they traveled."

"Wait, I know this." I thought of Ryan, the man I'd been dating until he'd disappeared on an extended business trip. "They buried their things – money, jewelry and silver – somewhere on their property." My words were tumbling out in excitement. "And everyone knew that if the wife stayed home while her husband was away, he wouldn't even tell her where he hid them. That way she was protected and so were their things."

"It was a common practice, but there was a downside for one family," Janet added. "One man buried their valuables then went to Philadelphia on business. He came down with a fever and died there. They say his wife never found them. I'm sure there are a lot of things hidden here on the Shore. That's why you see people wandering over fields and through wooded areas with metal detectors, looking for treasure."

My curiosity was piqued. "Has anyone found anything?"

"If they have, they're keeping it a secret," Janet crossed her arms. "They probably don't want competition in the hunt."

Lorraine looked off in the distance with soft eyes and said in a dreamy voice, "The pieces in that painting might be right here on Bruff's Island or even in St. Michaels."

More silver in St. Michaels? "Really, where?"

"The Bruff family built one of the oldest houses right in the center of town." Janet gazed at the painting, almost longingly. "Those pieces could be anywhere."

"At least we have proof that they existed. He must have crafted them or why would he have them placed so prominently in his portrait?" Lorraine said with certainty.

I looked at the painting with new interest. "It would be worth the effort to find them, if they still exist."

A man with coal black hair walked into the room and gave Janet a peck on the cheek. His pearl gray silk sports coat, expertly tailored to fit his barrel chest and broad shoulders, accented the gray at his temples. "I thought I might find you looking at Mr. Bruff's silver pieces, my dear." The crow's feet crinkled around his eyes as he smiled at his wife. The subtle creases across his forehead and the lines around his mouth suggested he was a little older than his wife. He turned to us and his gray eyes twinkled with amusement. "I think my wife loves silver almost as much as she loves art."

"Silverware is art, Anthony. It's just another form," she insisted. She turned to us, pushed her shoulders back and raised her chin. "Ladies, this is my husband, Anthony, chairman of the Plein Air-Easton Art Festival." Her pride was genuine. "If you have any questions, he's a good man to know."

He chuckled quietly. "My wife and my biggest fan." He gave her another kiss. "Don't misunderstand. I'm not artistic, but I can manage. That's how I got this job. If there's anything I can do, just let me know." Though his powerful build made him a strong presence in the room, his warm smile and modest manner drew us to him. "We're glad you could come for our opening event. Hope you'll participate in the sale later this evening. The artists are working all over the island, have been since early this morning."

"Even through that thunderstorm this morning?" Lorraine asked. "Wasn't that dangerous?"

"We have people assigned to do nothing but watch the weather. When the storm moved our way, we ferried the artists and their equipment to shelter and, after the deluge, we returned them to their chosen spots. I'm afraid they found some impressive puddles and mud everywhere, but it didn't seem to slow them down. These artists are very committed to painting en plein air—in the open air. To them, it's more than art. It's a lifestyle. It gives them an opportunity to paint, travel, socialize… and make a little money."

Janet laughed. "For some, it's a nice income. Many artists who are here will sell between $10,000 and $20,000 worth of paintings by the end of the festival."

I was surprised and impressed.

The chairman of the festival was delighted to give us a little more background. "The plein air festivals began in the late 20th century and are usually associated with large cities."

"I wouldn't call Easton a large city," I said carefully so I didn't offend him.

"You're right, it isn't. The population of Easton is around 18,000 and Talbot County is less than 40,000 people." He held up his index finger to make a point. "BUT… we have two valuable assets: a community that supports the arts and an incredible landscape filled with historic homes, boats and more. The Eastern Shore offers many intriguing subjects and places to paint, don't you agree?"

I nodded enthusiastically. "I certainly do. I've only been here for a short time, but you never know what you're going to see as you go around a bend in the road or look over your shoulder. Whether it's a breathtaking water view or an osprey diving for dinner, it's always a pleasant surprise."

"Would you like to take a little tour to see some of the artists at work?" Anthony offered. "A golf cart and volunteer driver can take you around."

Intrigued, I looked to Lorraine for an answer.

She patted my arm. "You go along. After that walk from the car in this humidity, I'm going to find a tall glass of ice tea. Is that possible, Janet?"

Janet said, "Absolutely. Come with me."

"And I'll get Abby on her way." Anthony led me outside to a golf cart.

A compact-figured woman with sable-colored hair, marked by a ribbon of silver, sat at the wheel. Dressed in the typical all-black uniform of people in the arts, her intense focus on her volunteer responsibilities barely allowed her to smile. The one playful thing about her was her earrings. The huge triangles of blue mottled metal surrounding smaller triangles were mesmerizing as they danced around each other.

"My name is Sara V. Gordon. Everyone calls me Sara-V so I'm not confused with my cousin, Sara-Bee." She stuck out her hand. "Good to meet you."

Anthony suggested she give me a quick tour and, in very efficient fashion, the volunteer had me seated next to her. In moments, we were bumping along a path away from the main house and into the woods.

CHAPTER TWO

The table setting most often used in the dining room is the Service à la Russe. Each course of the meal is served in a specific order, using the appropriate serving pieces.

—"The Butler's Guide to Fine Silver" Mr. Hollister, 1898

Out here on the island, the artists had lots of sources of inspiration: flowers in the lush gardens, the water views beyond the tall trees, views of architecturally interesting houses and docks across the water channel and the blue heron and egrets dining at the pond not far from the road onto the island.

As we moved to flat open ground, my volunteer chauffeur talked about the island from an artist's viewpoint. "It's getting late in the day so the artists are chasing the light, one of the true meanings of painting en plein air. Once, all still life, portraits, even landscapes were painted in the studio."

"Landscapes? Wouldn't an artist want to be inspired by the actual scene?" I asked.

"I'm sure, but there was a problem. An artist had to make the paints from scratch by grinding dry pigment and adding the right amount of linseed oil, a process that took time and expertise. Once someone made oil paints and stored them in tubes ready for the palette, everything changed. And that someone must have made a bundle."

She shook her head and her earrings jingled. "I have to stop doing that, thinking in terms of money and return on investment. I was a mortgage banker for a lot of years, but I'm retired now. It's hard to break old habits."

She tapped a finger on the steering wheel. "Back to the artists. They headed outside to paint en plein air. They had to work quickly or the shadows would change so they changed their focus to capture the essence of something instead of the detail."

"That sounds like Impressionism, if I remember my art history class."

"That's right. You'll recognize the names of early plein air artists like Claude Monet, Winslow Homer and, of course, Renoir." She pulled to a stop near a forest-green pickup truck with a California license plate. Not too far away, an artist worked at his easel. When the man waved, Sara-V set the brake. "Let me introduce you to one of the rising stars on the plein air festival circuit, Seth Myers."

The man's muscled body almost dwarfed his easel. His khaki shorts exposed chiseled calf muscles. His broad shoulders and trim torso showed he liked to work out.

Sara-V lowered her husky voice as we made our way across the wild field grass. "He's one of the lucky ones. He quit his regular job and does this for a living now, along with giving art lessons."

The man put down his brush and took a step toward us. He flashed a big smile and I could see the sun and wind from painting outside had taken a toll, giving him a permanent weathered look. His eyes, the color of ebony, danced with excitement and pleasure.

"If you have a minute, Seth, I'd like you to meet a new friend of Plein Air."

Seth took off a beige canvas hat and dark, shiny hair fell in waves around his face. "Any friend of Plein Air Easton is a friend of mine." I didn't groan at the weak joke because I wouldn't mind being his friend, not at all.

Sara-V said, her gray-green eyes dancing, "I was just telling Abby about plein air painting and how you're always chasing the light."

"You're right," said Seth. "It is all about light and its effect on shapes. A plein air artist has to make quick decisions about what to paint and how. Then, he has to get the paint on the canvas fast to capture the light and shadows and values because, in moments, everything changes." His enthusiasm was almost contagious.

I stepped back and studied his work. "When I look at your painting, I see big, bold shapes of color with details added here and there. It's easy to see that you've captured the feeling of the river scene."

He laughed with relief. "I thought you were going to say you hated it."

"No! Not at all. It's a remarkable painting. My congratulations."

"I have to be honest. It's one of my warm-up paintings. After hours of traveling, moving in with my host family and getting the lay of the land, so to speak,

I try to do a couple of paintings to get the creative juices flowing. Like an athlete stretching his muscles before a game."

I could have listened to the artist's deep resonant voice for hours. It was nice to receive the attentions of a good-looking man, though I felt a tiny stab of guilt. I'd been dating Ryan, a tall, hunk of a man with a great personality, for several months when he was called away on family business. The last I heard, he was in Hong Kong.

Sara-V stepped forward, glanced at her watch and said crisply, "We really must let you get back to work, Seth. It's almost time to gather for dinner."

As I was hurried back to the golf cart, Seth called out, "See you under the tents."

On our way again, Sara-V apologized for interrupting our conversation. "The evening events start soon. We volunteers have a lot to do in a very narrow window. We must move all the canvases to the gallery tent for the exhibit and sale. That's not as easy to do as it sounds."

"Why?'

"The paintings are still wet, of course."

"Would you like me to get out here and walk back?" I asked.

Sara-V looked at me with a shocked expression. "I couldn't allow that. I was assigned to guide you around and I shall return you to our starting point."

So there. I thought, the banker was back. I'd better make nice. "I certainly appreciate it. I must admit I had no idea this was such a major undertaking."

My guide leaned toward me and said in a soft voice. "Between you and me, I think everybody is feeling the stress tonight. The first event sets the tone for the entire festival. There's a little extra pressure this year." She sat up straight. "This is the tenth anniversary of our plein air festival and there are a lot of special aspects this year."

"Like?"

"Well, the first prize in the competition is $10,000 – that's double what it was last year. It's a nice payday for one week of work, don't you think?" I nodded. "The money and the national recognition have attracted an outstanding field of artists who deserve to be treated well. After all, a top international art collector selected fifty-eight artists to compete. Not all the festivals do it this way. Plein Air Easton is always juried to get the crème de la crème.

I looked at the fields and wooded area nearby. "It must be hard keeping track of so many artists on such a large property."

"We've devised a clever system to monitor everyone. When each artist picks a spot, a call goes to the Information Center. Markers on a map of the area show where everyone is working. That way, we can deliver water, food, art supplies – whatever they need. And members of the public know where to go to see the artists at work."

Shocked, I had to ask, "The artists want people to watch them paint?"

"Oh yes, that's part of the plein-air experience. Many times, the artists will talk about what they're doing, what inspired them, techniques – that kind of thing.

Tomorrow, the artists are allowed to paint anywhere on the Delmarva Peninsula so the map is really important. Then, on Monday and Tuesday, they're limited to Talbot County. On Wednesday and Thursday, they have to stay within the Easton city limits."

"It sounds like a coordination nightmare."

"I guess it could be, but the people who run the festival have it well organized." He/she chuckled. "We haven't lost an artist yet."

I pointed to an area up ahead on the right. "Looks like somebody is looking for something." An older man was emerging from a stand of trees, swinging a large metal detector back and forth just inches above the ground. When we were talking by Bruff's portrait about people looking for buried treasure, I never expected to stumble across one so soon.

"What the…Hey, hey you!" She called out.

"I don't think he can hear you. He's wearing serious headphones." Clamped to his head, they looked like large pillows covering his ears. His body had shrunk with age and the extra weight had gone to his waistline. He was wearing jeans with suspenders along with a belt. The electronic device was strapped to his upper arm and he kept his eyes trained on a box close to the hand grip. The man moved it in a lazy arc, intent on not missing a spot.

"Great, now we're really going to be late." My guide steered the golf cart straight toward the man, without a care about the bumpy ground. I grabbed on with both hands. I didn't want to bounce out of the cart while she was in hot pursuit. Her artsy earrings clattered, setting my teeth on edge.

"He's not supposed to be here." She mumbled. "How did he get on the island?" We rapidly bore down on the man with the metal detector and stopped just feet away, much to my relief. Our sudden arrival got the man's attention. He slipped the headphones off his head.

"Just what do you think you're doing here?" demanded Sara-V in her official boardroom voice. Her polite manner had evaporated.

"What are you doing here?" the man countered. His grizzled gray hair was neatly combed and he was clean shaven. His thick glasses magnified his watery blue eyes.

"I belong here," she snapped. "… and you don't!"

"Not so. I paid my money and I am a guest. Now, if I may get back to what I was doing." The funny little man started to reposition his listening equipment over his ears.

"Wait just a minute. What are you doing with all that gear?" She said, not willing to let things go.

"If you must know, I'm a hunter and I'm looking for silver. This island is Bruff's Island." Sara-V gave him a blank look. The man responded with intensity, as if it would help us understand. "Bruff, the family of silversmiths? They settled here and worked on the Shore for some two hundred years?" The man looked skyward in frustration. "Never mind. Word is, there are silver pieces buried around here and I'm looking for 'em"

"He's right," I said. A silversmith did settle here. Back in revolutionary times and before, people buried their treasures. We might be sitting on top of a teapot or a spoon.

"Thank you," the metal-detector man said, with a little bow. "Now, if I can get back to work."

"No, you can't," Sara-V declared, her earrings clanging as she shook her head. "This is private property."

"Yes, it is. I figure if I find something, I'll show it to the owner and I might get myself a reward. At least I'll get some recognition from my detecting group."

Sara-V half stood in her seat and her head pivoted around like a periscope. "You mean there are more of you out here? Where?"

Losing patience, the man barked, "There's nobody here but me. I work alone. If I find something, I take pictures and such to document the find."

"You mean the way fishermen do when they have a great catch and then release it?" I hoped to help diffuse the situation. "For you, the thrill is in the hunt."

"You're not helping," My chauffeur muttered through clenched teeth.

The old man ignored her. "The thrill of the hunt — and the finding. I've made a nice bit of change over the years. In fact, I found —"

Sara-V raised her voice and laid down the law. "Sir, we don't have time for this discussion. You can't do that detecting thing here, not now."

"I figure I can and will. Now, you run along." The interloper fiddled with a knob and the detector squealed.

"You might check out the Bruff House in St. Michaels," I called out quickly. I turned to find her glaring at me. I tried my innocent look and settled back in my seat as meek as could be. "Just trying to help." It didn't work with the retired banker, but the old man waved as he walked back into the woods where we couldn't follow with the golf cart.

As Sara-V kicked the cart into gear, she yelled out, "I'm going to report you!" We roared away.

Back at the main tent, Sara-V stopped the cart just long enough for me to jump out before charging off to make good on her threat to report the weird metal detector man.

Chimes rang and everyone hurried to find their places at the large round dinner tables. I was scanning the crowd to find Lorraine when Seth appeared with a broad smile on his rugged face.

"I didn't think I'd find you in this crush of people, but I'm glad I did. We—"

A soft, feminine voice with a thick Southern drawl interrupted him. "Why, there you are, Seth."

After looking up at my new friend, I had to look around and then down to find the woman speaking. She was a little thing, several inches shorter than five feet with curly white hair and blue eyes that sparkled with mischief.

The little lady looked at me while she said, "Why, Seth, I thought I was the lady in your life." She tittered and held out her hand to me. "Hello, I'm Filomena Hopkins, but everybody calls me Filly…with an F, because I'm so frisky." She smiled and I was completely charmed.

Seth introduced me, and Filly said, "I'm so sorry to

intrude, dear." She put a hand on Seth's arm. "I was sent to find you and bring you in. They want us all together for something or another." She gave me a sincere look of regret. "I'm afraid I have to steal him away, but you can have him later."

"Promise?" said Seth with a laugh.

I had to laugh. This man was making me feel like a giddy schoolgirl.

"It's up to the lady, young man. It's always up to the lady." Her Southern upbringing was shining through. "Now, we should go before they send out Sherman's army. Nice to meet you, Abby."

I was alone again with people milling all around. Lorraine had promised to find out our table assignment, so all I had to do was find her. Easier said than done. The crowd parted for a moment and I caught a glimpse of Lorraine – tall and tan, gently shaking her shoulder-length light brown hair, the highlights dancing in the soft light. Lorraine was involved in a lively conversation while sneaking glances, searching the crowd for me. Once again, Lorraine made me feel like I belonged on the Eastern Shore, thousands of miles away from the city of Seattle where I was born and raised.

Our eyes met, we both waved. We worked our way through all the people and sat down with strangers at a huge table with an artful and dramatic centerpiece. The table setting suggested it would be an elaborate dinner that required extra forks and spoons. It would be nice if they were silver. Not for an art festival with hundreds of people. It seemed that only heads of state had place settings for large groups anymore. Because of the sheer size of the table for ten and the live background music, I was limited to talking with the men seated with me.

The one on my right jumped right in with introductions. His yellow sports jacket of raw silk along with the pale yellow shirt and tie with shades of gold made him look like King Midas. "Name's George Plummerly, Plummerly Real Estate." He thrust a beefy hand in my direction. "Did you know you're sitting next to a winner, young lady?" He motioned to the skinny man sitting on my left. "He won our first prize last year, didn't you, Paul?"

I turned to Paul, who wore wire-rimmed glasses, a neatly-trimmed moustache, and short salt-and-pepper beard. He gave me a tight smile as George leaned forward to look down his bulbous nose at him. "He even looks like an artist, don't you think? Paul, didn't they name that beard you have after an artist?" The side of the tablecloth danced as Paul's leg started jiggling from nerves.

George didn't let up. "Too bad the money was only half as much as this year's purse. Maybe you'll repeat, though no one has at Plein Air Easton."

This was not the time or place for a confrontation. Sitting between the two men, I waded in to break the tension. While making a grand show of admiring Paul's face, I said, "I think it's called a Vandyke. The artist was Flemish, I think."

Paul nodded, gratefully. I thought it was too early in the festival for a winning artist to look so stressed. The mantle of success must weigh heavy, especially when a bombastic supporter like George added to the load.

Paul blinked a few times, scrambling for something to say. "George is a big supporter of Plein Air. In fact, he bought my winning painting last year."

George smiled triumphantly. "Indeed I did! It's hanging in my office. You should come by sometime and see it. I show it off to our clients who want big-ticket homes. They connect with the artsy atmosphere we have here on the Shore. I guess you could say that we're bringing in new potential buyers of your artwork, Paul, every time we sell a home." He laughed so loudly at his own joke, people turned around to stare. It didn't faze him a bit.

The waiter arrived offering red or white wine. The options didn't seem to please Paul. He responded with a plaintive, "No beer?"

George leaned across me. "Still a beer snob, Paul? I bet if this guy wasn't a painter, he'd travel from one microbrewery to another."

"Everybody's got to have a hobby, George. Yours is collecting."

Interesting observation. A point for Paul.

As course after course of the dinner was served, the mood of the gathering became impatient. It wasn't the service, which was good. It wasn't the quality of the dinner, which was delicious. It was all about the art. People were anxious to get to the gallery tent. Seeing the volunteers moving back and forth just outside the dinner tent heightened everyone's anticipation. They were ferrying canvases into the display area for the sale.

George pushed back his chair and stood. To Paul, he said, "Don't worry. I'm only going to the men's room, wherever that is. I'm not going to the exhibit… yet." He chortled as he walked into the semi-darkness.

Paul's nervous twitches – his jiggling leg, tapping fingers – seemed to calm down. "He's talking about how everybody wants to get to the paintings first. The sale is first come, first served. Collectors like to snap up the work of their favorite artists. They won't be able to buy again until the Collectors' Preview Party on Friday evening."

My eyes trailed over to the place where George had disappeared. "An early peek…"

"Would be valuable," Paul finished. As they served dessert, he excused himself. "I want to check on my paintings. See you later."

I saw other artists slipping away and presumed it was to check their paintings. If they were still wet and a volunteer wasn't careful, an artist might be able to repair a smear before the sale. George hadn't returned as he'd promised. Left on my own, I enjoyed the delicate custard with fresh strawberries, blueberries and raspberries along with a fresh glass of champagne filled with effervescent bubbles.

That's when the woman screamed. And screamed and screamed.

CHAPTER THREE

Remember the silver pieces entrusted to your care represent more than things important to the House. Learn the history of silver that reaches back to ancient times. In the Bible, vessels of silver are named more often than gold.

—"The Butler's Guide to Fine Silver" Mr. Hollister, 1898

Everyone froze—then the place erupted in chaos. Many jumped up and ran toward the screams, some grabbed to the person next to them and held on tight, still others hid their faces in their hands, willing the fear away. Lorraine and I exchanged glances to be sure that we were all right, then we bounded out of our chairs and joined the throng headed toward the covered boathouse beyond the main house. We didn't get very far. It wasn't long before the organizers and volunteers were gently redirecting guests away from the water and back to the tent. They tried to reassure us that everything was under control and "Would you all return to the dinner tent, please?" They herded us toward the tent while the caterer scrambled to make more coffee.

I listened as others confidently traded suppositions about what happened: Someone was attacked. Someone fell in the water. Chessie, the legendary monster of the Chesapeake Bay had appeared. Then, real information filtered through the crowd. The police were coming. It wasn't long before we heard sirens in the distance.

Lorraine and I settled down at our table that the waiters had partially cleared and we sipped a watery glass of tea. Soon, we saw the emergency vehicles – both police and ambulance – threading their way to the dock area behind the house. Their blue and red emergency lights flashed off the leafy canopy over the house.

"This is more than a drunk guest slipping off the dock," whispered Lorraine.

Anthony, the chairman of the festival, stepped up to the podium and tapped the microphone. His lips were pressed together and perspiration glistened on his forehead. Janet, concern etched on her ashen face, went to her husband, gave him a little hug, then moved off to the side.

Anthony tapped again. "Is this on?" When his voice cracked, he cleared his throat, hoping to sound as relaxed as he had while making his welcoming remarks earlier. "Ladies and gentlemen, thank you for your patience. I'm afraid there's been an accident."

There was a collective gasp, followed by a low hum of speculations. "Please, please," Anthony tried to continue, the strain making his voice crack. "I've been told by local law enforcement to ask each and every one of you to remain here until you meet with an officer."

The air was peppered with complaints, though I suspected many of them would have spent another hour or two viewing and buying paintings or walking the grounds under the light of the full moon anyway.

The chairman raised his hands to soothe the crowd. "I know it's an imposition but, under the circumstances, we have to comply. More officers are on their way. It really shouldn't take too long." Someone appeared and whispered something in his ear. He brightened. "Yes, good idea. Ladies and gentlemen, let me invite you to our gallery tent to see this year's first works of this year's Plein Air. But, please, do not leave the premises until you've spoken with an officer. Thank you." Quickly, he stepped away from the dais and walked toward the flashing lights, leaving questions from the guests in his wake.

"I guess we might as well look at the paintings," suggested Lorraine.

We joined the crowd moving toward the gallery tent, but the urgency and anticipation were gone. As we lumbered along, a chilling piece of information interrupted every conversation: "They found a body floating in the water."

Now, everyone was asking questions: Who? Who died? Who was involved? How did it happen… an accident, or Lord forbid…?

We entered the gallery tent and gravitated toward a small group gathered around a painting in shades of silver with musky green tones. Someone whispered it was the Larry Chambers standing next to the easel answering questions about his work. His name didn't mean anything to me, but the others were paying rapt attention to the tall man in his 50's with thinning light brown hair. He wore cowboy boots, a hefty belt buckle and a white cowboy hat. Somehow, it all worked and didn't scream cliché.

Larry gestured toward painting. "We don't get a lot of rain in Phoenix. When that thunderstorm blew through here this afternoon, it was a rare opportunity for me. I had to work quickly before the sun burned off the mist."

I didn't want to think about what had happened elsewhere on the island that required the police. It felt so much better to focus on the artist's technical discussion about how he mixed his palette. A short woman with dull brown hair cut close to her head stood a few steps behind him – quiet, not really part of the group. A volunteer discreetly pressed a small red dot on the frame of the painting: Sold. The group of collectors applauded and moved on to other works.

The woman glanced down, saw the dot and came alive. She stepped forward, grabbed the artist's arm and looked at him with adoring eyes. "Honey, it sold already!"

Tenderly, he patted her hand and said quietly, "That's the idea, honey. My wife, Rebecca."

She extended her hand. "Rebecca Prager-Chambers, actually. Hello."

Larry explained, "She gets a little exuberant when I make a sale. Means we can pay the bills this month." Rebecca gave him a playful slap on the arm.

Lorraine smiled. "Paying the bills must not be a problem. You're very good."

The man looked down and put his hands in his pockets. "And you're very kind. Thank you, ma'am."

George, my bombastic dinner partner, hustled into the group. "I got it, Larry! It was me." He pointed at the little red dot. "And just in time. Some woman was sniffing around it, but I zoomed in and grabbed it… another addition to my Lawrence Chambers collection." George slapped Larry on the back and strutted away.

A deep resonant voice whispered in my ear. "Hello, again."

I turned to find Seth, the artist from my field tour, and introduced him to Lorraine. As we explained how we met, I felt a little thrill – funny, happy and appreciated. It was hard to hide my delight.

"Larry is a top contender for the big prize this year," Seth said.

Feeling a little protective, I asked, "What about your chances? They must be good, too."

"I'm doing okay on the plein air festival circuit, but I'm still new. Larry has been doing it for years. His wife is an attorney in Phoenix."

We talked as we walked and looked at paintings. "I got the impression she was a little concerned about money."

Seth shook his head. "He's prolific, but not enough to flood the market. His early paintings are inching up in value, too."

"You seem to know a lot about the business side." It was more of a statement than a question. Lorraine narrowed her eyes and looked at him closely. I'd never seen her act like this before. I didn't want to think it was because this man was showing an interest in me. Was she thinking about Ryan, gallivanting around Asia? Surely, she didn't see Seth as competition for my affections. I'd just met this man.

"Yes, ma'am, I'm kind of a hybrid. I used to be a commodity trader. Now, I'm a full-time artist."

Lorraine continued, "Isn't it unusual for someone who worked with trends and analytics to have such a creative side?" Seth stiffened a little, but Lorraine didn't notice or chose to ignore it.

"Not that unusual for someone who didn't enjoy working long hours at odd times, where the only visuals were the trending charts and pricing graphs."

We stopped at an easel holding a painting of a barn with a bright red roof and two sailboats at the dock. It was the same scene we saw when we drove on the island.

"Oh, you finished it!" I said and turned to Lorraine, "Seth was painting this canvas when we met."

She frowned at me then raised her hand to her chin and looked closely at the painting, evaluating it. "I must admit, you're very good."

"Thank you." There was little warmth in Seth's polite words. He reached out and gently grabbed the arm of an older woman hurrying by.

"Here's another artist you might like better who is in contention for the big prize. Margaret—"

"Sorry, can't stop. Somebody said a volunteer smudged my painting." She was gone.

Different expressions moved across his face. It was clear that he wanted to follow Margaret since this must be a calamity for an artist, but he also didn't want to be rude.

I reached out and touched his arm. "Go, if you

have to."

He paused, considering, then said good-bye to Lorraine and whispered to me, "Thank you" before he rushed away.

As we walked along the lines of easels holding landscapes, blooming roses and more, Lorraine quietly confirmed everyone's worst suspicion. Old friends drew Lorraine into a conversation. I continued along. Police officers walked by with important places to be. Some leafed through small notebooks, others compared notes or talked on the radio. I turned back to the paintings to blot out thoughts of the dead body found floating in the water.

Finally, I'd had enough of paintings and casual comments from strangers. That's how I ended up in the dinner tent by myself. I just wanted to be alone and have a cup of coffee or something stronger. The tent was empty, except for the catering staff clearing things away. I lingered over a fresh glass of champagne and watched them work. That's when I noticed a solitary figure sitting in the far corner.

It was Filly, the petite and lively artist I'd met before dinner. She sat staring straight ahead at nothing. Only her hands were moving, shredding a tissue. Some of the tiny pieces were carried away by the wind. When her fingers ran out of tissue, they continued to shred the empty air. I approached her slowly and held out a clean tissue from my purse.

"Looks like you might need this," I said gently, but she still jumped. "I'm sorry. I didn't mean to startle you. I'm Abby. I met you earlier with Seth."

I saw recognition on her face as she made the connection. "Yes, yes, of course…" Her voice trailed off.

"It's just that you seemed to have run through your tissues and I thought you might need another."

Filly looked at the few bits on her lap. "Oh, dear." She gathered up the torn pieces in a little white pile and deposited them in a pocket. She took a deep breath and let out in a long sigh. "Oh, dear."

"Is there anything I can do for you? I'm sorry. I should have realized that you're one of the artists. Should I get the festival chairman or a volunteer? "

"What?" She tore her gaze away from the empty place in mid-air where she'd been staring and reached up to touch her Plein Air identification card with her name and picture, her lower lip trembling. "Yes, yes, I am. I have my badge now. They want us to display our badges so the police…" Her voice caught on the word. "The police can identify the artists. It's my fifth year here. It's such a wonderful festival." Her eyes wandered back to the empty place.

I was about to leave her to her private thoughts when tears welled up in her eyes again. I couldn't just walk away. Maybe it would help if we talked about something neutral. "Um, that's a very unusual necklace you're wearing." The words must have penetrated for she reached up and touched the green frog hanging from a silver chain at her throat.

Stress eased from her face and her mouth turned up in a peaceful little smile. "Isn't she lovely? She's made of green fiery opals from Australia. The detail work is sterling silver and 14K gold."

"Spoken like a true artist. You notice the details."

Her smile broadened. "I like her big eyes and the way she lays against my skin, as if she's giving me a hug."

"It's very sweet."

"She's very important to my work. I guess you could call her my talisman or creative amulet. It's not easy putting yourself in front of an easel, especially when you have to paint every day at a festival and the work has to be good. It's not like being a bookkeeper, adding up numbers with a calculator: push the buttons, get a total, go on to the next column. Sometimes, the creative muse wants to sleep late when she should be inspiring me. So, I've trained myself that when I put on my necklace, my little frog, I'm awakening my creative spirit to go to work and do the best I can."

She sat back against the chair and her shoulders relaxed. "It would be nice to sit and wait for a creative idea to strike. When I paint in a plein air festival, I don't have that luxury. When it's time to work, it's time to work, ready or not. And this week was so full of promise."

Tears started to trail down her face. "Especially for him. To see him staring up at me from the water. It was awful."

"Y-you found the body?" She nodded. I rubbed Filly's back a little to offer comfort. It was something Lorraine did when someone was upset. It had helped me a time or two. "I'm so sorry." I wanted to ask her for details, but resisted the urge and tamped down my curiosity.

"What an awful thing to happen here and to such a nice man," she said, wiping her nose.

"You knew the—" I didn't know what to call him that wouldn't upset her.

"Walt? Oh yes. We met years ago at a plein air festival, of course." She cocked her head and tapped her chin with her index finger. "I'm not sure, was it in Alabama or Richmond? Oh well," She rubbed her temple and blinked her eyes several times. "Sometimes, the details run together. All the festivals are wonderful, though this is one of my favorites. He used to come regularly in the late spring and during the summer. Walt was a wonderful painter. Won competitions, was always busy with commissions." A sad frown formed slowly on her face. "That was before."

"What happened?"

She took a deep breath. "His dear wife, Joyce, came down with cancer. Awful thing. He didn't want to leave her for more than a day or two and, of course, the festivals run about a week. When she got worse, he laid down his brushes. He didn't want to miss a moment with her. He was planning a 50th birthday surprise party for her. When the time came, he was planning her funeral instead."

She started sniffling and I handed her a fresh tissue from the stash I kept in my purse against the effects of summer allergies. She blew her nose and continued. "I encouraged him to come, thought it would help him to get out in the fresh air and sunshine. Joyce died about a year ago and he thought she would want him to start painting again. It's not fair. "

She looked down at her hands now quietly clasped in her lap. "It took a lot for him to come, to even apply. You know, an artist can't just send in an application fee and be part of Plein Air Easton. You have to be chosen. I was afraid what it might do to him if he wasn't selected, but he was. He was so worried about painting again at such a prestigious festival he started getting headaches. He needn't have worried. When he picked up a brush this morning, I saw the sadness drop away and a blanket of joy wrap around him."

I asked, softly, "Will you stay… and paint in the competition?"

She turned her head quickly, determination burning in her eyes. "Oh yes, of course. Bleakest black is part of the palette just as death is part of life. We can be sad, but we have to paint with what life puts on our palettes."

A uniform officer walked up to us. "Excuse me, Miss Hopkins? The detective needs to talk to you again. If you'll come with me."

"Of course." She patted my knee. "Y'all come by my easel this week and we'll chat some more." She followed the young man out of the tent, leaving me alone with a lot of dirty dishes and linen.

CHAPTER FOUR

The work of the silversmith is related to the art of the sculptor. Each must rely on the ability of his hands and the keenness of his eye.

—"The Butler's Guide to Fine Silver" Mr. Hollister, 1898

"Don't you look like a lost soul?" Anthony walked toward me with a compassionate smile on his face. "Fear not, dear lady. I've come to rescue you."

"Don't you have a thousand things to do with the police, being the chairman?" I said, meekly.

"I've done everything I can for now. I think they're glad to be rid of me for a while. So, may I do something for you?"

I jumped to my feet. "Oh, yes please."

He put a hand on my elbow and guided me outside. "I saw you sitting there looking so forlorn. I couldn't just walk away."

"I'm so glad you came. I don't know where Lorraine is and all I want to do is leave."

"Have you spoken with the police?"

"No, not yet. It feels so strange that we're confined on this island with hundreds of people and one of them may be a murderer." I slowed to a stop and looked around. He had led me to a wooded area. I could see people milling around in the lights of the main house and the tent that blazed in the distance. Here, it was more like twilight with a few squirrels in the branches overhead.

Anthony must have read my mind. He dropped his hand and took a few steps away from me. "I didn't mean to make you nervous. If you want to go back to the tent, I'll understand."

I thought for a moment, then shook my head. "I'm sorry, I guess I'm a little jumpy."

"Everyone is. It's understandable. It's all very upsetting with the police here and all," Anthony said calmly.

"That's right. If it was an accident —"

"They would still be here to make sure it was just an accident."

I sighed. It was stupid to be nervous around Janet's husband. After all, she was friend of Lorraine's... and president of the Friends. "I guess you're right. It's the 'not knowing' that's wearing me down."

He clapped his hands together and said with renewed energy, "I don't know any more than you do about what's going on around here now, but I do know a thing or two about what went on here centuries ago. Can I interest you in a little history while you're waiting to see the police?"

I nodded.

"Good, follow me."

He kept several feet apart from me as we

walked. It was a very thoughtful thing to do under the circumstances.

I began to relax. "I've always loved history, not the parts about dates and royal lineage or who blew up what. I want to know how people lived and why they did what they did. I even wanted to major in history in college. The only thing was, I couldn't figure out how to support myself unless I earned a Ph.D. and entered academia." I shook my head. "No, that wasn't the life for me."

"What did you do?" He asked.

"Studied computer science and went into software development."

His head jerked in surprise. "That's a big switch."

"Yes, I suppose, but it worked," I said, sounding resigned.

"Too bad you didn't foresee the big interest in historical fiction books. If you liked to write, you could have combined it with your love of history and made a living."

"I used to write a lot, as a matter of fact." The memories came back, dusty and distant from my life in high school and college. "In school, I wrote for the newspaper and the yearbook. Even cranked out short stories, usually late at night. I liked the challenge of taking an idea, developing out the plot and characters, then mixing them all together."

"Were you good at it?" His smile flashed in the moonlight. His question wasn't meant to be obnoxious, just curious.

A playful, embarrassed giggle slipped out. "Yes, I

thought so … and so did my teachers. Later in college, I didn't have time to work on stories, so I started a journal." Without warning, I felt empty inside as I remembered why I'd stopped journaling. Grief could do that. After Gran died, it was too hard to put my thoughts down. I stopped writing… and I missed it.

Anthony didn't notice my reaction and went right on. "Now, you're researching the history of sterling silver."

"And really enjoying it. Enough about me, what about you?"

'Oh, there's not that much to tell. Janet and I moved here five years ago. Now, among other things, my favorite hobby is history."

"Where are you from?" I asked. "You have an accent that doesn't sound like it's from around here."

"Whaddaya mean, I have an ak-cent? I'm from Joisey." He grinned and held up his hand. "And before you ask, yes, I am the living cliché—an Italian kid, born in Joisey, who went into his father's concrete business." I tried to swallow my smile. "It's okay, you can laugh. You have to hear it all—my dad was a great guy. He shortened the name, the one from the old country, to Bruno so it would fit on his trucks. He used his fists and people called him Bruno the Bruiser. He didn't care, said it worked because guys thought twice before trying to mess him over." He rubbed his palms together and a slow smile crept over his face. "He was a good dad and gave me a good life. Now, we can live on the water and go to New York, Philly and D.C. for the arts."

"You weren't far from those places when you were

growing up, were you?" I asked.

"No." His face took on a pink tinge barely visible in the moonlight. "My dad was so busy teaching me the business – Tony, do this; Tony, do that – I didn't have time to learn about those things." His laugh came out more like a huff. "If we'd ever gone to a museum, he'd have asked who poured the foundation. When I met Janet and could get out of the business gracefully, I did."

We stopped above a line of riprap designed to hold back the water. The breeze was a welcome relief from the humid evening.

"This is the Wye River. It's narrower and twists more than the Choptank or the Miles. We built our place up the way. When we moved here, the history of the area became my hobby. That's when I found out about the pirates."

"Pirates! Here?"

"Yes, ma'am. In the late 1600's, this was a port to ship out tobacco on three-masted schooners."

"I thought pirates went after gold or jewels or spices."

He smiled. "In those days, tobacco was money. The British pound sterling was scarce over here."

"Maybe that's why Thomas Bruff didn't work as a silversmith when he came here. There wasn't enough silver."

"Maybe he exchanged his craft for religious freedom and land."

I brushed away a mosquito. "Tell me more."

"With pleasure. He was part of a Puritan rebellion led by the man who lived over there." He pointed to the land opposite where we were standing on Bruff's Island. "That's Bennett's Point named for Richard Bennett who stirred up a whole lot of trouble. His compatriot was Edward Lloyd."

"Wait a minute, I know that name. Isn't it connected with Wye House?"

Anthony nodded. "Very good. Mr. Lloyd who built Wye House, got himself into a situation of Just when you think you're safe, you're not. To escape religious persecution, he moved to the New World from the Wye River Valley in Wales early in the 1600's. That's how the river here got its name. But first, he went to Virginia and established a good life for himself and his family. Almost overnight, things changed there."

I was intrigued. "He wasn't safe?"

"No, they had to run for their lives. He came here just before Mr. Bruff arrived and had to start all over again. Together, they led a Puritan rebellion against Lord Baltimore. Talk about biting the hand that feeds you." He shook his head. "But it didn't take those fellows long to realize that money, land and their way of life were more important than imposing their religion on others. They adopted a live-and-let-live approach and their families thrived. Wye House, one of the most beautiful mansions in the area, is still in his family."

My phone vibrated in my pocket. The text from Lorraine read:

Police ready. Meet me at Bruff's portrait.

It was time to face the reality of murder.

CHAPTER FIVE

A monogram may consist of a single initial of the family or the three initials of the lady. If the continental style of dining is used, the monogram is placed on the back of the fork handle because the tines are held in a downward position while eating.

—"The Butler's Guide to Fine Silver" Mr. Hollister, 1898

Back in the dining room, Lorraine introduced me to Detective Mike Ingram from the Talbot County Sheriff's Department, promised to meet me at the tent, then slipped away. The man wasn't much taller than my 5′8″. His gentle, almost unobtrusive manner was so different from the usual macho attitude of the police I'd met. He was older and, if the lines on his face came from experience, this man knew what he was doing.

"So, you are Abby Strickland?" I nodded. "The woman who has been so helpful to my good friend, Chief Lucan?"

I smiled and nodded. He was referring to the police chief of St. Michaels, the village that I now called home.

"We've faced a few tough situations together. I was happy to help when I could." Eager to see a familiar face, I asked, "Is the Chief here?"

"No, I'm afraid not. Out of his jurisdiction. The body was in the water so it falls under the Natural Resources Police. They don't have the manpower to interrogate more than two hundred people so I'm here with my officers."

"Interrogate? That sounds a little extreme," I said.

"Extreme?" He shook his head. "An artist with a gash on his head, in the water? Drag marks from his easel to the water's edge? No, this was no accident. I have two hundred suspects."

"Suspects? You mean… why would someone…"

"Murder an artist? Money. National attention. Respect. Those are good for starters."

The thought of someone in the arts killing one of their own brought bile up my throat. "Mrs. Andrews must have given you our contact information. We didn't see or hear anything, so what do you want from me?"

"I hear you pick up on things, sometimes get involved somehow in an investigation. I don't want you getting in the way, all right? If you come across something during the festival, pass it along to me. That is, if I don't cancel the whole thing first."

"What?" I blurted out. "You can't cancel the festival."

"Yes, I can and I will. A man lost his life. My investigation trumps any painting contest," he said with steel in his voice.

"I understand, but that's such a drastic move."

"Murder is a drastic event," he said.

A thought hit me that might prove useful. "If you cancel the festival, all your artistic suspects will scatter.

Isn't it better to keep them here, doing what they're supposed to do, especially if there's a way to monitor their movements?"

He looked at me with quiet interest as I explained about the map, the way the volunteers kept track of the artists when they were out painting. "If you let the festival go on as planned, you'll have more time to gather information with your suspects close by."

He looked at me, thinking. The look on his face gave nothing away. It probably never did, which was an advantage for a police detective. "It's one way to proceed. I'll think about it. If anything else occurs to you, you tell me. No running off on your own. Nothing more. Understand?"

"Yes, sir." I almost felt like I was talking to my dad, who was a Navy man.

Detective Ingram extended his hand to shake mine. "Thank you, Abby." Then, he lowered his voice so the officer standing by the door couldn't hear. "You know if I take your advice and let the festival continue, some innocent person's life may be in jeopardy. If a killer strikes once, it's easier for him or her to strike again."

The truth of what he said struck me like a hot knife. I didn't want the responsibility for anyone's safety. Before I could say anything, he announced to the officer, "She is free to go, along with her friend." I rushed away to find Lorraine.

I went outside and a tall, lanky man, not much older than a teenager, blocked my way. "Excuse me, ma'am." His wire-rimmed glasses with smudged lenses slid down his nose and he jammed them back in place.

Imagine, a young man calling me ma'am when I hadn't even celebrated my thirtieth birthday. My guard went up.

"Jack Humphreys, from the Star." He added, "The local newspaper."

I knew the paper, of course, but I didn't know Jack. Plus, reporters always made me nervous. He didn't build any trust when he stuck a recorder in my face.

"What can you tell me about your conversation with the detective?" His serious expression showed his supreme confidence that I would tell him everything I knew about anything he wanted to know.

"Nothing. There's nothing to tell," I replied with a shrug.

His eyes narrowed in suspicion. "But, but the detective sought you out. He—"

"The police are talking to everybody. If you want to know what the detective said, I suggest you ask him." I started to walk away.

He caught my arm. "But, I'm working on my narrative report. The death will be the talk of the town. I need—" Finally, he noticed I was staring at his hand on my arm and quickly removed it. "Sorry, it's just that with everything shrouded in secrecy, I can't get my story."

"Then I suggest you wait for a formal statement and ask your questions then." As I walked away thinking about the tough Detective Mike Ingram, I said, "Good luck with that."

Just outside the big tent where we'd had dinner – it felt like days ago – I saw Larry, the artist I'd met earlier, talking to his wife Rebecca with the hyphenated last name. I wasn't sure why that grated on me. I'd never been married, so I've never faced the question, but I suspected that if my maiden name was so important, I'd keep it all by itself. Or I could use it in professional situations. But, this was an event for her husband. Why wouldn't she use her married name or go by Rebecca, Larry's wife? Why make life more complicated?

As I got closer, I heard Larry say, "I have to talk with the police. I'll be back as soon as I can. Will you be okay here?"

His concern impressed me. It wasn't lost on her, either. She rose on her toes and kissed his cheek before he left. Then, she went to one of the tables and used a napkin to wipe a clump of mud off her shoe. She started to wobble. I rushed forward and caught her arm.

"Oh, thank you," she breathed. "I don't know why we have to get all sloppy. Sometimes, I wish he'd paint in a studio – preferably with air-conditioning. The heat is worse here than in Phoenix."

"The locals say it's not the heat, it's the humidity. The breeze off the water saves us from the worst of it."

"I'm not sure I feel saved. I should be used to hot weather, living in South Texas. The humidity here is draining the strength right out of me."

I was confused. "I thought you said you were from Phoenix."

"We are… now. We spent years in Dallas while Larry worked in management and I went to law school at SMU. Then I joined the prosecutor's office – criminal cases mostly. When we found out we couldn't have kids, we decided to start over. We moved to Phoenix and both shifted careers."

"That was a gutsy move," I said, impressed.

"Yes, I guess it was. I joined a firm as a criminal defense attorney."

"That was a switch."

"I learned a lot from prosecuting cases that helped me on the defense side of the table. Larry made an even bigger change. He started painting for a living. It was always his first love. We figured, why not try it?" she explained.

"From what I hear, he's very successful."

She sniffed. "This plein air circuit takes him away from home too much. While I was settling into my new job, I didn't mind, but now, it's hard coming home to an empty house. It's almost as if we're living apart." She looked off in the direction Larry had gone. "I can't let that happen, that's why I came to this festival," she said with a sigh.

"It's nice you could join him."

"Yes. I can't always get away. This time, I made it happen." An icy glint in her eye suggested that she usually succeeded at what she set out to do.

"Well, I hope it's a good festival for you both."

"It hasn't started off very well," she said, with a scowl on her face.

"No, it hasn't, especially for Walt. Well, I have to find my friend. They said we can leave and I'm more than ready."

"No husband?" She said with interest as she glanced at my left hand that didn't have a wedding ring. "No boyfriend?"

"Not right now."

"A girl should always have a man around she can call her own. Don't let him get away."

Her interest in my love life and what sounded like Southern rules for young debutantes were making me uncomfortable so I said good night, eager to find Lorraine.

It wasn't long before Lorraine and I were walking toward the car. Since we were alone, I told her about my conversation with the detective.

"Thankfully, your reputation for working with the Chief got us an early release," Lorraine said, with a sigh of relief. "It's going to take them hours to get everyone's contact information, let alone finding out who saw what, when. At least they're interviewing the artists first so they can get some sleep before painting tomorrow... that is, if they don't cancel the festival all together."

"I hope they don't. The detective suspects it is a case of one artist killing off the competition for the big prize and prestige."

"That sounds a little extreme," she said.

"I agree."

I went on to tell Lorraine about my conversation with Filly, the artist who found the body.

Lorraine took a ragged breath. "She must have been walking on the dock by the pretty dark green boathouse with white gingerbread trim. It must have been awful for her, to find a body of a friend like that." I could feel Lorraine shudder in the dark. "His body was caught in the branches of a dead tree that had fallen into the water."

I gasped. "How do you know that? You didn't—"

"No, no, that's not something I'd want to see. The son of one of our farm workers is in the sheriff's department. He said it was a sight that would stay with him for a long time."

We walked along in silence trying to erase the picture our imaginations painted. My thoughts started to wander. "Rebecca is interesting. She was complaining about her shoes. I wonder how they got so muddy."

"You're seeing the boogey man everywhere. The grass is still soggy from the cloudburst earlier today. Look at your own shoes." Lorraine sighed. "There's the car, at last."

I looked down at my shoes and groaned. "You're right, I'd better let them dry out when we get home and clean them in the morning."

I drove slowly toward the entrance to Bruff's Island, scanning the shadows for Helene of the golden hair. Tonight, she had the ghostly company of a gifted artist. The reason why remained to be uncovered.

CHAPTER SIX

Ancient Greek artisans were the first to do Repoussé work on silver pieces. A small hammer was used to beat a thin sheet of metal to create different shapes on the surface. The same techniques are used today to create this artful form of ornamentation.

—"The Butler's Guide to Fine Silver" Mr. Hollister, 1898

The next morning was a lazy Sunday at Fair Winds. Lorraine opted for a nap. Even my young black Labrador Retriever Simon and his three buddies, Lorraine's huge Chesapeake Bay Retrievers, stretched out under the shade trees, instead of scampering around. I didn't feel like working on the silver collections. The online auctions didn't need my attention. I took my tablet outside and, after clearing my email, poked around for something about the beautiful Helene with the golden hair. After all, one doesn't visit the haunting grounds of a ghost every day.

After some serious searching, I realized I should never have doubted Lorraine. A portion of a memoir written by Elizabeth Lloyd Schiller mentioned the elusive lady. She wrote that Helene, known for her beauty, was once mistress of Bruff's Island. She would ride sidesaddle over to the Wye House in the afternoons and join Elizabeth's father on the porch for a glass of Madeira.

I gazed at the river, daydreaming. I loved my electronics, but the charm of those bygone days – when one had the time to ride over to visit with a friend or neighbor – was appealing.

I scrolled through other search results to find out that the lovely Helene was married to an eccentric man. He wanted to live in a world that was black and white, literally.

Elizabeth wrote:

"...the chickens were black and white; the turkeys white;

two beautiful big white barns were built. They added a guest house,

a tenant house and an enchanting little creamery – all in pristine white."

The heat was getting to me. I figured I could take a nap for the rest of the afternoon or ... I had a better idea. I put my things away, dropped the top on my Saab convertible and headed up to Easton and the headquarters of the plein air art festival.

The information center was upstairs in the Avalon theater building. I waded into a room of busy people. Volunteers were moving about with cell phones glued to their ears. Visitors were easy to spot because of the lost look on their faces. It was the first public day of the festival and we all had to find our way around.

"Hi, can I help you with something?" The friendly volunteer bubbled with excitement.

I wanted to ask if she'd heard anything about the murder last night. Instead, I stammered, "W-well, this is my first plein air festival and —"

"Say no more. Follow me." She carved a path through the crowd and, in moments, I had pamphlets, a map, and more. "Now, you're ready to go out and visit the artists."

Had she read my mind...that I was curious to know where Seth was painting today?

"Oh," I sputtered. "I couldn't intrude."

"Of course you can," insisted my friendly volunteer. "That's the whole idea of the plein air festival. It's for art lovers. The artists have agreed to allow people to visit their easels and watch them work. You'll see a painting take shape right in front of your eyes. Keep in mind that not everyone is willing to chat while they're working. Many would rather wait until they take a break to talk to visitors, but there are ways to tell that you are welcome."

"Really? What are the secret signals?"

She chuckled. "Oh, they're not really secret. The important thing is to pause before you approach a painter at work. If someone has set up an easel in a high traffic area – right in the middle of things – he is probably willing to talk. If an artist is wearing bright colors and maybe fun jewelry, she cares how she looks and that means she's interested in talking. Some artists strike up a conversation with a visitor and, before you know it, the painting is sold right off the easel." She leaned close to me. "Remember, don't creep up on an artist and scare her to death." She lowered her voice. "Especially after what happened last night." She pursed her lips and gave me a knowing nod. "All the artists are a little nervous, but every one of them is out there painting today."

Everyone but Walt, I thought. "Have the police found out—"

"Oh, I wouldn't know about that," she said quickly, brushing away any thoughts about the murder. "Now, let me tell you what you need to know about approaching the artists. If someone has on a big hat pulled down..." She tapped her head like a kindergarten teacher. "Or is wearing sunglasses..." She moved her finger to her eye. "Or is using earbuds..." She touched her ear. "Keep your distance. The creative juices are flowing and the painter shouldn't be disturbed."

"Got it."

She led me over to a map of the area. "Here is the map that shows where the artists are painting today."

I was glad to see that Filly had overcome her tissue-shredding and was out in the field. I hoped it wasn't obvious that I checked out where Seth was working. I turned to thank the volunteer, but she was welcoming another visitor, Detective Mike Ingram.

"No, thank you." He pointed at me. "I just want to talk with her, if that's all right." She walked away to help someone else.

I greeted the man. "Good morning, detective,"

"It's afternoon," he shot back. "And there's nothing good about it."

"No new developments?"

He took a small step back and examined me. "The Chief was right about you. You don't quit."

I held up a hand in apology. "I didn't mean to

overstep. Sorry."

He paused and then, as if he'd made a decision, he touched my elbow and steered me to a quiet corner. He took up a position with his back against the wall so he could watch the comings and goings behind me while we talked. "I talked to Chief Lucan last night. He said you could be trusted to keep quiet."

Caught off-guard by the comment, I almost couldn't hide a smile of pleasure. I respected the St. Michaels Chief of Police and secretly wished he was involved in this investigation, but rules were rules and this crime was outside his jurisdiction. I waited for him to continue.

"A preliminary report came in about the body found in the water last night."

"Walter." He looked a little surprised. "I talked with Filly last night." He didn't make the connection. "Philomena Hopkins, the artist who found the body."

"Filly?"

I filled him in, hoping to lighten his mood. "Yes, she said her daddy gave her the nickname because she was as frisky as a young horse."

"She wasn't very frisky last night. Devastated was more like it."

"Walt was a good friend of hers," I explained.

"That's what she said." He paused and looked around to make sure no one was listening to our conversation. "Her friend didn't end up in the water by himself. It looks like he had some help."

My stomach clenched. "You mean…?"

"The paramedics found a section of his skull caved in from a blow to the head," he continued.

"Maybe he slipped, fell and hit his head on something on the bank. It knocked him out and he rolled into the water." I rushed on with another alternative to murder. "Or maybe he slipped, fell in the water and hit something—" The detective was shaking his head the whole time I talked. "What? It could happen."

"Yes, but I don't think that's the case," he said. "The injury was deep, too destructive to be an accident."

"But—"

He motioned like a traffic cop for me to stop. "Abby, you don't give up, do you?"

I bit my lip. "I'm sorry." He was right. I was eager for Walt's death to be a freak accident. I didn't want a murder to mar the art festival.

The detective continued. "It's not about speculation or how we'd like things to be. It's about facts and evidence. The paramedics reported their findings to the medical examiner and they agree that I should proceed as if it's a murder investigation unless the autopsy shows otherwise."

I let out a sigh that went all the way to my toes.

He scanned the busy goings-on in the room. "I saw the map showing all the artists' locations." He shook his head. "This case has some firsts for me… a bunch of creative types and a map that may lead me to the murderer."

"So, you still think it was one of the artists?" I whispered.

"Works for me. Kill off the competition, claim the big prize." He ran his hands through his brown hair. Look, I want you to keep this information quiet for now.

You seem to get along with these artistic types, so let me know if you come across anything interesting." He shifted his eyes and they bore into mine. "And, I repeat, under no conditions are you to do anything. I don't need another victim, understand?"

"Yes, sir." The formal response slipped out without a thought. I had no desire to get involved in another police matter when, not so long ago, I'd almost lost my life. "You can count on it."

He gave me a quick nod and walked into the crowd. I went to follow him and walked right into Jack, the eager reporter.

When he recognized me, his face fell. "Oh, it's you again. My uncooperative source."

"You're still here," I shot back. "What are you doing, tailing the detective?"

"Of course. It seems like that's the only way I'm going to unearth any information." He paused to look at me closely. "Unless you're going to shine a spotlight on what's going on. I need to get my story before this becomes a feeding frenzy with those obnoxious reporters muscling in from the Western Shore." He was referring to the media from Washington, Baltimore and Philadelphia, all within a two-hour drive of Easton. He watched silently while a volunteer walked by. "The scuttlebutt is that it wasn't an accident."

I tried very hard not to react. "What, the body in the water?"

He took a deep breath and let it out in a burst. "Of course, the body in the water." He moved his face close to mine. "I hear it was..." He paused, hoping to shock me. "Murder."

I gave him what I hoped was an innocent look. "I thought you wrote about news events, not fiction." I breezed by him to talk to Janet and Anthony who'd just walked into the room.

Janet met me halfway, grabbed my hands and gave them a gentle squeeze. "Oh, Abby, It's so good to see you."

"This is a bustling place." I did a quick survey of the room to make sure that the reporter wasn't lurking close-by.

Anthony, the festival chairman responded. "More like organized chaos. It works, and that's what's important. We're very proud of our volunteers and staff."

"I thought you might be researching our Mr. Bruff's sterling silver," Janet suggested as she gave me a sparkling smile.

I hesitated to say something then decided that Janet would appreciate knowing the truth about the Bruff silver. "Actually, it probably wasn't sterling. All the silversmiths at that time used coin silver."

Janet gave me a blank look. "Isn't that the same?"

"Not really. It all has to do with the chemistry. As you probably know, pure silver is very soft. Another metal has to be added so it's strong enough for silverware or silver coins."

"I know it sounds funny, but isn't coin silver used in coins?" asked Anthony.

"Yes, but it wasn't that simple back in merry ole England. They made it rather confusing. In Bruff's time, people used silver coins as money. Silversmiths melted them down to make silverware like knives, spoons and teapots. When they started running out of actual money, they raised the percentage of silver required for silverware. The term coin silver was used to show the difference between early silver actually made from coins, the higher-content silverware made later, and sterling silver, which has the highest silver content of all and came along much later. Sorry, I didn't mean to get so technical."

"Not at all," Janet said lightly. "You taught us something that even I can understand."

A lady rushed up, looking very concerned. "Excuse me, Mr. Anthony. We need your help at the desk."

"I'll let you get back to work. See you later." I took another quick peek at the map to confirm Seth's location and went to my car.

CHAPTER SEVEN

Living life is like sketching what you hope will be a beautiful picture...without the benefit of an eraser.

—Walter Stanton, Artist

The directions led me down a single lane road in the middle of nowhere, only earth and sky around me. The only signs of humanity were an old barn of weathered wooden slats that was slowly falling apart and a green pickup truck that belonged to Seth. I pulled in behind it and looked around for him. The afternoon sun glinted off the water making it hard to see. Using my hand to shade my eyes, I looked around again. There, in the shade of a tree made crooked by the wind stood a single man, intent on the scene, his palette and his painting. There was something captivating about the way he squared off in front of his canvas and, with great care and consideration, captured his interpretation of the scene. Though powerfully built, with a broad chest and well-developed shoulders, he was gentle as he touched his brush to the paint and then applied it to the canvas. Gentle, controlled and confident. Clearly, he was comfortable with what he was doing. As if he could hear my thoughts, he turned around and, when he saw me, he raised his hand in welcome. Feeling the effects of the heat and humidity as I stood in the open sunlight, I moved forward quickly to share the shade with Seth.

"This is a surprise," he said. "I'm glad you came and found me."

"I checked with the information center and found you on the map." Why do I suddenly feel so shy? I hope I'm not blushing.

I picked a safe topic to discuss. "You certainly picked a beautiful spot here. Is that an old tobacco barn?"

"I have no idea. I picked it because, in this natural setting, it stands as a memorial to man's efforts long ago."

I looked at him in surprise. He laughed. "If you must know, I just like the composition. I confess I find it hard to find a place to paint when I'm here on the Eastern Shore."

My mouth fell open in shock. "What? The Shore is beautiful and interesting almost everywhere you look."

He threw out his arms wide. "That's the problem. I should have said I find it hard to settle on one place to paint. I want to paint everything."

I laughed with relief. "That's something I can believe."

"And the concept of painting en plein air – in the open air -- doesn't make my job any easier," he complained with a little pout playing on his lips.

"And why is that?"

"The whole idea is to chase the light. Outside, the

light changes as the sun moves across the sky or when a cloud floats by. It all has an effect. I can't freeze the light as you can with a photograph. I must paint quickly, confident in my technique. As the light changes, it brings out new details and shadows that attract me. I want to pull out a new canvas and start again. That's why Claude Monet painted the Haystack Series, simple haystacks in a field, so fascinating to see as the light changed. Some people thought he was crazy to keep painting the same subject, but it was brilliant. His techniques and work were part of the foundation of Impressionism and painting en plein air."

Worried, I asked, "You have to paint fast as the light changes and here I am distracting you. You should be working instead of talking to me."

He glanced at his painting, and then at me. A slow smile formed on his face and I felt a thrill. "I think I've got the important parts down and my memory can fill in gaps." He motioned me to the easel. "Come here and stand where I stand so you can see what I see. There are browns and silver and a touch of red in the boards. I softened the contrast of the barn a little to create the peaceful effect of this place. Painting is very much like life. You have to find the right elements and fit them together to make something beautiful. Now, wait and watch for a few minutes. You'll see the shadows move, some of the colors intensify and some fall into the mud. It's all because the light is changing."

I could feel him standing behind me though we did not touch. The air around us was almost crackling. I swallowed. "I guess I understand what you're saying intellectually, but I never stood still long enough to see it."

"People are so caught up in the busyness of life that the world looks the same all the time. If you look, you'll see it changing, nature is always changing." He sighed.

"You're right, we need to slow down, or stop in order to see it." And, I stopped and really looked at what was in front of me: the wild grasses waving in the breeze, the water reflecting the blue sky, and the barn standing alone, probably once a place of great activity. It all felt so right, as if it was all connected.

A feeling of peace settled over me as we stood quietly, watching the scene change, together.

Slowly, I felt something stir deep inside me, a welling that would not be denied. It grew, insistent. I couldn't wait a moment longer.

I grabbed a tissue from my pocket and sneezed.

Sniffling and wiping my nose, I mumbled, "I'm so sorry. It's my allergies. What you were saying was so serious, so true. I didn't mean to ruin the —"

He started laughing. It began with a chuckle and grew to a roar that was contagious. I joined in until tears were running from my eyes. In the joy of the moment, Seth threw his arms around me and I was engulfed in his warmth.

"Oh, Abby! You're wonderful! Where have you been all my life?" He laughed again, not in fun, but in true happiness.

As the moment passed, we both felt a little self-conscious. After all, we'd only met the night before and didn't know each other at all. We moved out of the embrace and I hoped I wasn't blushing.

He salvaged the moment. "I have to thank you. You've done something wonderful for me. After what happened last night, with Walt dying because of a stupid accident, I dashed out here this morning, desperate to escape reality. I worked frantically. One canvas is already finished and this one is well on its way. I didn't want to think about Walt and how unfair the fates could be." Seth shook his head sadly. "He was such a good guy and so talented." He waited a moment to get his emotions under control, then looked up at me. "But, a lovely lady came to visit and renewed my faith in the world. She showed me it's safe to stop and look again."

His words brought me great joy, until I realized that he was looking at the situation from a false angle. The world was even harsher than he imagined, because someone chose to violently strike down a creative individual. I didn't want to tell him the truth about the situation for fear it would affect, even destroy, his drive to paint during the festival.

"What is it?" He frowned. "Has something happened?"

The reality must have shown in my face and he caught the change. Why was I surprised? He was a trained observer.

He put his hands on my shoulders and held me at arm's length, searching my face. "There's something you're not telling me." He waited, but I couldn't bring myself to speak. "Abby, please? It's better to tell me than let my imagination run wild."

I pulled away gently and walked to the trunk of the

tree. I studied the bark, not wanting to see the pain on his face that my words would cause. He came up behind me and gently turned me around to face him. His eyes were pleading.

"All right, I'll tell you, but you must not say a word to anyone else," I let out a long sigh.

"Wait! Is it something that someone told you not to repeat?" I nodded. "Then, let me try to guess so you won't violate a trust." He looked away, thinking. "It must be about Walt and it must be worse than I've imagined." He looked to me for confirmation and read it in my eyes.

He looked up to the jade green leaves fluttering high above our heads. "Something worse than an accident," he said slowly. "That can only mean that somebody caused him to fall in the water." His eyes, haunted with grief, searched mine.

In barely a whisper, he said the words I could not. "Someone killed him."

I closed my eyes in confirmation and to take away the sight of his sadness. When I opened them again, silent tears were making tracks down his cheeks. I reached out and held him while he cried.

When he was calm, we walked in silence back toward his easel. I felt so guilty. I'd destroyed his concentration. My revelation had taken away his enthusiasm for painting.

"I shouldn't have come. I'm sorry."

"Nothing to be sorry about. It's not your fault. It is what it is." His steps were slow.

I stood in front of the easel. "Will you finish it?"

He joined me in looking at the painting. "It's really quite good, you know."

He looked at the scene and back at the canvas. "The light has changed."

"You said it would. You said you had it in your memory."

"Did I?" He sounded distant as his eyes darted from one element of the scene to another...

I tried a little playfulness to lighten his mood. "Yes, you did. And I believed you or I would have left long ago." When I didn't get a response, I said. "I must admit I'm in awe. I don't know how you do what you do, but I do know that it would be a shame to walk away from this painting. I can't imagine how you can capture such beauty so quickly."

He paused and cocked his head to the side a little, the same way Simon does when he's curious. Tentatively, he asked in a serious tone, "If you're really interested, I mean, really...would you like to meet me early tomorrow morning?"

It was more than an invitation. It was time for him to make a decision. Would he keep his commitment to the festival or give up? I could see the battle going on inside his head. Did he have the courage and strength to continue his work this week, even with all the sadness and emotion he felt?

"Will you be painting?" I held my breath as I waited for the answer.

Slowly, he smiled. His uncertainty was gone. "Yes, I'll be painting for the festival competition."

Relief flooded through me. "If I won't be in your

way, I'd be honored to meet you."

We exchanged cell phone numbers and made a plan that he would text me in the morning when he had settled on his first spot to begin painting. I would meet him to watch how a subject took form on the canvas.

I started to walk back to my car. "I'm leaving now, so you can get back to work. Do you mind if I bring my roommate?" The smile slide off Seth's face. "I promise Simon will be good." I paused for effect. "He's very well-behaved for a black Lab puppy."

As he realized what I'd said, his smile crinkled his eyes, sparking with fun. "Of course. Maybe I'll even put him in the picture."

Our laughter rippled across the field.

CHAPTER EIGHT

One specialty serving piece is for honey. The design may suggest a hive. It may include a small spoon with a deep bowl and a bee on the handle. One must never use a specialty item for the something other than its intended use.

—"The Butler's Guide to Fine Silver" Mr. Hollister, 1898

The next morning, I was up early and in the kitchen with the Fair Winds cook, Mrs. Clark. I wanted to take a few things with me in case Seth was hungry. She found a wicker basket that was perfect to hold a large thermos, cream and a variety of sweeteners because I didn't know how he drank his coffee. She packaged up a few pieces of country ham, a couple of boiled eggs and some of her jams and jellies. We were waiting for a batch of her famous biscuits to finish baking when Lorraine appeared in the doorway.

"My goodness, this is a lot of activity so early on a Monday morning. What's going on?"

Mrs. Clark avoided looking at her, as she answered, "Miss Abby is going on a picnic."

Lorraine looked at the pile of goodies in the basket. "You must have quite an appetite, Abby?"

"Oh, it's not all for me. Simon and I are going out for breakfast," I said, feeling shy suddenly.

Lorraine turned toward the ovens. "Do I smell biscuits, Mrs. Clark?" The cook nodded. Lorraine looked at the goodies again. "Since when does Simon eat biscuits with jam and honey?"

I tried to laugh, but it sounded more like a nervous giggle. "Simon is spoiled, but not that spoiled."

"I'm confused," Lorraine said, looking from me to Mrs. Clark and back again.

Dawkins, who now managed the main house of Fair Winds, floated into the room. Wearing, as usual, a dark jacket and a plain tie, he spoke in an equally muted tone. "It seems we are preparing a breakfast picnic for Miss Abigail to take on her visit with an artist working somewhere in the county. A Mr. Seth Myers, I believe."

I rushed to explain. "He's one of the plein air artists. You met him the other night at the party on Bruff's Island. He's going to show me how he starts a painting."

Why was I trying to justify an innocent little visit with an artist? Did Dawkins just sniff his disapproval? Usually, he didn't express an opinion about anything. I peered at him, trying to gauge his reaction, but he was as unreadable as a slab of cold marble.

Instead of clarifying things, he ignored me and asked Lorraine, "Madam, would you like some coffee?" He moved to the coffeemaker and, seeing how I'd seriously depleted the supply, glanced my way. "It won't take me a moment to make a fresh pot, since it's almost empty."

I'd been chastised in a most genteel way. Without another word, he went about the preparations.

Lorraine's gaze made me feel a little uneasy as she said, "Thank you, Dawkins."

Thankfully, she didn't ask me a direct question, though I knew what she was thinking, what they all were thinking. What about Ryan?

Ryan and I met during my first visit to the Eastern Shore, a time filled with secrets and events too tragic to dwell on. Lorraine took me to the Tilghman Island Day celebration and introduced me to her young friend – a tall hunk of a man about my age, with light brown hair, kissed by the sun. Over the last months, we spent a lot of time together and a strong relationship was developing between us, when he was called away on family business without a moment's notice. His father needed him, but he'd been gone for two months and contact with him was sketchy, even in this day of email, texts and sky phones. I wasn't sure what to think. There was no understanding between us, as Jane Austen might say.

Was it my fault that I was enjoying the company – and yes, the flirting – with a creative and accomplished man like Seth? It made me uncomfortable to think that Lorraine might not approve, but I didn't want to meet the question head on. I busied myself rearranging the contents of the basket, careful to leave room for the biscuits. I caught Lorraine and Mrs. Clark exchange a look in the mirror by the door. I needed to pack up and go before —

The timer dinged. Thank goodness, the biscuits were done. At the same time, my cell phone chimed.

Feeling a little guilty though I really shouldn't, I explained, "It's Seth. He said he would text me the directions to the place he's going to paint this morning." No one said a word.

I scurried around Mrs. Clark as she took the golden lovelies out of the oven and wrapped them in a tea towel. I carefully laid them in the open spot inside the basket, clamped it closed and rushed for the door.

"Abby," Lorraine sounded tentative, as if she wasn't sure she should say something. Then, it all came out. "Please be careful. The man is older… and stronger than you are. Someone was killed last night and—"

I turned to give her a smile. "I know, I always take care of myself. See you later. Come on, Simon." I fled to the car with my dog on my heels.

The sky was an achingly blue dome that extended all the way down to the horizon, marked here and there by a thin line of dark green or gray. High wispy clouds did nothing to dissipate the cooking rays already bearing down. It promised to be a hot one, but I was only feeling the warmth of excitement as I stowed the picnic basket in the trunk, clipped Simon into his harness and sped off with the top down. We were headed to Oxford, a little town about twenty miles from St. Michaels. This was another time when it was faster getting around by water than using roads. I had an option: take the ferry from Bellevue to Oxford. It would be a short, pleasant trip, but I wasn't sure how Simon would react to the grinding engine of the ferry boat. It could be a stressful crossing and I was in no mood for that. Instead, I turned on Route 33 toward Easton, and, at the light for the bypass, turned right and right again for the Oxford Road.

Going to Oxford was an adventure by itself. The

closest I'd come to the little town was hearing its bells across the water last fall while working on an obituary with Lorraine at Harraway Hall, her father's farm. Lorraine had told me that Oxford had once been a major commercial center that pre-dated the Revolutionary War and had gone through economic ups and downs over the centuries. Now, it was a tight-knit community with a character that was very different from St. Michaels and Easton. I was looking forward to seeing it… and meeting Seth.

The ride in the early morning air was refreshing. A lane for bicycling, a favorite pastime of both residents and visitors, paralleled the main road and wasn't for the faint of heart as it squeezed between the car lane and thick metal rails of the bridge as we crossed Peachblossom Creek.

Two large white horses having an early morning nibble ignored Simon's crazy barking as we whizzed by. A sign that read Country Club Road was like a last touch of civilization. Soon, the drive felt like an endless trip passing split rail fences, random houses and open fields of corn when another sign grabbed my attention. HELS HALF ACRE ROAD. It was either a misprint or the name of a family that settled on that bit of land. I'd have to ask Lorraine about it.

A sign warned that the speed limit was dropping to 40. I'd lived on the Shore long enough to know that when a town posted speed limits, they were strictly enforced by the local constabulary, and I slowed down. In front of a house, a man was sitting on an overturned bucket, putting a fresh coat of white paint on an old-fashioned wood fence with a trefoil at the top of the broad slats. Just a block further on, the road ran past a strip of water crowded with massive power cruisers and graceful sailboats tied up to rows of docks. I followed the bend and was greeted by quaint homes, their porches decorated with gingerbread trim and blooming flower gardens.

Seth said to watch for the Oxford Market on the right with its colorful display of plants and hanging baskets. I saw it and pulled in. Seth's truck was parked on the other side of the street. As I got out of the car, I spotted an artist across the street, standing like a scarecrow with a brush in one hand and her palette in the other. It took only a moment to back up and out of the way of her picture. She gave me a little wave in gratitude and went back to work.

Picking a place to paint is more than having a great view. At least she didn't set up in the middle of the street. I hope she can paint quickly.

"Okay Simon, we have arrived."

I took the blanket and picnic basket from the trunk and unhooked Simon from the back seat. "Be a good boy, please. No pulling or jumping, okay?" As if I'd given him the idea, he dragged me across the street to the grassy lawn of the park. A granite headstone emblazoned with a bright blue star and a black plaque read:

BLUE STAR MEMORIAL BY-WAY
A tribute to the Armed Forces of America
Oxford Garden Club
National Garden Clubs, Inc.

Again, I faced the challenge of finding Seth. The park was large with tall, leafy shade trees, benches, picnic tables, a play area with swings and a slide and the wide river beyond. Light posts with lanterns on top dotted the area. No sign of Seth. I gave up and somehow juggled my phone to send him a text. My phone signaled in response.

I see you. Keep coming toward the river.

It was slow going. Simon wanted to sniff every blade of grass, leave a calling card at every tree and generally thwart my forward progress. I didn't want to yell at him to hurry, but I was eager to get to the water's edge… and Seth. Instead, I kept up steady pressure from my end of the leash, that turned into tugging – he in one direction, me in another. It was an ordeal until we got to the edge of the grass where a little sandy beach with rocks and wild grasses grabbed his attention – and a handsome man caught mine. Seth was standing at his easel, his painting supplies set up next to it, ready to go to work. There was something about his smile as I approached that made the trip worthwhile.

"Good morning!" He called. "I was beginning to think I'd have to start without you."

"I'm sorry, it was — OH!" Simon pulled the leash right out of my hand and scampered over to Seth, madly sniffing his shoes and pant leg. I introduced them and smiled as they made friends. In moments, we spread out the blanket on the sand and ate until I thought I'd burst. Seth looked at the position of the sun and checked his watch.

"You said you wanted to see how an artist goes

about starting a new painting. Are you sure you want to know?"

Simon responded with a belch from too many bites of biscuit and plopped down on the grass. "Well, I would like to know," I said, a little embarrassed by Simon's manners, or lack thereof.

"All right, then," he said, getting up. "I'll try to keep it short."

"Of course, you have to work," I said, a little worried that he might think I was wasting his time.

"Well, there is that, but for someone who doesn't paint, it will probably sound like a dissertation. Okay, here goes." He started to pace. "When I think about setting up an easel at a certain spot, I've got to figure out what caught my eye. What is it about that view that I want to paint for someone else to see?"

"That carries a burden of responsibility, doesn't it? To think that you can capture something that someone else needs to see."

"And," he added. "A certain amount of narcissism, that I can do a painting that someone should see and even buy." He laughed, a little self-consciously. "I hope my ego is still under control. Many painters are so obnoxious. I can't stand to be around them."

"I know what you mean." He raised his eyebrows to encourage me to explain. "I saw it all the time when I was in software development in Washington, before I moved here to the Shore. It took a lot of confidence to tell a client that this was the way a program or website should work. The field was still evolving. We were breaking new ground with new code and applications almost every day. It seemed that the more arrogant a person was, the greater the chance that the system would fail."

He agreed. "Many of the successful artists who win competitions, awards and commissions are nice, supportive and fun."

"Like they really don't have anything to prove?" I suggested.

"That's it! That's exactly it."

I suggested, "People like Larry who I met at the party?"

"Yes." Then, his face lost its brightness a little. "And Walt."

"Have the other artists said anything about his death, like who they think might have killed him?"

He stared at the ground and slowly shook his head. "No, everybody loved him. They were so glad he was painting again." His eyes glistened with tears as he looked out toward the horizon. "I just can't believe it was one of us." He turned his back to me and wiped his eyes with his sleeve.

"He was the one who helped me improve my technique of organizing the scene in my mind. It's not an easy thing to do. You have to get the structure right or the painting will fail."

He held out his hand and pulled me to my feet. Simon raised his head, snorted and resumed his position on the cool sand.

At the easel, Seth pointed at the scene down the shoreline. "Let me show you. See the patch of grass in the foreground contrasting with dock after dock jutting out into the water and the buildings in the distance?"

I nodded. I was starting to see what he saw.

"What attracts you to this scene? Is it the light? The shadows? The boats and the water? The colors? A painter has to figure that out in the beginning. Then, he uses the light and dark values and colors to guide him throughout the process, the same way notes and rhythm lead you through a piece of music. You can't get distracted by the details in the beginning."

He moved me in front of the canvas.

"I'll show you something Walt taught me." His enthusiasm for his subject carried him past the pain of losing his friend. "Stand here. Look at the scene again, and squint. When your vision blurs, it's easier to see the values or intensities."

He led me away from the easel to an open view of the sky. "Here's a little trick for seeing color. Look up. The sky is blue, right?" I nodded. "But, it's not all the same blue. One area may have a little more red in the blue. Another has more green. That's what makes a painting interesting."

I squinted up at the clear blue sky. "How can you tell where the color changes?"

"Do this." He held his index finger up toward one area of the sky. "Now, focus on your finger and let the rest go out of focus. Do you see the color in a different way?"

"Yes," I wanted to see it as he did, but felt unsure. "I think so."

"Now, swing around and do the same thing. Are the blues the same?"

"No...no, they aren't." I was starting to see what he saw.

"They are not the same," he confirmed. "It's all in the light."

"Like you said yesterday." He smiled, pleased that I had really listened.

"We owe a lot to Sir Isaac Newton. He discovered that light was made up of all the colors of the rainbow. To work out the questions of color, artists took that spectrum of red at one end and violet at the other and joined the ends to make the color wheel. Every artist uses it to this day. You know, you might try your own hand at painting."

I laughed out loud. "Oh, no! I'm about as artistic as that oak tree, but I can appreciate good quality, design and craftsmanship. I'm working on the large sterling silver collection – knives, forks, teapots and the like – owned by my friend Lorraine who you met at the party. I'm cataloguing, replacing, filling in the gaps. We hope many of the pieces will be incorporated in a museum collection in Baltimore. And, I'm dealing with the massive inventory I inherited from my Aunt Agnes. After she died, I found out she was a closet silver dealer. But, that's a story for another time. You have work to do."

He looked around at the scene he'd chosen to paint. "I think you're right. The light is changing and I'd better get to work. This was a great picnic, thank you. I'll help you pack up."

"No need. I thought I'd sit there and finish my coffee, if that's okay?" I said.

He smiled again. "No problem at all. In fact, if you really like listening to painters ramble on about their art, you should come to Banning's Tavern in Easton. We gather there every afternoon to wind down from painting all day. Maybe you could tell me your story tonight."

"Maybe."

"Thanks again for breakfast. See you soon, I hope." He patted Simon on the head and went to his easel.

I poured myself some more coffee, closed my eyes and let the place have its way with my senses: the water lapped in a lazy rhythm on the sand; seagulls and land birds squawked and chirped in a raucous conversation; the leaves rustled over my head. It was getting warmer. I opened my eyes to see the effect of the sun's rays on the lazy Tred Avon River. Lorraine had said during our visit to Harraway Hall that there were all kinds of historical names and spellings for this river, including Third Haven, Tread Haven and Trade Haven. I heard the drone of a lone power boat on the river. I shielded my eyes to spot it in the glare. Instead, I saw Seth looking at me.

Even if I sat quietly, Seth wouldn't concentrate on his work the way he should. It was time to go. With a little wave, I got up and packed up the basket. I had the urge to kiss him good-bye, but grabbed Simon's leash instead and headed toward the street.

Simon was eager to cross the street and climb into his spot in the back seat.

I gave him a cookie and said I'd be right back. The artist trying to paint the market had disappeared, but someone else was working down the way. I made some noise as I walked up to her.

She raised her head when I said, "Good morning, Filly."

"Oh, Abby. What a surprise!"

"I saw you and wanted to say hello. Is that all right?"

"Of course. I'm past the age when I take a festival so seriously that I can't take a moment to talk to someone." She smiled, but there was a touch of sadness in her eyes.

"I see you're wearing your frog necklace." The fiery opals winked in the sun.

Her hand went to her neck. "You remembered! I wear my talisman whenever I work."

I looked at the beginnings of the work on her easel. Seth's painting lesson had opened my eyes. "Was it the black wrought iron fence that caught your imagination?" I asked.

"Yes." Excited, it was more of a trill than a word. "And the building has such strong lines. Someone said it used to be a bank."

The broad white lintel above the double front doors and the painted gray brick gave the building a solid and impressive appearance. It looked like it could weather any storm – economic or natural.

"It's not a bank anymore." Filly gave me a mischievous grin. "I must admit it was the name of the business that's there now that captivated me. It's a bookshop called Mystery Loves Company. Isn't that wonderful? It has a strong look yet, somehow, invites me in."

"You should paint the interior," I suggested. "There

must be lots of books inside. At least you'd be in the air-conditioning."

She frowned. "No, I can't do that. This is a plein air art festival. I have to paint outside for the canvas to qualify."

"Well, maybe you'll find an intriguing and cooperative proprietor who will pose outside… or at least, offer you a glass of water?"

"That's the spirit, Abby. You're catching on."

"Um, have you heard anything else… about Walt, I mean?"

Her shoulders slumped. "No, nothing. I think everybody's afraid to say anything in case the police jump to the wrong conclusion."

"Well, I'm glad to see you're doing better." Simon barked, scrabbling to get his feet up on the back of the seat. "Oops, I'd better leave you to it. My companion is getting impatient." We promised to stay in touch.

When I saw who was coming toward me on the sidewalk, I quickened my step. Jack, the local reporter, was spying down each street and alleyway, looking for Lord only knows what. I skipped into the street, hoping the cars would give some cover. Simon started to bark.

"Sh-h-h," I said, though it sounded more like a hiss. "Be quiet." He barked louder, of course. "Cookie." The word floated to his ears and he sat down, panting in anticipation.

I slide into the driver's seat and slipped him the promised cookie. As I put the car in gear, Jack spotted me.

His hand flew up in the air. "Hey, Hey!"

Would he jump into the street to make me stop? Not wanting to find out, I swerved down a side street and, after meandering among the one-way lanes, I was on my way out of town.

Is that how a famous star feels with the paparazzi on her trail, I wondered.

To celebrate my escape, I cranked up the radio and sang all the way back to Easton.

CHAPTER NINE

The silver traveler, an inkwell for used when travelling and about the size of a thumb square, presents potential problems. Often ornate, the intricate scroll work requires patient polishing to remove oils and tarnish in the crevices. Gently use a small natural bristle brush.

—"The Butler's Guide to Fine Silver" Mr. Hollister, 1898

After I got back to Fair Winds and emptied the picnic basket, I felt guilty. Not about meeting Seth. It was Monday, the beginning of the work week, and I'd played hooky. Armed with a cold bottle of water, I went to my office to find the top of my desk.

Someone once said that organization is the key to efficiency. It was a good rule to follow, especially when juggling so many different projects and details. Today, none of the items on my list of things to do sounded intriguing. Maybe the summer doldrums had set in. I did a few odds and ends, then tackled the endless filing. My heart wasn't in it. The only thing that was tickling my curiosity was the assortment of silver pieces in the Bruff portrait. I decided to do a little poking around.

Right away, I stumbled across an interesting

tidbit. Thomas Bruff was the first in a family of nine silversmiths who worked their art over the next 150 years on the Maryland Eastern Shore, in Baltimore and New York. Pieces made by his descendants appeared on auction, sales and museum sites, but I could only find one spoon by the first Bruff. That made the pieces in the portrait even more interesting.

There were three items in the Bruff portrait: a tankard, a covered bowl and some spoons. I might as well start with something easy, so I searched spoons.

The results were pretty basic: the concept dated back to prehistoric times when man drank using a shell. The Greeks and Romans developed the basic spoon shape. It wasn't until the end of the 14th century that the English reproduced it, but in wood. A little more reading revealed that word spoon came from an old English word, spon, which meant a splinter of wood!

Ouch!

A drawing of a metal spoon that resembled the Bruff spoons in the painting appeared as I scrolled down. It seems that type of spoon was very important to wine drinkers. Though a common drink, making wine wasn't a refined art in the 1600's. People would have to add as much as an ounce of sugar to a pint or sixteen ounces of wine, just to make it palatable. I winced at the thought.

Scrolling down a little further, there was a picture of a specialty spoon sitting next to the same type of covered bowl that was in the portrait. It wasn't a bowl at all. It was called a porringer. Today's experts claimed they weren't exactly sure about its purpose, but it was a very popular item during the second half of the 17th century, the time Thomas Bruff was working. The ones made in the New World were about four inches deep with a flat bottom for easy heating. A triangular-shaped handle or two on the side made it easy to feed stew or broth to a child or sick person. Goldilocks-style porridge was also an option.

What I read next made my stomach flip. An old medical procedure called bleeding often used a porringer. Someone would press it tightly against the skin to catch the 'bad blood' causing the illness as it flowed out of the patient.

Bled one day, fed the next. Yuck. That search definitely turned up more information about silver than I wanted.

Wait. Search. Silver. Searching for silver.

It hit me. I was back at the party, zooming around in the golf cart. The creepy man with the metal detector appeared in my mind. Did he have something to do with Walt's death? Maybe the man wanted to search the area where Walt had set up his easel? Maybe they got into an argument? His electronic device looked heavy. If the man lifted it and swung, it could do some damage to the artist's skull. Plus, it was a small island. It wouldn't take long for him to kill Walt, drag him into the water then walk to the place where Sara-V and I saw him. Did Detective Ingram know about him? Did he know he even existed? Somebody should tell him.

I looked at my Piaget watch. Most people my age rely on their phones for the time, but this watch had sentimental value. Gran gave it to me when I graduated from college, just before she died. It read just past five o'clock. Too late to call the detective's office? A new thought came to me. The artists would be gathering at Banning's. I bet the unassuming detective wouldn't be far away. I shut down my computer and slipped Simon only one cookie so it wouldn't spoil his dinner. Back in the car, speeding down the road to Easton, I refused to admit that I was making the drive to see Seth as well.

The doors at the entrance to Banning's Tavern were made of beveled glass set in intricate designs. They gave me the feeling that I was entering a very special, very unique place. I had to push hard to open the heavy door. Once inside, the warmth of an unspoken welcome reached out to me. Maybe it was the old wood of the bar area with its golden patina. Maybe it was the collection of people enjoying lively conversation or playful banter. It didn't feel like a tavern, it felt more like a club where people were friends and cared about one another. Plein air people, wearing festival ID's on lanyards around their necks, blended in with Banning's regulars at the bar during Happy Hour. A lady bartender, statuesque and attractive, handled each customer with ease, warmth and friendly chitchat. Anthony and Janet were sitting at a table, deep in conversation with some important-looking people I didn't recognize.

In that awkward moment of figuring where to sit, a voice from behind me sent puffs of air against my ear and chills down my back.

"Gotcha! You gave me the slip this morning. You are not going to do it again." Jack, the reporter from the local paper, had slipped up behind me.

"Look, I don't know what—"

"It's okay, I get it all the time. I'm a reporter." He shrugged, dramatically. "Goes with the territory." I tried to move away but the crush of the crowd was too much. "Want to get rid of me? Give me something I can use and I'm gone. Easy as that."

I doubt it, I thought. If I give you anything, you'll latch on for more and then, I'd have to punch you in the nose to get rid of you.

"Let me tell you what I think," he said. "Seems to me that the investigation is at a crossroads. Why don't we take a table, have a drink and do a little creative thinking outside the box?"

I didn't hold a whole lot of hope for this man's career if he used as many clichés in his writing as he did in his speech. I wanted to get rid of this guy. Looking as earnest as I could, I said, "Look, I don't know anything you don't. I'm just interested in the art festival, that's all. There's no other connection."

He narrowed one eye and looked at me with suspicion. "Yeah, the same way you weren't connected with the communion chalice in St. Michaels?"

I shook my head. "This isn't St. Michaels. It's a whole different ballgame." Wow, is it possible to catch a cliché bug? I shook it off. "You need to talk to the police here, not me. Good-bye."

A group at the bar raised their glasses. Someone made a toast, "To Walt!"

"To Walt!" they said as one. The artists were remembering one of their colleagues.

I felt like I was intruding and turned to leave when I felt a tap on my shoulder. Certain that it was Jack again,

I started to snap, "Leave me..."

"Hello again." It was Larry, the artist holding a cowboy hat. "You were at the party on Saturday, weren't you?"

"Yes, I didn't mean to—"

"Butt in, as we remember one of our own? Nonsense." He raised his voice to get the attention of the others at the bar. "Hey, make room for one of our Friends." He was referring back to Saturday's party for the Friends of Plein Air. "Remember, we all need our friends."

Everyone laughed as they shuffled around to open up a bar chair for me. Larry stood behind me and made sure I was served a glass of white wine and met those around us. In moments, everyone seemed to settle in.

I had to lean close to Larry so he could hear me above the hum of conversation and music. "It must be hard for you and your friends to paint after... after what happened."

He took a deep drink of his beer. "Well, we had to make a choice. We could all give up on the festival, go home and be sad or we could stay, console one another and paint the very best we could. We talked about it and decided that Walt would want us to celebrate life and the art he loved. So, here we are." He raised his glass a little and murmured, "To Walt." I too raised my glass to drink to his friend.

I explained that this was my first plein air festival and I was still trying to learn the guidelines. "I understand you have to complete two paintings for the competition by Friday at noon, is that right?"

He nodded with a smile. "Most everybody does more than that."

I shook my head. "I'm not an artist so I can't imagine how you do that."

He shook his head and smiled. "I guess if I focused on the time factor, it would make me crazy. I can't wait for the muse to show up or I'd be sitting beside the river for months. No, I set my easel and let the energy, the feeling of the scene—its challenges and unique aspects—boil up and I'm off into a world that is the art. I focus on what I'm doing and somehow, it all comes together in the time allotted. Though, I must admit that as things tighten up…" He tilted his head to the side and raised his eyebrows as if facing something inevitable.

I didn't understand what he was talking about, so I asked. "Do you mean your muscles tighten up after all that time at an easel?"

"No," he laughed. "Well, maybe. This body isn't as flexible as it once was. I meant that as the geographical restrictions they put on us tighten up, so does the strain. On the first two days of the festival, we're allowed to paint anywhere on the Delmarva Peninsula, from the Bay to the ocean beaches or everywhere in between. Of course, attendance at the Friends party last Saturday was mandatory, but that was all about access to a private place, meeting people, good food and fun… at least it was supposed to be fun." His eyes clouded as he remembered what happened to Walt.

I hoped to lighten the moment. "Where did you paint today?"

"Here in Talbot County. Same is true for tomorrow."

The man sitting on my other side turned and joined our conversation. It was nice to see another familiar face: Paul, my amiable dinner partner from Saturday night. "This county is a big, beautiful area with lots of possibilities – street scenes, waterfront, boats – there's almost too much so it's hard to pick a subject and stick with it."

A woman squeezed into our little group to order a refill and add, "You can't forget the one iconic subject of Plein Air." To the bartender, she said, "Can I have another Harp, please?"

Larry introduced Claudia Wainwright, an artist in her 40's I guessed, from Ohio. Her face had a calm expression, as if she'd been caught in a storm and survived.

I asked her. "What iconic subject is that?"

"It's the one thing that everyone seems attracted to paint at some point or another: the cows, those black and white cows at Cooke's Hope Farm outside Easton." Claudia continued, in a low whisper. "Though I can't imagine why." Her laugh was like a tinkling bell. "Why paint cows when you can paint water vistas and boats? Boats are everywhere. There's everything from little well-worn rowboats to big modern sailboats."

Paul added, "I like the simple lines of workboats and the skipjacks are elegant in a strong sort of way." His index finger tapped the bar, another nervous habit. "You only find them on the Chesapeake Bay, right?"

"Yes, I think so," I answered.

Claudia picked up her beer and held the full glass up to her nose. "I love that sweet aroma. This is a great beer for a day like today." She dove back in the crowd.

Larry brought up a favorite subject of his. "I like the old buildings by the drawbridge. They're so weathered and rustic. They look like they've been there forever."

An older woman, who wore her black and gray hair pulled back into a bun on top of her head, wedged herself into the narrow slot left by Claudia. "Larry, you and your boats and falling-down buildings," she teased. She waved for the attention of the bartender. "Another Corruption, please. It's a new craft beer for me – thanks for the suggestion. I love the name, too."

"And a good evening to you, Margaret," Larry said.

"If you're talking about painting in Easton, you can't forget the little gardens tucked away here and there. There's always something blooming this time of year. You can never lose with flowers, as I've proven time and again." And with that, she left.

"I leave the flowers to artists like Margaret. They have the eye and the patience for all those petals. Give me my boats and buildings like the ones on Tilghman Island. There are some gems just waiting to be discovered. I'll be down there tomorrow before the crab feast."

"That's right, the island is in Talbot County."

"We don't get reined in again until Wednesday and Thursday when we have to paint inside the city limits of Easton. You'll see easels lining the brick sidewalks so people can try their hand at the old buildings and street scenes."

Larry continued. "The shop owners are very patient as we clutter up the sidewalks."

Paul picked up the thread. "It will seem like we're

everywhere. When you've got more than fifty artists vying for the best spots and subjects, it gets a little crazy. You can see what your competition is doing just by walking around. You might even have to share your spot."

"But, you're all friends, right?"

He thought for a moment. "Yeah, I guess so. Some have known each other for years, others are more like acquaintances. As the deadline gets closer, collectors and visitors start arriving. The tension builds until it's like the heat and humidity hanging in the air, making us all sweat. Everything comes to a head on Friday night."

"Time for another big party," I said, getting caught up in the momentum of the festival.

Paul didn't look so happy. "Yeah, the Collectors' Preview Party is on Friday evening when each of us can offer up to ten paintings for sale. Only two of them must be done during the festival. Many of the artists bring the additional paintings with them. Others like to do all ten during this week. It's a great way to take advantage of so many buyers in one place. The big guys have their followers so they'll have good sales."

"Do you?" I asked.

His reaction lacked enthusiasm. "I did last year. All my paintings sold, because I won first prize. I don't know what will happen this year."

Larry said, "The pressure's on this year. They've doubled the cash prize for the tenth anniversary of the festival."

Sounding almost depressed, Paul went on. "People are buzzing already about who will win. I've even heard that some of them are betting each other on who will win. Everything tightens up: The area where we can paint is smaller. People will start talking about the paintings they've seen and who will win the big money. It will be in the air and we'll sense it. Announcement of the winners and the sale are almost a relief."

"I see what you mean." I glanced over Larry's shoulder as we talked over the noise and saw his wife Rebecca breeze in and look around the bar. When she spotted us, her face went dark.

I pulled away from him. "I think your wife is here."

CHAPTER TEN

A silver lorgnette requires special attention since the handle is exposed to skin oils when the spectacles are held up to the eyes. The solution used to clean the glass must not harm to the silver frames.

—"The Butler's Guide to Fine Silver" Mr. Hollister, 1898

Rebecca made her way to us and stood close to her husband who kissed her cheek. She smiled at me with her thin lips. Time in the sun had given her a warm glow. In moments, she had maneuvered him to a table by the window where they could sit alone.

I don't know why, but I felt a little embarrassed that Rebecca caught me standing close to her husband. How much it would help Larry to have his wife with her little jealous streak at the festival? I nursed my wine, played with the napkin and avoided eye contact with the people sitting around the rich wood bar. Seth wasn't there. He probably decided he had better things to do, like painting a prize-winning picture.

What am I doing here? I don't belong to this group. I can't even draw stick figures. I had just about made up my mind to leave when a woman a few seats away said something that rose above the din.

"...and there is that lovely pine tree that I want to include as an element." I didn't know her name, but it was obvious that a day of painting en plein air had taken its toll. Her dull brown hair hung around her face and her nose was sunburned.

Margaret had moved into Larry's vacant seat and ordered another refill. "It's a great tree with some interesting lines. Don't forget to include the wasp's nest that's hanging in its branches."

The other artist went pale. "Wh-what wasp's nest?"

"The one in that tree. Didn't you see it?" The woman took a deep drink of her dark beer.

"No-o, I didn't. I should have noticed it since I'm so allergic to bee stings."

"I know, that's why I brought it up. Just watching out for you." Margaret toasted the woman and took another swig of her beer while watching the other artists gathered around in the mirror behind the bar.

The woman raised her glass in return. "Thank you, Margaret. I had no idea." She gathered up her things and slid off her stool. "I guess I'd better take another look around now, so I don't waste time in the morning looking for a new place to paint."

"See you later. Good luck." She swiveled in her chair so she could get a good look at the artists, as if she was taking roll.

I felt compelled to say something. "I heard what you said just now. That was a really nice thing for you to do. I guess you all try to watch out for each other."

Margaret studied my face as if it was under a

microscope. "You're not one of us. Are you with the local festival?"

"I'm just a friend. I went to the party on Saturday and met some of the artists, like Larry and Seth."

"And I bet they weren't together when you did," Margaret said with a little huff as she lifted her glass.

"Ah, no, now that I think of it, they weren't."

"Figures. Oh, they'll be civil to each other in public, but they shouldn't push it. It's too soon."

"What happened?" I asked, not sure I really wanted to know. The festival was supposed to be about the art, not petty emotions. "The festival just started on Saturday."

Margaret put her elbows on the bar and got comfortable. "It started long before we got to Easton. All the festival organizers on the circuit try to make sure there's enough area with interesting elements for all the artists so we're not working on top of each other. I think the trouble started at a Plein Air event out west. California, I think. I wasn't there. Too far for me to travel from Massachusetts."

"What did you hear?"

Margaret hung her head and moved it slowly back and forth as if exasperated by the story. "What always happens when two people think they have to paint the same scene from the same spot to get the same angle. What are we, in kindergarten? But boys will be boys and they got into it a little bit, at least that's what I heard."

I stared at her as I thought about the mild, sensitive man I'd had breakfast with that morning. "Did it come to blows?"

"Oh no, we don't hit, but we can get nasty. It happened again at a festival a few weeks ago. I heard it got hot. Remember, I'm not speaking from firsthand experience, but that's what I heard."

"Why does that happen?"

Margaret pushed back some strands that had escaped from the messy bun on top of her head. "Larry and Seth have similar styles and are attracted to the same types of subjects. That bodes well for Seth because he may follow in Larry's successful footsteps, but the guy has got to understand that we're all in this together. Give a little, take a little."

"Is that why you told that other woman about the wasp's nest?"

She wiggled her eyebrows. "Maybe there's a nest, maybe there isn't. I like that tree and want to see what I can do with it. Don't want to get in a spitting match like Seth and Larry." She drained her glass and pushed herself up from the bar. "I've gotta get going if I'm going to set up to do a nocturne tonight." She snickered. "Sounds fancy, doesn't it?"

"Isn't that a type of musical piece?" I asked.

"Could be. Not smart about music. To us, it means a painting done at night: nocturne… nocturnal. Get the connection?" I nodded. "Lord knows, it will be cooler than painting during the day. One thing we can always count on at Plein Air: the heat. Thought I'd try one to see if I could get ahead. If I'm going to make some money next weekend, I have to finish ten paintings this week. Ten!"

"I understand you only have to do two for the

competition. You could have brought other paintings to make it easier on yourself."

"That's right, but I've got too much stuff to get my finished canvases into my car. Do you know how much it costs to ship paintings? It's robbery, I tell you. I'm allowed to sell up to ten paintings here and I mean to have ten for them to buy." Margaret turned on her heel and muscled her way through the crowd.

The plein air art festival certainly had its share of personalities.

CHAPTER ELEVEN

Some tankards are made of bone, horn or crystal using silver only for the lids, bands and feet. It is believed that poison in the drink will cause discoloration. Keep polish only on the silver.

—"The Butler's Guide to Fine Silver" Mr. Hollister, 1898

"Look who's here." Paul bellowed over the noise. An older couple was making their way to the bar. "Come on over," he said, gesturing madly. "Take my seat. Barkeeper, give them whatever beer they want and put it on my tab."

As everyone shifted around to accommodate the newcomers, Paul explained that he'd stayed with them last year during the festival. "They were my host family. I wish I was with them this year. They were my lucky charm."

The woman leaned over and put a comforting hand on Paul's arm. "They said they needed our extra room for Larry since Rebecca came with him."

Her husband joined in the conversation. "She brought some work with her – files and papers and a computer and he has his painting supplies, of course."

"They're such a lovely couple," she added. "His wife gets up early every morning, gets his coffee ready, makes sure he eats something, even lays out his pills and vitamins. She doesn't want him to feel like he's dealing with it alone."

"Yeah," said her husband. "Larry and I are both dealing with high blood pressure. I think he's doing better than I am."

"Another glass of wine?" the pretty woman tending bar asked me.

"No," Paul said. "Give her your list of craft beers. If you learn about them, you'll learn to love 'em, I guarantee it."

"Thanks, but I don't drink beer very often."

"That's because you don't know about it." He ordered up a beer sampler. "And pour one for me, too," he said to the bartender. He grinned at me. "That way I can drink right along and help you identify what you're tasting."

He had to twist his short, pudgy body up and on to the bar chair. The extra weight, probably from his preference for beer, didn't help. It wasn't exactly a beer gut around his middle, just some extra padding. I did a quick scan of the artists at the bar. They all had a little cushy look to them, a result of sitting or standing for long hours at the easel. The sheer nature of plein air artists meant they worked outdoors which gave many of them a warm, healthy glow. For some, their skin hadn't fared as well and tended to look a little weathered. For the men, it gave them a rugged look – like Seth. The effect on the women was a hard, not ladylike appearance

– like Margaret.

The bartender put down two trays of four small glasses filled with different beers. Trying to be polite, I sipped the one with the lightest color.

"You know I won this Plein Air competition last year, right?" Paul said.

"Yes, someone mentioned it."

He pressed his hands onto the rich wood of the bar, spread his fingers apart and looked at them. "These hands set up the canvas, mixed the paints and used the brushes that created the painting the judge announced was the best." He folded his hands together and set them down on the bar. "The question is, can they do it again?"

"I'm sure they can," I said, not knowing exactly what I was supposed to say. If he was like some ultra-sensitive artists, one comment from me might skew the whole festival for him. Being supportive seemed the best approach.

"Some say they can't." With a big breath, he broke his hands apart and dropped two fists back on the bar. "They're wrong. What do they know? They've never won the prize. They don't know what it's like." Slowly, he raised his eyes and they went soft, remembering. "There you are in a packed room of artists, collectors, the media – people who know and love art. Know what I mean?"

I quickly took a sip from another sample glass to buy time to come up with a good comment. The bitter taste made my mouth pucker. I fought the reaction, worried that Paul would think I was reacting to what he said instead of what had attacked my taste buds. "Um, I can only imagine."

"It's a thrill unlike anything else you've ever experienced."

"I'm sure."

He really wasn't listening to me as he plowed on. "To hear your name announced in a packed room. It was the greatest feeling I've ever had in my life. Do you know what I mean?"

I shook my head slowly. "I'm afraid I can only imagine."

He pointed his index finger around the bar of artists happily chatting in small groups. "That's all most of them can do, imagine what it feels like." He jabbed his index finger on his chest. "I know." He drooped in his place. "I should win this year's prize. Prove to them that I'm that good. They jacked up the prize money and they all came out of the woodwork." His eyes traveled around the room. "Like they'll only paint for big money. Me, I paint because it's in my soul."

"I'm sure." My fingers edged toward my check sitting on the far edge of the bar.

"Last year was a breakthrough for me." His words were starting to slur.

"That's good."

"But the judge…"

I perked up. "What about the judge? I haven't heard about him."

"Oh, he's known internationally. I don't want to think that he'd award the prize based on somebody's reputation, rather than the quality of the paintings done during this festival."

"I doubt that would happen. Favoritism would harm his reputation as well as the prestige of the festival."

He tightened his lips and gave me an appraising look. "So you say. We'll see if they appreciate my work or if they try to push me aside. Mark my words, when it comes to my art, I can push back. I can do this. I just need the right inspiration and for people to get out of my way." Paul was slurring his words more, which made me wonder if a lesson about beer was only an excuse for him to drink. "Shall we try another sampler?"

"No, I think I've had enough." I stood up.

"You're right." Without another word, he staggered away.

A tug on my arm made me turn. Filly had materialized next to me. It was good to see her smiling. "Hello again, it looks like you're feeling better than the last time I saw you."

"Oh yes, I'm doing much better now. I'm worried about Paul. I saw you talking to him just now. Did he say anything to you about leaving the festival?

I jerked my head back in surprise. "No, he was talking about winning the whole thing again. You need to tell him not to go. It will look suspicious."

"It's not as easy as that." Filly's eyes darted around to be sure no one was listening to our conversation. She moved in closer and lowered her voice. "Paul has a secret. You're not one of us. It shouldn't matter if you know." She flicked her eyes up and stared deep into mine. "If you tell anyone, even if I'm dead, I'll come back and haunt you."

That was a little dramatic. I raised my hands in submission. "My lips are sealed." Unless, I thought, it's important information to the murder investigation.

She leaned closer to me and mumbled, "Paul is blocked."

"Blocked? Blocked from the festival?" It didn't make sense.

"He got an automatic invitation to this year's event because he won last year."

"That's bad?"

"In his case, yes it is. He says he's been limping along with his work ever since. He says his creativity is drying up. I've seen it happen time and again. Artists aren't sure they can live up to the hype and they freeze."

"It sounds serious."

"Oh, it is," she said. "I told him to forget about expectations and enjoy the moment of creating a painting."

"Maybe he doesn't have anything to worry about. George, the collector, said that no one has repeated a win at this festival."

"That's true. Walt got close once. Years ago, he won the festival's first prize then, came in second the following year. I don't think any of that matters," Filly added in a strained voice. "He told me that he's thinking of leaving."

"That's not a good idea." As soon as the words were out of my mouth, I knew I'd made a mistake.

Filly searched my face. "It's the police, isn't it? They would make certain assumptions, wouldn't they?" Her face was tight with worry. "Because somebody killed

Walt, didn't they?"

Me and my big mouth. Too late, I clamped my mouth shut.

"I knew it!" She squealed, though no one heard her over the noise of conversations and loud music. Self-conscious, she moved closer to me. "I knew it. Walt would never do anything so stupid. When his wife got sick, he started obsessing about safety. It changed him." She shook her head so hard, her curls danced. "No, he would never walk so close to the water's edge that he could fall in. Never." She took a sip of an amber liquid in a small glass. Filly would take her liquor neat. No froufrou drinks with little umbrellas for this lady. She'd analyzed the situation and reached a logical conclusion, at least the one that worked for her.

Around us, the room grew quiet except for the music playing from overhead. All eyes were trained on the front door of the tavern, locked on Detective Mike Ingram.

CHAPTER TWELVE

Now that the strawberry is a favored fruit, inspect the silver pieces purported to be a strawberry spoon. To meet the demand for pecuniary gain, unscrupulous proprietors are selling the bowl of a plain, old spoon welded onto a handle embossed with fruit and foliage.

—"The Butler's Guide to Fine Silver" Mr. Hollister, 1898

The detective worked his way into the room and signaled the bartender.

"National Bo?" she called out and he nodded.

Paul stumbled back to the bar. "Is that a local beer?" Paul asked the bartender as she pulled a glass.

"It sure is. If you like just plain beer, you should try it."

It's funny how people react when there's a police officer in the room. Even if they haven't done anything wrong, they do things that suggest they are guilty …of something. I glanced around the bar and saw signs of it: one woman was biting her lip; Paul had a thin film of perspiration appearing on his forehead. Most people kept their eyes down, captivated by the drink in their glasses.

The bartender held up the full glass high in the air and put it down next to me. I was surprised to see that Filly had melted away. I caught a glimpse of her bouncy white curls outside as she slipped around the corner. Had she run away from the cop? Why?

It didn't take Ingram long to slide through the crowd since it seemed to part for him. He was in the chair next to me, taking a drink of his beer. This is what I wanted – to talk to him about the creepy metal detector man – but I felt awkward in front of so many people. Gradually, people relaxed and restarted their conversations.

"That's the best part of a cold beer," he said, without looking at me. "The first drink."

How do I start a conversation that might point a finger at an innocent person with a man I barely know?

There was no need to worry. Detective Ingram took another swig and said, again without looking at me, "You get around, don't you? Find out anything?"

I took a sip of my wine and noticed my hand was a little shaky. With my elbow planted on the bar and my chin in my hand, I said, "I want to ask you something about last Saturday."

"And I thought I asked the questions. Ask away. If I can answer I will." He realigned the napkin under his glass.

"Did you know that there was a man on the property that day who wasn't an artist or with the festival?" His eyes shifted toward me with interest. "The man paid his way into the Friends of Plein Air organization and into the event so he could wander around the property with a metal detector."

Ingram sat up like a shot. Seeing that people noticed, he eased back against the chair again. "And you waited until now to tell me? The man could be on the moon by now," he hissed, just above a whisper. "You think this is helpful?"

"I'm sorry. I thought —"

"You thought… what? That I knew? How… if no one tells me? I wasn't there, but you were." Casually, he looked at the people around the bar who were involved in their own conversations, but glancing over at him from time to time. He passed his hand over his hair and took another sip of his beer, trying to appear calm and uninterested. "Do you have anything else, like a name?"

I described the man as best I could, but it was very general.

"Well, that fits about twenty percent of the men in this county, let alone the Shore." He picked up his glass and finished his beer.

"Wait, the volunteer who took me around that day in the golf cart… oh, what was her name? They had words. She thought the man was trespassing and reported him to the festival people." The name floated to the surface and I was surprised that I could have forgotten it. "Yes, you should talk to Sara V. Gordon."

He placed his empty glass back on the bar. "That's better than nothing. Thank you."

The bartender, good at her job, was right there offering a refill. He shook his head, then turned straight at me and raised his voice. "If Walt was such a good guy and a great friend, as everyone says, people should help us find his killer."

Killer. The word fell like a rock in the pool of water, creating ripples of silence. He pulled himself out of his chair as he looked from one person to another. He walked slowly to the door, a murmur of voices following him. At the door, he looked around at everyone in the bar.

"Yes, you should help. I'm around." The detective waited for a response. There wasn't one. He pushed open the heavy beveled glass door and left.

Curious eyes swung back in my direction. With that announcement, Ingram had drawn me into the circle of suspicion. I didn't know Walt, never even met him. The others didn't know that, but I wasn't part of the artists' circle. They turned away, wanting nothing to do with me. Walt's apparent murder and the police presence were affecting the festival and poisoning the atmosphere. A voice next to me confirmed it.

"Nobody will talk to you now that they know you're friendly with the police," said Claudia. "But I will. Walt was my friend. My Midwestern values tell me to dive in, not walk away. This matters. Not only does the Sixth Commandant say, Thou shalt not kill, this isn't good for the arts or our creativity. Rumors were flying around before that policeman dropped the bomb. People will be too busy wondering who and why. It will be amazing if people can work at all."

"Why do you think Walt was killed?" I asked trying to ignore the sly glances aimed our way.

At first, Claudia seemed uncomfortable with my question. I watched as her jaw set and she nodded her head once signaling she had made a decision. "I'll tell you that last Saturday night, when we heard that Walt had been found floating in the water, people started wondering if it was more than an accident. They didn't use the word murder, but they danced all around it. They were thinking it's all about the prize."

"Because of the money?"

She nodded. "The money and the prestige. They're saying somebody is killing off the competition." She laughed a little at the irony, no happiness in it. "They forget there are more than fifty artists in this competition, many of them very good. The killer…" She tripped over the word. "Whoever did this would have to knock off at least a few more to improve his chances of winning."

"Or her," I added. She gave me a quizzical look. "It could have been a woman."

Claudia paused for a moment to consider what I said, then nodded. "You're right, of course." A shiver ran through her body. "It's so ridiculous. We're getting distracted. The police think we're here for the fame and fortune. They forget that it's about the art. If you do good work, you've already won, no matter what the judge thinks." She shrugged. "But, that's something even the artists forget sometimes."

I was impressed by what she had to say. "Have you been at this a long time?"

"Yes, it's a little harder now that I'm older and shouldering all the responsibilities of being a single mom." She checked the time on her phone. "As a matter of fact, it's getting late for me. I still have to get ready for tomorrow's round of painting and I want to call my boys. If you're leaving, you can walk outside with me."

It was a relief to leave all those inquisitive eyes inside the bar. As we strolled along the brick sidewalk, a breeze rustled the leaves and brought a little respite from the July heat. We walked in a relaxed silence. Maybe that's why she felt comfortable asking a personal question.

"I couldn't help but notice that you were keeping a close eye on the doors into Banning's. Were you waiting for someone?" Claudia asked. "Were you waiting for Seth?"

I didn't respond, but the answer must have been all over my face. She put her arm through mine and patted my hand. "Don't worry. Seth is a friend. He said he'd met somebody special and you stood out. When you've been doing plein air festivals as long as I have, you start to recognize the same faces from one season to the next. But you're a fresh face. I wouldn't have thought I'd find one here at the Easton festival. Tell me, who is Abby?"

I almost sighed with relief. I thought she wanted to discuss Seth or give me a warning. Instead, she wanted me to talk about myself. That was easy. "I'm new to the Eastern Shore, as well as Plein Air. After graduation, I left my hometown of Seattle and came to Washington, D.C. to work as a software developer for government contractors, like so many other people. I took a gamble and signed on with a startup that met hard times. Just as I was dealing with unemployment – resumes, job interviews and all – I discovered that my great Aunt Agnes had been a dealer for many years."

Claudia looked at me with a barely-veiled look of shock.

I really have to stop playing to people's natural assumption that I mean a drug dealer. But it's so much fun.

I shook my head. "Not what you think. She bought and sold fine sterling. I had no idea until the estate attorney had eight large cartons of silver delivered to my doorstep."

"It sounds like a queen's treasure," she said, her eyes wide.

"I guess it was. I was out of work and second-guessing my chosen career. It wasn't fun anymore. If I'd been really honest, it was never a red-hot reason to get up in the morning. I was just making a living."

"What did you do? Did you keep the silver for your own use?" she asked, eager to know.

I couldn't suppress my giggle. "No, no. I have my family's silver and that's enough for any girl. I started offering pieces on eBay and that's what led to my move to St. Michaels. A woman here won an auction for an angel food cake breaker. One thing led to another. We became good friends and she hired me to sort out her huge collection that's come to her from mothers, aunts and cousins. It should keep me busy for a while."

I skipped over the part about how my cake breaker was used as a murder weapon and all the secrets that came to light.

"Funny how things work out," she sighed. "You're lucky to be doing something you enjoy, all the time. I wish I could make a living with my art. I'm getting closer, but I'm not comfortable quitting my day job, not yet."

"I'm happy here, doing work I enjoy and learning about this area."

"It's always been a favorite area of mine," she said. "There are almost too many subjects and scenes to paint. If you don't like what you see, just walk a little farther… or just turn around."

"I don't paint, but I know what you mean."

"Did you first meet Seth at the party on Saturday?" she asked.

Oops, I didn't expect that question. "Yes, I did. He seems to be a very talented artist."

She nodded slowly. "He is. Growing into his potential, I think. He's very fortunate to be able to devote all his time to his work. I usually wait for a festival that's closer to home or go off someplace for a few hours to paint by myself. It's a little hard for me to get away with my two kids. Family and friends volunteer to help. Even their dad takes them sometimes though he still doesn't understand why I have to paint." She looked down at the pavement. "He thought I should concentrate on him, all the time. I made a nice home for us all, but he wanted more."

She put her hands in her pockets. "Once, after the boys came along, he went with me to a weekend festival, a wonderful gathering of creative people interested in the same things I was, like composition, values, painting techniques, you know. He was bored out of his mind," she said with resignation. "But he saw how friendly the artists and collectors were and got the crazy idea that we were all sleeping together." She scratched her forehead, as if she was still getting the idea through her skull. "It made sense to him that he could play around while I was away. He found Tiffany, a blonde twenty-something who saw her chance and had him in divorce court almost before I knew what was happening." She gave me a big smile. "It's okay, it's really better for me. Now, I make arrangements for the boys to do something fun and I get to paint… without all the fighting."

What do you say when someone tells you such a terrible thing? I kept walking and glanced up at the trees arched overhead, as if they were the most interesting thing on the planet.

She went on. "I tell you all this, because things are not always what they seem at these festivals. I don't want you to get the wrong idea."

"Do you think that's why Larry's wife is here? Does she have the wrong idea?"

"I hope not, because Larry really loves her and is so happy she's here. He spends a lot of time on the road and in his studio. It's his career now. Of course, I'm sure he'd be glad to have her find something else to do during part of the day, instead of following him around everywhere. It can get boring to watch paint dry, as they say." She chuckled at her own joke and I relaxed.

"Do you need a ride back to your host family's house?" I asked.

She squared her shoulders. "No, the walk will do me good. It's close. I need to focus on what I did today and what I'm going to do tomorrow. Just like everything else, it's all about putting one foot in front of the other." Even in the soft light of the street lamp, I could see the color coming back to Claudia's cheeks. "I never expected things to turn out this way. I'm thriving and so are my boys. That's what is important. I better get going. Tomorrow is going to be a busy day. Maybe the police will come up with some answers. Good night, Abby." We hugged and went our separate ways.

CHAPTER THIRTEEN

Silver is a soft metal. It must be combined with another metal to craft silver serving and flatware pieces for the dining room. An older piece may contain more silver than pieces made today and require special care to prevent damage.

—"The Butler's Guide to Fine Silver" Mr. Hollister, 1898

When I got back to Fair Winds, I went into the main house looking for Simon. I followed my instincts and made my way to the library.

"I should have known I'd find Simon here in the library, curled up at your feet, Lorraine. Sometimes I wonder if he's really your dog and sleeps at the cottage only to humor me."

She laughed with delight, because dogs were dear to her and Simon was a favorite. "Oh Abby, if you only knew how he pouts when you're not here. When he heard the kitchen door open, his head popped up off his paw and his tail wagged like it was going to fly off."

"That's not what I saw when I came in," I responded.

"Maybe not, because I think your puppy is becoming coy and calculating."

Simon raised his head as if he understood

everything we said and made a little whimpering sound. "See?" Lorraine continued. "He's acting as if I've falsely accused him. What an act."

We laughed together and I sat down on the floor next to Simon who promptly climbed into my lap. "He's too big to sit in my lap anymore. He hangs over."

"Wait until he hits eighty, ninety pounds or more. Then, you'll really have something to complain about."

Simon nuzzled and gave me a long, wet lick on my face. As I reached for a napkin, I noticed the breeze cool against my skin. "You've opened all the windows to catch the breeze instead of relying on the air conditioning?"

"There's something refreshing about a summer breeze off the water after the hot sun has gone down. I thought I was going to melt away today. But I suppose it wasn't too hot for your breakfast picnic this morning."

It seemed that Simon wasn't the only one in the room who could be coy and calculating. "No, it was really nice, though this evening things were a little testy among the plein air people." She gave me a quizzical look. "I went to Banning's where everybody tends to gather after a hard day of painting."

"Everybody?"

It felt like she was asking about Seth, someone I wasn't ready to discuss. Instead, I swung the conversation in a different direction. "I saw Janet and Anthony busy with some important-looking people. I didn't go over to say hello. To be honest, I was afraid she'd ask if I'd learned anything new about Bruff's silver.

"Oh, speaking of silver." She jumped up and went to her desk. "Look what I have to show you."

She handed me a spoon. "All the talk that night about Thomas Bruff reminded me of a piece I inherited from my mother's sister."

The spoon looked like an early version of the modern teaspoon, same oval-shaped bowl with a plain handle, but there was something a little off about it. The size of the bowl was larger, but not as large as a soup or serving spoon. The angle of the handle in relation to the bowl was flatter, straighter than a modern spoon. On the back, it was marked with the word, COIN.

"We should try to date this piece at some point. There might be some interesting history behind it," I suggested.

"Why don't you look into it when you get a minute and let me know?" Lorraine sighed. "There's always more to learn when it comes to sterling."

"Oh!" She jumped and so did Simon. "Sorry, it's just that I forgot to tell you. I found something about why it's call sterling."

She sat down to listen. "Tell me."

"The reference said the word referred to a group of Germans who immigrated to England and called themselves Easterlings based on where they lived in relation to the city."

Lorraine jumped in. "That sounds a little strange, doesn't it? I've heard people living in the east end of London refer to themselves as Eastenders, but not Easterlings."

"That's what I thought, too. I did some more digging and found that around 1300, King John asked this group to refine some silver that met the purity standard set for coinage. It seems they knew what they were doing and the quality they produced became the basis for a law passed in 1343 that referred to sterling silver. For some reason, they dropped the first two letters and created the word, 'sterling.'"

Lorraine thought about that for a moment. "The word was probably in common use. Over time, people got sloppy and slurred over the 'ea' of easterling until it disappeared. Same thing happened here with the name of our St. Michaels River, now known as the Miles."

"I love how historical tidbits from thousands of miles away fit with local knowledge to make a more complete picture," I said.

"That's one of the things that fascinates me about silver." She yawned. "I think I'll go to bed. It's going to be a long few days, starting tomorrow. I don't know why I made the arrangements so I'd have to leave so early."

"Leave?"

"I must have forgotten to tell you. I'm going over to Baltimore tomorrow for a day or two. We're moving my aunt, Momma's oldest sister, into an Alzheimer's unit."

I felt a chill from the memory of Aunt Agnes moving into an assisted-living residence. Aunt Agnes couldn't stay in our large Victorian house, and she didn't want to, now that Gran had lost her battle with cancer. After I helped her settle in, it was hard leaving her there and going back to the real world. The least I could do for Lorraine was to be a good friend. "Is there anything I can do to help?"

'No, but thank you. It's the best we can do for her." She gave me a weak smile. "I'm planning to stay a few days to help ease her transition. In her more lucid moments, which sadly are now fewer and fewer, she seems to respond to me. I may be able to help in some small way. The place has well-qualified caregivers and they're on the cutting edge of treatment, though I fear it's too late for my aunt. It's rather advanced." She sighed. "Well, that's what I'll be doing this week. I know we'd planned to start tearing through those trunks and boxes of silver in the attic, but I need to do this right now."

"Of course. Don't think twice about it. The break will give me time to organize some notes and find the top of my desk." I chuckled. "I'm beginning to think that writing software was easier than working with sterling silver because everything lived in the virtual world. Now, my office is littered with real pieces of silver—forks tied with little identification tags, boxed sets, so many things, plus the notes and scribbles and the reference books with slips of paper sticking out. I really need to do some organizing."

She was about to get up from the chair when she remembered something. "Speaking of getting things organized, did you tell the detective about the man with the metal detector?"

"Yes, I did." I let out a long sigh. "To be honest, he got mad at me, wanted to know why I didn't tell him on Saturday night when it all happened."

"Maybe you were distracted?" She asked.

"Right! Imagine how awful it was talking to Filly who knew the victim… who found him floating in the water?" I knew I sounded a little defensive.

"It certainly wasn't the evening I was expecting. I

thought we'd talk to some people, have a good dinner and chat about all the paintings. I didn't think we'd finish off the night with a chat with the police about —" She paused. Her expression was pained. "Abby, was it an accident?"

I shook my head. "No, the detective said that his initial impression was correct. It was murder."

"Does he have any idea who would do something like that? I hope he doesn't suspect someone from the festival."

"He does, I'm afraid. He hasn't come out and made any accusations… yet. He came into Banning's and looked around and watched. I think he's convinced it was one of the artists."

"What do you think?"

I shook my head. "I have no idea. While he was in the pub, the artists and festival people acted a little uncomfortable, as if they were under surveillance."

"Well, I guess they are." She turned her head a little, trying to act nonchalant as she asked, "Was everyone there?"

Simon worked his way off my lap and barked. I was glad he gave me an excuse to avoid her question. "You know, you can almost set your watch by this dog." The old grandfather clock down the hall started to chime the hour. "See? It's ten o'clock and he's ready to go to bed, as usual." I stood up, realizing that I was sleepy, too. The morning picnic with Seth felt like it was days ago.

"Well, it promises to be an interesting week for both of us – me in Baltimore, you with the Plein Air festival," added Lorraine.

I sensed something more in what she said, but I didn't want to face Lorraine's questions about Seth. I didn't even want to face my own.

"Yes, it should be an interesting week." I walked to the door of the library. "I hope all goes well in Baltimore. If you need anything, just give me a call."

Simon and I headed back to the cottage for our nightly ritual: a last romp outside, followed by a search for the hidden cookie. When we went upstairs, I'd stash it someplace and watch Simon sniff the sheets and comforter of the bed looking for the treat. When he found it, he'd throw his head back, to show off his prize, before settling down to eat it. We had such fun that I was happy to live with the crumbs. Oh, what I do for this new pal of mine.

CHAPTER FOURTEEN

One test to determine if a piece is sterling silver is to hold a magnet to it. It should not be attracted since silver is not magnetic nor is copper, a metal commonly combined with it for strength. Be warned that the best test is to find a stamp or hallmark to identify the piece as sterling.

—"The Butler's Guide to Fine Silver" Mr. Hollister, 1898

It was late morning by the time I dragged myself into the office. So many things were stacked up, I was tempted to turn around and close the door behind me.

It will only get worse, I lectured myself. Get started with something.

What was it that Claudia said last night? "Just like everything else, it's all about putting one foot in front of the other."

That's what I needed to do, start with something. Anything. My mind started working: something small, something easy. I remembered the Bruff portrait. I'd researched two out of the three silver pieces in the painting. It was time to finish this mini project. Tankard, went into the search engine.

The word itself had a somewhat romantic origin. It

referred to clumsy hollowed logs bound with iron used to carry water. So, tankard was used to describe a large one-handled drinking vessel with a hinged top to protect against spills. The thumbpiece used to open the lid was called a purchase. It could be a simple knob, like the one in the portrait, or a fancy lion or eagle.

Then, a fun fact surfaced. It seemed that many tankards had a whistle built into the handle so it was easy to call the server for a refill.

I bet that kept sales lively at the bars and pubs.

Just as I was about to close the reference site, the word poison jumped out. At one time, people thought that a tankard made of bone or horn would turn cloudy if there was poison in the drink. Crystal was used for the same reason. I had no idea if there was any truth to that idea and didn't have the time to do the research.

With all the sites closed, the to-do list loomed large. It was a relief to hear my phone ring. When Chief Lucan came up on the caller ID, I grabbed it.

"Sorry to bother you, Abby," said the Chief. "I've got a little situation. I have a Mr. Jones in my office. He was brought in on a complaint about trespassing. He says you told him to go on that property."

"First, I don't know a Mr. Jones. Who is he?"

"He says you told him to look for some antique silver at the Bruff-Mansfield House here in town." The Chief didn't sound convinced that the man was telling the truth.

It was coming together in my mind. "Jones must be the weird metal detector man."

There was a silent moment, then the Chief

continued. "Well, he does have a metal detector."

"I never told him he should trespass on the property. I only mentioned it, that's all."

The Chief cleared his throat, a sign I'd come to recognize meant that he felt uncomfortable. "If you're not too busy, could you come by the office so we can figure this out?"

I wanted to agree, but the echo of Detective Ingram's warning echoed in my head. If anything comes up, you tell me. Nothing more. No running off on your own.

With regret, I told the Chief that I wasn't coming. "You need to call Detective Ingram. He's a friend of yours, isn't he? He'll want to know you have that man in custody."

"Why?"

"I think murder trumps trespassing. Call him."

Regretfully, I put down the phone and went to work.

Hours passed. My efficiency level was low. It was a struggle to strike even a few things off the list. My mind kept wandering back to the festival and one artist in particular: Seth. I was flattered by his attention and I started wondering…

Don't be ridiculous, I scolded myself. He's older than you are and so dedicated to his art that he spends months traveling around the country from one festival to another. I thought about Ryan who was somewhere on the other side of the world, doing who knew what. That's all I need, another man in my life who's far away. I pushed those thoughts aside.

I looked at my list again and another distraction

popped into my head. What was happening with the investigation into Walt's murder? I groaned. Another bad topic. Ingram was clear that I should stay out of it. Easier said than done. And, what about this Jones person searching for old silver at Bruff House? Had he found something? If he did, would the Chief know what it was and what to do with it?

It might be interesting, I thought, to see the little house on the park, now that I knew about its connection to the Bruff family. And I'd be close-by if the Chief called, needing to see me.

I couldn't stand it anymore. My rationale worked. I grabbed my keys and ran outside. It was a sunny afternoon with a cooling breeze. What a shame to stay inside and miss it. Yes, a travesty not to come out and enjoy it. I loved to feel the sun on my skin. Other people wore hats and slathered high SPF lotion on every exposed surface of their bodies. Not me. My curly auburn hair should have come with milky white, highly-sensitive skin. I got lucky. The red tones came with skin that could tolerate sun and give me a warm glow. Sure, by the end of the summer, I'd have a crop of freckles across my cheeks, but it was a small price to pay. I put the top down on my car and roared down the driveway to St. Michaels.

There were plenty of parking places in the lot at Muskrat Park only because it was a weekday. The newly-landscaped area looked lush, even in the hot sun. The object of my visit was on the other side of the park: the Bruff-Mansfield House.

The white structure was tiny, especially by today's

standards. According to the description I'd read, it was built at the beginning of the 1800's and was known for the fine woodworking on the mantel and raised paneling inside. I sat down on a picnic bench and tried to imagine what it would be like to live right in the middle of a bustling shipbuilding town. The sounds of hammers and saws must have drowned out the water gently lapping against the bulkhead. Today, the songbirds were the ones making the racket.

The heat was baking me alive. I couldn't sit there anymore—waiting, hoping for the Chief to call. There was no way I was going back to my office today. I called the art festival's information center to find out if any of the artists were painting on Tilghman Island. It seemed like a logical assumption because everyone was invited to a crab feast tonight.

The volunteer who answered the phone laughed when she heard my question. "Almost all of them are working there right now. Why don't you go to the island and drive around? It isn't a very big place. I'm sure you'll fall over them."

I headed down Route 33 and when I came around the bend, the drawbridge over to Tilghman Island was just coming down after a big power boat with a high fly bridge pass. The woman at the information center was right. There were easels everywhere. Many of the artists had opted to paint on the island to be close to the crab feast planned for that evening. Nobody wanted to miss out on the seafood and shellfish pulled out of the Bay waters earlier in the day.

I cruised the streets and saw that the heat was

taking its toll on the artists. Volunteers dashed around delivering water and ice to them. The local siren started to wail. There was some kind of a code to let people know if it was a fire or ambulance call. I couldn't tell, but I hoped it wasn't an emergency involving one of the artists.

I turned a corner and pulled to the side of the road. It was the same harbor where I'd watched my first boat-docking race. I smiled and closed my eyes as I remembered that clear fall afternoon, the first time I met Ryan. I was so taken with him that I called him a hunk, right out loud. My little laugh at the memory turned into a sigh. I was surprised how much I missed him.

What could be keeping him away so long? He said it was family business, but it must be more than that. His emails are so short. I wonder what will happen and how I'll feel about him… and how he'll feel about me, when he comes back… whenever that might be.

Well, it wasn't going to be today. I didn't want to waste my time pining for a guy who was just a friend. No, he was becoming more than a friend.

It finally registered that two artists had set up their easels near the bulkhead and were standing with their heads together, conferring over a canvas. They moved apart, laughing. I realized with a jolt that it was Larry with a young woman. They were looking very friendly together. She flipped her long, naturally blonde hair over her shoulder. She laughed at something Larry said; it sounded like small bells caressed by a breeze. I sat up and searched the area for Larry's wife Rebecca. I couldn't imagine this scene would make her very happy.

She must have found something else to do rather than sit in the afternoon heat watching paint dry. Nobody was around except the three of us. As I watched, Larry seemed to be mentoring the young artist. She followed his hand when he pointed to something, maybe a boat tied up across the water. His hand moved to an area of her canvas and, after she looked at the real-life scene, she dabbed some paint on her picture with a long brush. After a few minutes, he nodded and went back to his own easel.

If Rebecca had seen the friendly mentoring session, would she have jumped to the same conclusion I did? The woman was young and eager. They looked very relaxed together. They were having a good time. Maybe too good. Claudia said that things happened at art festivals. I wondered if Rebecca had come to this festival to check up on her husband.? Jealousy was a mean emotion that could eat one alive. I eased the car around toward the main road. I didn't want to be drawn into their story.

It wasn't long before I saw another easel set up facing west. The head of silver curls bent over a painting was familiar. Filomena must have felt me watching her. She looked up, recognized me and waved. I parked the car and walked over.

"I didn't mean to disturb you," I said.

"Oh, don't worry about that. You are very welcome at my easel any time." Her bright manner made me feel so welcome. I could understand why she was so popular at art festivals: she had a fine artistic talent and was fun.

"You know what I'm doing." She gestured at the painting of one of the rustic old buildings that looked like it would fall over if you sneezed. "Now, tell me what you're up to on such a fine afternoon." She pulled up her shoulders in anticipation of hearing something wonderful.

"I'm playing hooky," I announced.

"Oh, what fun! What should you be doing?"

"I should be doing research and organizing my files."

Filly dropped her shoulders as if a bubble burst. "That sounds ghastly. No wonder you're out here with us. I tried working in an office once." She wiggled her eyebrows. "The boss couldn't wait to fire me. I was a disaster… and I hated every minute of it. Now, I can do what I want. At the ripe old age of 78, I think I've earned it."

"78?!" I blurted out in shock. "You can't be."

"Don't let these curls fool you. I've earned every one of those silver hairs."

"But…" How could I say that she didn't act like a really old lady?

She read my mind. "You want to know why I don't act my age?" She hunched over and gave me a look with a slack jaw.

Her pose made me laugh. "Oh, stop! You're nothing like that."

She popped up, straight and tall again. Her only concession to her age was a little grunt that maybe she'd moved a little too fast for her body. "I work hard not to be like that. In fact, I know people who are ten, even fifteen years younger than I am who struggle just to get around."

"Maybe they —"

"Nope, it's nothing like that. They've decided to be old, so they are. I decided not to be old. Of course, I don't do the crazy things I did when I was in my sixties, but I've barely slowed down. My goal is to die with a brush in my hand." She held one high in the air.

"And I hope that is a long, long time in the future," I said, and truly meant it.

"Me, too." Her laugh was infectious. "When I'm at a festival, I focus everything on my work."

I gestured at the pendant on her necklace. "I see you're wearing your frog.'

Filly touched it lightly. "Oh yes, my direct connection to my creativity. When it's time for me to paint and I put it on, I think it sends a signal to my right brain that it's time to do something wonderful. Some people call it getting in touch with their muse. I don't care what you call it. My frog helps me get the work done. It's like as if it stokes some engine inside me. Sometimes, it boils up so much energy that I almost have trouble keeping up!"

"It must wear you out. Are you always like this?"

She chuckled, "Oh no. When I'm home, I sort of… oh, not swoon, it's more like wilt. I guess I naturally do that when I'm not working at a festival, so I can recharge that engine."

"It sounds like you know how to manage yourself. Were you always able to do that?"

"No, no. So many years I languished, from bed to chair to kitchen, taking pills for this and that… likely, nothing serious. When I started painting, I learned to listen to my instincts: stop and paint from this spot;

go with the more transparent paint to give the colors a different effect.

"When I was home, my body would tell me to sit and read a book, do the grocery shopping later. It works because it seems to revitalize my work." She shrugged. "I had to teach myself to pay attention to… me!" She looked down, almost shy. "And sometimes I pay attention to someone else."

"Your husband?" I asked.

"No, I'm afraid I lost him a long time ago." She pursed her lips as if she wanted to tell me, but …

"Filly, do you have boyfriend?" I hoped the sudden surprise in my voice didn't embarrass her… or me.

She gently nodded. "Even at my age. Who would have thought it?"

"Oh, Filly. That's wonderful. Does he travel with you or do you leave him at home?"

"I leave him at his home. We just, how do you young people put it? We have a good time together. That's all." She giggled. "Why don't we walk a little? There are some painters working down the way and I'd like to see what they're doing. These old legs could use a stretch." I was relieved that she wasn't pointing in the direction of Larry and the young woman.

We ambled along the road and soon saw three painters working at their easels set far apart. There was no conversation. They were each lost in their own thoughts, all but one. He was staring into the foam of his beer, as if the secret of life was hidden there.

Filly leaned close to me and lowered her voice. "That's Paul over on the far right. I'd recognize him anywhere, the way he is always hunched over. I don't know why he doesn't just stand up!"

"Maybe he has a problem," I suggested.

"Oh, he sure does, but it has nothing to do with his back. His problem is all in his head. He's worrying himself into a snit. I'm beginning to worry that he might not get his... oh, what do they call it?" She tapped her nose, straining to remember. "Mojo. That's it! I wonder if he'll ever get his mojo back. Look at him. His movements are tentative, too careful."

As I watched, Paul touched his brush to his palette and moved the paint toward the canvas where it hovered. He looked at the scene again, dropped his eyes to his picture, then raised them again to reconsider the live scene. Back and forth, back and forth. "I see what you mean. It's almost painful to watch him struggling."

A male voice whispered, "Hello, ladies."

CHAPTER FIFTEEN

Inspect the inside of a silver traveler inkwell carefully. The stopper for the glass reservoir must be in excellent condition or the ink will leak out and create havoc.

—"The Butler's Guide to Fine Silver" Mr. Hollister, 1898

"Jack! You have to stop sneaking up on people!" I demanded.

"I'm a reporter." He raised his chin and looked down his nose at me. "How else to you expect me to get the scoop?"

I put my hands on my hips and wanted to tap my foot. "Are you kidding? You really said scoop?"

"Well, yeah. I'm here to get a story. I need the inside scoop," he said, not having a clue what I meant.

"You might raise your credibility if you didn't sound like you're Clark Kent working for the Daily Planet," I shot back.

Sounding defensive, he went on. "According to what I learned in J-school, I —"

Filly held up her hand. "Stop! What is J-school?"

He rolled his eyes and pushed his glasses up on his nose. "Journalism school, of course."

Filly nodded her head as if to say, Oh, I see, and started to walk down the road again. I joined her with Jack scrambling along behind us, talking to our backs.

"Look, I have a unique opportunity here to see the real goings-on of a prestigious art festival. Add the suspicious death of an artist and I have the makings of a real story."

I noticed Filly bite her lip when he mentioned Walt's death. How unfeeling could this cocksure kid be? I started to give him a tongue lashing, but she touched my arm and gave her head a tiny shake.

I took a deep breath and tried to sound light and interested. "Jack, you may be right. This could be a big story. It might even lift your career into the big leagues."

I heard him gasp in surprise. "You agree? That's great. Maybe you could give me your insights, to help me in my investigation."

Filly looked at me, perplexed. "I thought it was up to the police to conduct the investigation?"

Now, it was my turn to shake her off. She caught my cue and dropped it.

I spoke up quickly. "Jack, I do have some thoughts. You might not find them helpful, though."

He rocked on his feet for a more stable stance so he was ready for anything. "I'll certainly consider them, but I want you to know that I can't share a by-line, I never share a by-line. This is my story, agreed?"

"Of course, Jack." I fought the urge to flutter my eyelashes at him, as if he was my hero. "I was thinking that if the death on Saturday was murder —"

"Do you think it was?" He interrupted.

"Let's just suppose it was. There might be a sinister plot, worse than we thought. The detective suspects the artists, of course. What if it was someone else, somebody totally unexpected?"

Jack sounded like he was slobbering in excitement. "Who, who do you think it might be?"

"The situation reminds me of a story I read about a man in France who committed a crime and almost got away with it. The same thing could be happening here."

"Who? Tell me, who." His voice was thin with the strain of anticipation.

I stopped and looked him square in the eye, which was hard to do because he was bouncing on his toes. "Jack, I think it's you!" His mouth dropped open. "There was a retired crime reporter in France who fell on hard times. He'd covered the stories of master criminals for years and knew the mistakes they made that led to their arrests. He went on a crime spree of his own and pulled off a series of armed robberies. The local cops were stumped. The story was picked up all over the country. They caught him when a camera caught him in the act and one of the older police officers recognized him, even though he was wearing a wig, a fake mustache, glasses and all when he committed the robberies. It seems to me that if a reporter here on the Eastern Shore got tired of covering little no-nothing stories, why couldn't he concoct a dramatic crime, so he could report it and further his career? What do think, Jack? Did you do it?"

He sputtered. Anger grew in his eyes. He said through clenched teeth, "You're making fun of me. Not taking me seriously. I'll show you. I'll shed light on what's really going on here, just wait." He stomped off.

Filly could barely contain the giggles. "Oh Abby, that story about the reporter was too much. You shouldn't have been so hard on him." Her laughter broke through and it rang out. "Really, a reporter committing a crime so he could cover the story? How rich. You should be a writer."

"I must confess that most of that story is true. The reporter was retired, needed the money and committed five or six robberies in all. Is the possibility that Jack could be the killer so farfetched? Competition is fierce in the news business. Maybe Jack is creating the story as a springboard to a major media market. Reporters have faked stories before. Why couldn't he commit a real crime and report it?"

As my words sank in, her laughter petered out. "No, please tell me you're kidding." She looked at me as her eyes began to fill with tears. "Please tell me Walt didn't die, because some snotty kid wanted to make it to the big-time."

I wrapped my arms around the tiny woman, hoping to offer comfort. "Filly, I'm sorry. I was just trying to get him to back off, so he'd stop bothering us, stop bothering everybody. It was the first thing that came to mind. I didn't mean to hurt you."

Slowly, the shudders stopped and she drew away from me while reaching for a tissue. "I'm the one who is sorry, Abby. I don't know where that came from. I guess, I guess…"

"I guess you needed a good cry. It's all right." We started walking back toward her easel. "Tell you what.

Whenever you feel like stopping your work for today, I could drive us over to the place where they're having the crab feast. We could get a glass of wine and —"

"Bourbon. Not wine." She shook her head and made a face as if she'd tasted something nasty. "Bourbon. Yes, I think that's just what the doctor ordered."

"Yes, ma'am." I scurried after her as she marched back to her things.

CHAPTER SIXTEEN

The seafood fork is unique. It is the first piece of flatware used and its proper place is to the right of the knife and spoon arrangement at the right of the plate. If it is placed with the other forks to the left of the plate, the entire setting is incorrect.

—"The Butler's Guide to Fine Silver" Mr. Hollister, 1898

Filly and I weren't the only ones to call it quits early and head for the bar at the crab feast. When we got to the covered dining area built over the water, many of the artists, volunteers and guests were milling around. As we waited our turn to order our drinks, Filly greeted friends with a peck on the cheek and a promise to find one another later to catch up.

"It's such fun to see everyone again. I don't know what I'd do without the plein air festivals. You know, Abby, by the nature of our work, we each spend a lot of time alone. It all comes down to the artist and the canvas. When we get together, we thrive on the human interaction that everyone needs, of course. But there's something more, something special about spending time with people that do the same thing I do, struggle with the same questions of light and color and... I don't know, the whole experience. We help nourish each other's souls and grow as artists, together." Her little laugh almost sparkled in the air as a pink tint rose in her cheeks. "Oh, listen to me waxing philosophic. I didn't mean to…"

I thought of Claudia and her story of how her painting changed her whole world and not in a good way. "Don't apologize. It's interesting. I guess whenever you get deeply involved in something -- no matter what it is -- you have to block out the whole world. If you're not careful, you become a recluse and that's not healthy for an artist, accountant or anybody."

She raised her glass and her smile lit up the room. "That's it! Here's to Abby, a woman who understands." We clinked glasses and each took a grateful sip – Filly had her bourbon, me with my icy cold beer.

She winked. "You and Seth just may go far."

Before I could ask her what she meant, we were jostled as people tried to get their orders to the bartender. "Let's find a better place."

"I'm with you as long as there's someplace to sit down," she groaned. "My feet are killing me."

We tried to make our way through the growing crowd. The problem, if you could call it that, was everyone wanted to say hello to Filly or to meet the woman who had quite a reputation as an artist and gained a new one as the woman who found Walt's body floating in the water off Bruff's Island. It reminded me of a high school reunion where people wanted to catch up on the latest and talk about the career-changing experiences. One large group pulled her in. Paul was there, fidgety as ever, along with Margaret, the very busy lady who had ten paintings to finish before the judging. I wanted to ask how she was doing since she only had two and a half days left, but there were too many other people between us and their discussion was spirited. I was content to listen to a conversation already in progress.

"I think plein air is all about connection with what you see right in front of you." Claudia straightened her shoulders. "An artist must be courageous. Never let the subject intimidate you. Just pick up your brush," she said, picking up an imaginary paint brush. "Dip it in the paint." She mimed the action. "And let it fly over the canvas, interpreting what you see on the canvas."

"Don't be tempted to get caught up in tiny details," said a tall, thin man. "Or you'll look up and see the light's changed. Then, you're sunk."

Several artists in the group nodded sadly in agreement. One person grumbled, "It happened to me today."

Filly's hands fluttered in front of her as if pushing away all the negativity. "That's all about technique. What's really important to me is getting to that special place inside where the art comes from when it's time to paint. It gives me so much comfort and joy, no matter what is happening in my life. When I am painting, I forget about any bad things going on and focus on creating something beautiful."

There was a murmur of agreement from the group. Filly's positive personality affected everybody.

Until Margaret spoke up. "That's all fine and dandy, but let's be honest. It's all about the bottom line."

She rubbed her fingers together to suggest money.

"Oh, Margaret. It's more than that," insisted the woman with long hair pulled back into a braid. "Why are you such a cynic?"

George, the collector, blasted into the group and stood by Margaret. "Here they are, my little painters. I hope you all got a good day's work done. Friday's coming, you know. You have to have something ready for me to buy...if you're really good! Ha, ha, that's a joke."

I had to look away. His comment was offensive. His outfit looked so ridiculous, I was afraid I'd start laughing. The plaid slacks in shades of pink and blue made him look like an Easter egg. But there wasn't anything cheap about it. The little woven logo on his pink polo shirt wasn't one you'd find at department stores. The knight riding his steed with his lord's pennant labeled it as Burberry.

"That's what we were talking about, George," Margaret said. "Art is about creativity... and the money."

George draped his beefy hand over her shoulder. "Margaret, you're one smart cookie. If an artist doesn't think about the money and the prices she charges, she won't be able to pay the light bill."

Everyone looked uncomfortable and who could blame them? Over the past few days, I'd learned that many of them struggled to make a living from their art and, for some, painting full-time was only a dream. Being a plein air artist wasn't supposed to be all about the money the way it was in George's profession, real estate. It was supposed to be about creativity and personal growth.

George didn't sense the mood of the group. He continued to pontificate.

"Pricing is important to collectors, too. I don't want to see my investment go down the drain. Of course, I won't have to worry about the value of one artist's work." He wiggled his eyebrows.

"What do you mean?" asked Paul, pulling on his earlobe. As usual, his hands were always moving.

"Don't you get it, Mr. Festival Winner? With Walt gone, the value of his paintings will go up 'cause there ain't gonna be no more." He laughed loud enough to shake the roof.

Filly gasped. "How can you—"

Lost in his own calculations, he didn't hear her. "That means that the two paintings I have…"

Filly stalked off in a huff. Others started to move away using the excuse that it was time to eat. I watched George for a minute and wondered. Could a collector go to the extreme of murder just to increase the value of the paintings he owns? No, I scolded myself. That's too hard to believe. The detective still believed it was one of the artists, but I couldn't accept that either. Sure, they were in competition with one another, but to resort to murder? The situation was so complicated, my head started to hurt. I could be wrong. Just in case, I promised myself that I'd remember what George said.

As if all that wasn't enough to think about, there was Seth, another knotty puzzle. I turned to make a quick survey of the large dining area, but came up empty. There was no sign of Seth anywhere. I shouldn't have been surprised to see Detective Ingram standing in the corner. He reminded me of a vulture the way he studied the festival people. It was obvious he was suspicious of everybody. I wished the St. Michaels Chief of Police was working this case. He had his hands full with the summer visitors. I suspected that he contacted Ingram about Mr. Jones, the man with the metal detector, but I hadn't heard anything more. Why should I? Ingram used a by-the-book method for his cases. The Chief took a softer approach to his investigations, but he got results and didn't make everyone feel defensive. I didn't want to spend time with the detective and felt relieved when his cell phone rang and he stepped outside to take the call.

Suddenly, I felt someone latch on to my arm. George leaned so close I could smell the alcohol on his breath. "These artistic types are wimps sometimes. They need a tough, aggressive attitude. They'd give away their work for nothing if somebody asked nicely. I admit it, art speaks to the soul, but you can always put a price on anything. And that's how we keep score, isn't it?"

Desperate to get away from him, I scanned the room again and was relieved to spot Claudia.

"Oh, sorry. Gotta go." I said, gently pulling my arm free.

I hurried across the room and in a moment, I sat next to my new friend, Claudia. "What a horrid man."

She gave me a weak smile. "He may be crass, but the reality is, he buys a lot of paintings."

"I know, but did he have to sound so pleased about how much Walt's paintings will be worth now that he's dead?"

Claudia shrugged a little. "Walt was very successful and had big price tags on his art before his wife got sick. No one knew what he'd do with this comeback. Now, we'll never know. He didn't have a chance to finish the painting he was working on."

"So, who…?" The words popped out of my mouth, much to my embarrassment.

"Who hit him over the head and threw him in the water?"

I was a little shocked at how blunt she was.

"You're really asking if it was one of the artists." Claudia rubbed her eye as if she didn't want to see the possibility, then her chest heaved with a sigh. "Yes, I think one or two – maybe even more might be capable of doing such a thing."

"Have you talked to the detective?" I whispered.

Claudia pulled away from me as if I had insulted her. "No, absolutely not."

"No, you're right," I said, quickly. "There's no reason to say anything if there's no proof. Oh, look!" I pointed to a line of servers marching toward us in a line from the kitchen, carrying trays of hot, steamed crabs held high as they passed an impressive buffet. Everyone applauded and jockeyed for seats at the many picnic tables set up all around.

Larry, carrying a plate piled high with food, said hello to me as he and Rebecca sat down on the bench on the other side of the picnic table. It gave me a little thrill that he recognized me from among all of his admirers.

"I couldn't wait. This is my second helping from

the buffet. I'm starved," said Larry, picking up a fork to enjoy some of the Eastern Shore specialties: stewed tomatoes, coleslaw and corn bread.

"You'd better leave room for some crabs," Rebecca said with a sweet smile.

Other guests settled at our long table. Daphney, the young artist I'd seen working with Larry, was all smiles as she headed our way. When she saw Larry's wife, her happy expression melted away and she veered off in a different direction. I peeked in Rebecca's direction to see if she'd noticed. There was a ghost of smile on her face. Or maybe I imagined it.

The memory of the first time I'd seen a pile of steamed blue crabs at the Crab Claw came back to me the first time Lorraine and I really talked. The shells were bright red-orange from the steaming process, and dotted with clumps of what I'd thought was dirt and grit. Since then, I've learned about Old Bay seasoning. Though I'd lived on the Shore for almost a year, I still didn't like "picking crabs" – the proper terminology for eating a steamed crab. Was it too much work for a few choice morsels or was it their beady black eyes staring at me? Gingerly, I picked up one, took a wooden mallet and crackers and went through the motions. I didn't want to stick out as an oddball. Maybe everyone else would be too busy wrestling their dinner out of the shells to notice I was filling up on fried chicken, French fries, rolls and coleslaw.

The server brought a platter of steaming corn on the cob and people pounced on it.

"There's nothing like Eastern Shore sweet corn,"

said a woman seated at our table. "Pass the butter please, not that it needs it."

"Honey, do you want some corn?" asked Larry.

"Yes, I—" Rebecca looked up at him and frowned. "Larry, are you feeling all right? You're sweating."

"It's the heat and humidity. This isn't the dry heat we have at home in Arizona."

His light comment didn't wipe away her conviction that he was dehydrated. She reached for the ice water pitcher and poured him a glass. "Larry, you need to drink some water. It will help."

"Oh, Becks. Don't fuss."

She thrust the glass at him. "Drink." That was my first glimpse at what she must be like with her legal clients and her steely attitude with the opposition. I bet when she got an idea in her head, it would take a bulldozer to move it.

"Really, it's just the heat," Larry insisted, but he took the glass and almost emptied it.

She looked at all of us sitting at the table and rolled her eyes. There was an unspoken word, Men. Their friendly little squabble was interrupted.

"Larry, tell me! Is it true?" boomed George, standing behind me. I didn't dare turn around since I'd probably be facing his belt buckle.

"Is what true?" Larry shot back, as he put down the glass and picked up a crab claw. He wasn't fazed by George's commanding attitude.

"That you're putting a cap on the price of your paintings on Friday? That you're keeping the price artificially low?" It was an accusation, not a question.

"I think we have to be aware that I'm selling these paintings at a summer festival and the state of the economy isn't great, George," Larry said between bites, not willing to let the collector spoil his dinner. "Some people are still recovering from the downturn. They deserve a little art and I think it's better for me to sell a painting than—"

George interrupted. "You need to think about the collectors who supported your career and bought your paintings from the very beginning. We don't need the value of our holdings to go down. Isn't that right, Anthony?"

The festival chairman was walking by and paused to look at George with his eyebrows scrunched together. "And what would that be?"

"You own Larry, too, right?"

I thought, What a funny way of referring to an artist's work.

Anthony nodded, "We have several of his paintings in our collection, yes, and enjoy every one." He tried to walk away from the bravado of George Plummerly, but the overbearing man blocked his escape route and put his arm around his shoulders to hold him in place. "Larry, if you don't want to consider my feelings, think of Anthony here. He's the chairman of the festival. You don't want to make him look like an idiot. He spent money on your work when you were an unknown. He helped make you the famous artist you are today." His voice grated like fingernails on a chalkboard. "Or you could give all of our holdings a big bump."

The last shred of politeness drained from Larry's

face. He took a quick, tense breath to control his growing dislike. He asked George, "And how would I do that?"

"Why, die, of course." His roar of laughter got everyone's attention.

Rebecca started coughing and choking. Her husband had to pat her on the back.

George ignored her. "Dying is doing wonders for Walt's prices, I understand."

"Isn't that a little extreme, George?" Anthony said, trying to defuse the situation. He had to calm Larry, one of the festival's most important artists, while placating George, one of the biggest buyers at the festival.

"Extreme situations create the biggest hikes." All the fun and hilarity vanished from George's face. "But, good old Larry isn't going to do anything to hurt his collectors, are you?" The nasty look on the man's face would have made a child cry. "You'll leave the pricing of your paintings at established levels, won't you, Larry?"

The only sound was the clinking of the silverware and glasses by the serving staff.

Anthony took a step forward. "George, all we want Larry to do is continue his wonderful work and the market will take care of itself." He held out his arm in the direction of the bar. "Why don't you let me buy you a drink?"

George stood rigid and glared at Larry for what felt like a long time, then broke out in such a big laugh that his belly shook. "They say the drama in finance is all on Wall Street. Ha! Those boys have no idea what goes on in the art world." George laughed again and began to move away from Larry's table. People were starting to breathe again when George let fly a final zinger. "Enjoy your dinner, Larry but watch out for those shrimp. They're so spicy they're called Killer shrimp." Ignoring Anthony, George laughed again as he walked over to sit at a table with other collectors who were smiling. They probably appreciated George's joke. The people at our table did not.

Larry broke the tension. "I swear you meet a lot of people on the plein air festival circuit. Most of them are terrific." He gave Anthony a quick nod who responded with a smile.

Larry, eager to enjoy the evening, picked up a plate of steaming yellow corn on the cob. "Now, how about some—" Rebecca was staring off into space, lost in her own thoughts. "Honey, don't let that blowhard upset you. Here, take some corn." She raised her eyes to him and looked like she was about to burst into tears.

He put an ear on her plate and passed the platter. Hands free, he threw an arm around her, pulled her close and kissed her hair. I couldn't hear what he whispered in her ear, but it made her eyes go soft.

It all made me a little envious. Someday, I thought. Someday I hope someone loves me like that.

Slowly, Larry's face shifted from a look of love to shocked surprise. He jumped to his feet, ready to run. He paused, confused. His eyebrows came together and his head tilted to the side. Then, fear drained the color from his face, even the rosy effects of the sun. He clutched his stomach. He folded over in pain. Desperate, he raised a hand and gripped his head. His breath came in short gasps. His eyes grew wide, the white showing all around. He tensed. His mouth twisted open and vomit spewed all over the table.

I sprang out of my chair, along with everyone else, and watched helplessly as the poor man gagged. He collapsed on the table in agony.

Rebecca's screams split the stunned silence. "Help him! Somebody help him!"

CHAPTER SEVENTEEN

Do not use a silver piece to serve table salt, olives, salad dressing, fruit juices, mayonnaise or eggs unless it has a glass liner. These foods will cause tarnish or damage. If you must, be sure the piece is washed immediately afterwards.

—"The Butler's Guide to Fine Silver" Mr. Hollister, 1898

Detective Ingram came out of nowhere, pushing everyone out of the way as he clamped a small radio close to his mouth and called for an emergency medical team. A siren wailed from an ambulance stationed nearby. Ingram stashed the radio and reached out to offer assistance to the man rocking back and forth in pain. His hands, trained to work in an emergency, hung in the air. What could he do to help? Pain and something more was consuming Larry's body.

In a blur, paramedics rushed to the suffering man, bundled him into the ambulance and raced him away with lights flashing and siren blaring.

I stared at the leaking, tangled mess of food, crab shells, medical trash… and more. Slowly, noises around me drew away my attention to see that Larry wasn't the only one suffering. All around the pavilion, people here and there groaned in pain, hunched over hugging their stomachs. Some, with sweat glistening on their faces, staggered toward the rest rooms.

Ingram was back on the radio, calling for assistance. More emergency medical personnel hustled into the crowd, administering to people who needed help.

"Are you sick?" a uniformed man asked me.

"No," I answered, a little surprised that I felt fine. The man moved on to someone else.

Slowly, I turned all the way around, taking in the chaos of sudden illness. Buffeted by people dashing around, I made my way to a table in the corner and sat down. Horrified, yet ready to help if needed, I watched as food poisoning claimed its victims. Then, I had an odd thought: We all were eating the same foods, but not everybody is sick.

Suddenly, Seth plopped down in the empty chair next to me. "There you are. Feeling okay?" His manner was calm.

"I'm fine."

"Good." He looked around the pavilion. "I guess others weren't so lucky. Looks like bad crab strikes again."

"What do you mean?" I asked in surprise.

"I mean that if the crabs aren't alive when they're thrown into the steam pot or they're not cooked just right, people get sick. Good thing I was late and missed it, but I'm starving."

Ingram surfaced from the chaos that was settling into an organized response. "Are you feeling okay, Abby?"

"Yes, I'm fine. What's making all the people sick, food poisoning? Are the crabs bad?"

"I doubt it," he said confidently. "The people here know how to handle crabs." He frowned. Did you have any?"

"No," I said, almost meekly. "I'm not a big fan of steamed crab and Old Bay seasoning isn't a favorite. I was filling up on the fried chicken and sides."

He straightened up. "Good, I'll file that away. It may be important."

I put my hand out and touched the table close to him. I felt my face grow warm in embarrassment. Just a little while ago, I thought he was a suspicious vulture, always eyeing the crowd. Thank goodness, he was right there to take charge. "I'm glad you were here."

He shrugged. "Just part of the job."

"But, getting the paramedics here so fast must have helped Larry." I swallowed. "Do you think he'll be all right?"

He took a deep breath. "Time will tell. I saw what was happening because I had news for the festival chairman who was standing right there."

"News…?"

I wanted to hear what he had to say, but Seth interrupted. "If you will excuse me, I have to find something to eat before I pass out from hunger." He stood up.

Ingram placed a hand on his shoulder and gently pushed him down in his chair. "Not so fast. I'm afraid you can't leave yet." He raised his voice so all could hear him. "Anyone who isn't sick needs to step outside and wait on the lawn." There was a collective groan, not from sickness, but frustration. "Take chairs with you, but don't eat or drink anything."

Uniformed police officers moved to create a human barrier to corral the people. The detective's eyes traveled over the collection of guests – artists, volunteers, friends and restaurant staff. "No one is to leave before you talk to one of my officers."

"Again?" The single word came from someone in the middle of the crowd.

"Yes, I'm afraid so." There was no apology in his words, only determination. He looked around quickly and pointed to a group of picnic tables by the water. "Form a line over there, please. We will process everyone as quickly as possible."

"But—"Seth began.

Ingram said quietly, "We'll process you first."

Like a shot, Seth was out of his chair and on his way to the designated interview area.

Anthony rushed up to Ingram. "Is this really necessary, Detective?" The man's face was wet with perspiration that wasn't from bad food. "These people —"

I watched as Detective Ingram slowly raised his chin to bring his full presence to bear. He was my height, but seemed much taller, all of a sudden. Enunciating each word carefully, he said, "Yes, sir. It is." There was no question that the detective was in charge. "I'm declaring this a crime scene."

Gulping air, Anthony slowly repeated the words "Crime scene?"

Ingram took a step back to extend the space between himself and the festival chairman. "Yes sir, I think a crime has been committed… attempted murder and right under our noses." Anthony looked at him with his mouth open in surprise. "Yes, sir, that's right. Attempted murder. Now, if you'll step back and…" He stretched out his arm and moved Anthony aside.

Claudia was waving from a table in the corner. I threaded my way through the churning throng of people and wondered what news Ingram had for the festival chairman. Everyone was frightened. You could almost feel it, touch it in the air. They were afraid for Larry… and themselves. If the police would let us, I think we'd all have fled the area. Instead, we had to beat down our emotions and make pleasant conversation.

I just wanted to see a familiar face. When I saw the person who always meant safety to me, I went to stand next to Chief of Police Lucan.

"Heard about the trouble on the scanner." He was calm and composed, as usual. "Not surprised to see you here. Never a dull moment when you're around."

Feigning shock, I shot back, "Hey, this isn't my fault. I came to have dinner with some new friends." The friendly banter was soothing.

He surveyed the milling crowd. "Who would have thought a group of painters, civic volunteers and art lovers would be so dangerous?"

His words slowly sunk in. I stepped in front of him and searched his face. "You don't think this was a malicious act, do you? People get food poisoning all the time." His expression didn't change one bit. Not even a twitch. "Tell me this was just an unfortunate accident," I pleaded.

He shrugged. "I've never lied to you. Do you want me to start now?"

The voice inside my head screamed, Yes! "Maybe Detective Ingram is overreacting. He's so intense."

He shrugged again. "Mike is a good man, has a lot of experience, and knows his stuff. If his nose twitches that something's not right, I gotta pay attention."

"How is his nose right now?" I asked, not really wanting to hear the answer.

"It's twitching like a dog on a hunt. He's already got one murder on his hands and no arrest. Who's to say that the killer isn't trying to bring down the whole festival?" The Chief continued surveying the group and I stepped out of his line of sight.

"Could it be that man with the metal detector? What was his name, Jones?" His eyes came back to me. "Ingram hasn't said anything to me. Is he a suspect?"

"I don't think so. All I could find out about him was the worst thing he's ever done is trespass on private property a couple of times. It's a giant leap to go from that to killing a man and poisoning a whole group of people." He ran his hand over the top of his head. "Anyway, I don't think he'd be interested in a painting unless it was buried somewhere. I'm being to think that Ingram is right. It all gets back to the artists."

"Chief, I'm having trouble getting my head around that."

"Artists targeting artists. That's a new one for me, too. Keep your eyes and ears open, Abby, and watch yourself." He walked into crowd.

With a heavy heart, I resumed my trip to Claudia's table.

As I sat down, the questions came fast and furiously. "What happened? You were right there. Are you all right? Is anyone else sick?"

With the Chief's suspicions fresh in my mind, I found I was looking at the artists in a different way. Watch yourself, he'd said. And I would.

"It was horrible, Claudia. One minute, he was fine. The next minute, the paramedics were all over him and rushed him to the ambulance."

"Did he choke on something?"

"I don't know," I answered carefully.

A soft, trembling voice asked, "D-do you know how he is? Larry, I mean. Weren't you at his table?" It was Daphney.

Claudia pulled her down to sit in a chair and we gathered to give her what consolation we could. There was no hard information, only hope.

"I just wanted this festival to be…" Daphney sputtered, barely keeping her emotions under control. "My whole life was supposed to… This was the turning point."

Had Larry declared himself? Were they making plans for a future together? Did his wife Rebecca ruin everything by coming to the festival? But, that didn't square with the way he treated Rebecca. Thanks to the Chief, my imagination was on fire.

Daphney's hands clenched so tightly that her knuckles were white. "I told David good-bye so I could concentrate on my art."

That threw me for a loop. "Who's David?"

She sighed so deeply that her shoulders seemed to sink into her chest. "He is ... was my boyfriend. He was hinting that he wanted us to get married." She turned her face to me, her eyes brimming with tears. "Do you know how exhausting it is to be on your guard—changing the topic all the time, so he wouldn't ask The Question? It was exhausting."

Actually, I didn't know. I'd never been that far into a relationship.

I tried to nod knowingly. "I thought you said he was your boyfriend?"

"He was, and these past few weeks, he was so loving and attentive. I couldn't focus on what I needed to do to get ready for this festival. You see, I want to quit my regular, boring job and support myself with my art. Larry said —" Her voice cracked on the name of her friend, but she held it together and went on with her story.

"Larry said he thought I was ready to..." She made air quotes around her next words. "'Make my presence known.'" Claudia raised her eyebrows in surprise. "Oh, he didn't mean that I'm good enough to win first prize or anything like that. He thought my work might catch the attention of buyers and that's how I should start building a following."

Claudia nodded. "He's right about that. It's a good way to approach things if this is what you want to do."

"It is." Daphney took a deep breath and hung her head. "That's why I broke up with David. I told him I never wanted to see him again."

"Wasn't that a little extreme?" I asked.

"If you want something, you have to do some extreme things. Isn't that right, Claudia?" She looked to the older woman for confirmation.

Claudia gasped a little. "Oh, um, you can't go by me. You have to do what's right for you."

"That's the problem," the young woman moaned. "I thought it was right to send David away. I thought I would do my best work so far at this festival. With everything going on, how can I even put two creative thoughts together?" She put her face in her hands and cried.

Claudia put her arm around the girl.

I had an idea of how Daphney felt. I was looking forward to a little fun, spending time at the festival with all these creative people. Now, I was looking at them in a different light: suspicion. The festival should be about creativity and doing good work. Instead, death and fear lurked in the shadows. The undercurrent of fear affected everyone. I felt desperate to get away from it all. I patted Claudia's arm and slipped away into the crowd. I caught myself speeding up the road toward Fair Winds. I wanted to get there as fast as possible: home.

CHAPTER EIGHTEEN

No man begins his profession as a silversmith. First, he must serve as an apprentice for years in order to learn the skills and techniques of the craft. Each silversmith earns the right to stamp his hallmark on a piece he has made.

—"The Butler's Guide to Fine Silver" Mr. Hollister, 1898

I picked up Simon at the main house, went to my cottage and closed the door. Once inside, that feeling of desperation was still with me. Why? I was safe at Fair Winds, safe inside Lorraine's little cottage that I now called home.

Why am I on edge now, I asked myself as I prowled around the cottage, from the living room which overlooked the Miles River, back to the kitchen with its little breakfast alcove, and out to the living room again. I realized with a shock that I'd locked and bolted the door.

That's weird. I never do that. It isn't necessary here. So, why?

I turned around and almost fell over Simon. "Don't do that!"

Wow! What's wrong with me? I know he loves the little stalking game he plays as he follows me around the cottage.

I dropped down beside him on the floor to make sure he wasn't hurt. He looked at me with those soft brown eyes filled with remorse and melted my heart. How could I yell at such a sweet boy?

"I'm sorry, I'm sorry, Simon. You're okay." I scratched his favorite place, right behind his right ear and he moaned in delight. I gave him a big hug and we were off to the kitchen and his cookie jar. Right on cue, he sat at my feet with his tail wagging.

"Good boy! You know what to do for a cookie, but you must stop walking in my footsteps. One of us could really get hurt." His response was to wag his tail even faster.

It was the best I was going to get. I dropped the dog cookies and went back to the living room. After taking a deep breath, I plopped down on the cushy sandy-colored leather sofa.

What's got me so wound up that I'm walking around here like a caged lion? Part of me is angry that the festival has a growing overtone of suspicion and ugliness where there should be only beauty and creativity. Do I feel threatened by all the unusual happenings at the festival?

I thought back to other things that had happened recently, even the situation that had brought me to the Shore. It was still hard to believe that someone used my silver angel food cake server as a murder weapon. If I hadn't sold it to Lorraine in an online auction… well, who's to say what might have happened?

No, something else is bothering me.

Then it hit me. With all the talk about composition and self-expression through art, the creative spirit of the festival had seeped into my bones. It was a shock to realize I was jealous… jealous of the artists and the work they were doing. I missed the thrill of creating, making something out of nothing. I did that all the time when I wrote software, but that was different somehow. I didn't give me the same thrill I got when reading a piece of fiction I'd written, that I'd created. I didn't do anything like that anymore.

Maybe that's what had me on edge. I wanted to recapture that feeling.

I went to my little desk in the corner of the living room and pulled out the top drawer. My bright fuchsia memory stick belonged with other important things tucked right in the front corner of the tray. But it wasn't there. I poked through the paper clips, pens and highlighters, nothing. I rooted through the index cards and memo pads, still nothing. It wasn't in any of the other drawers. A futile search of my computer case ramped up my anxiety. The stick was nowhere to be found.

Where can it be? Of course, where I throw everything I don't want to lose… the top drawer of my dresser.

I launched myself up with the stairs with my little furry cookie monster hot on my heels again. "Simon!" No, I didn't have the patience to train him now, so I stepped to the side and he streaked up the steps ahead of me. He sat patiently, while I pawed through the drawer. Maybe he thought I was looking for a cookie. Instead, I was finding things I'd forgotten were there. This dresser that came with the cottage was very tall. My toes were starting to ache as I stretched to see what was inside the drawer.

This wasn't working.

I pulled out the drawer and turned it over on my bed. As things tumbled out, I realized my mistake. Simon was already in mid-air, aimed for the center of the pile. Somehow I intercepted him and we fell together on the pillows. I shuffled him out of the bedroom and closed the door to the saddest whimpers I'd ever heard.

"This will only take a minute. Be patient, Simon." Ha, patience was not his strong suit, but he was very good at shedding. I looked at my pillows. His black hair was all over the pillowcases. Oh well, I'd deal with that later. Right now, I was on a mission to find my pink memory stick.

My fingers flew over the random collection of stuff. I pushed a hand under the stack and a smile spread slowly over my face as it closed around the memory stick. I closed my eyes and hoped, as I pulled it out. I opened my fingers. Yes!

Simon was so relieved when I opened the door that he raced into the room only to discover I was galloping down the steps, back to the living room and my computer. He reversed course and followed me downstairs.

I pushed the memory stick into the USB port and searched the file folders until I found the one labeled "Words." One click revealed two more file folders. I bypassed the one labeled "Journal" because I didn't want to stroll down memory lane of my last months in

Seattle.

I clicked on the other folder marked "Stories." It contained blogs never posted anywhere, essays, short stories, even the beginning of a novel. I slid into the chair and scrolled through the file listings as Simon curled up on my foot. I opened one of the documents and started reading.

This isn't bad. If I changed…

I moved the cursor and started typing in the middle of a paragraph. Two new lines appeared. Now where? I sat looking at the flashing cursor. It was waiting for my next words of brilliance. Flash, flash. Like fingers drumming on the desk, waiting. What are you going to do next?

I didn't know. I guess creative work isn't like a swimming pool where you can jump in anytime you want. That must be why Filly wears her little frog necklace to help her focus.

I'd try again another time. I shut down the external memory stick, pulled if from the port and put it in the drawer where it belonged. At least looking at my old writings got me thinking about positive, productive things again instead of all the confusing questions about Walt, murder, poisoning… and Seth.

A moment later, my phone rang, yanking me back to the here and now. Seth's name came up on the caller ID. My finger hovered over the buttons on the screen: Accept Decline. It wasn't that easy. Part of me was thrilled by his attention and being so close to a creative person, but there was something else. I felt a spark of loyalty to Ryan. Deep down, I felt it was something more than that. I felt uncomfortable. Close relationships always made me feel that way. Falling in love would be great, but in my family, it seemed to lead to sadness and heartbreak. I was scared. The phone kept ringing.

Seth. I had feelings for him, no question. Were they real or born from the glamor of the festival and excitement of his work? It would be easier to step back, not complicate my life. Then, Claudia's words about courage came back to me, how an artist had to put her fears aside and step up to the easel. I needed to do the same thing with my life.

My finger touched Accept.

CHAPTER NINETEEN

Any member of staff who handles the lady's jewelry must be properly trained in the care and handling of a silver piece.

—"The Butler's Guide to Fine Silver" Mr. Hollister, 1898

On the phone, Seth's voice was warm. He said he missed me, wanted to see me, asked if he could come to Fair Winds. Without thinking, I agreed.

It wasn't long before I saw the headlights of Seth's truck coming down the long driveway of Fair Winds. He followed my directions and we met in the little parking area by the main house. Simon came along but, after a sniff of Seth's pant leg, he trotted back to the cottage.

"It's a beautiful evening. Why don't we take a little walk," I suggested. "Have you heard any news about Larry?"

"No, they're still waiting for word from the hospital. I wouldn't worry. Painters go down all the time at these summer festivals, especially when it's so hot and humid." He shrugged. "It was probably food poisoning. Anybody can eat a bad crab."

"Not usually. Cooks are pretty careful about how

they're prepared."

We walked a little ways, enjoying the breeze off the water. "Speaking of Larry, somebody said that the two of you mixed it up at another plein air festival recently. What was that all about?"

Seth stopped. "It wasn't anything serious. It doesn't matter now. This is a whole new festival, a whole new competition, a whole new set of circumstances."

After a moment, he placed his hand at the small of my back and we started to walk again. "You know, Abby, I was so disappointed when they told me you left."

"That's sweet."

"No, you don't understand." He threw his arms open wide to embrace the rising moon and starry sky. He laid his head back and laughed with delight. "I have never painted this well in my life." He stopped and took my hands. His jet-black eyes gazed deep into mine as if he was looking into my soul. His voice went soft. "Do you know why?"

I was afraid to say anything.

"It's all because of you." His face shone with confidence and pleasure. "With you, I am whole because you are my muse."

I broke away gently and resumed our walk. "I've been a lot of things in my life, but never a muse. It's probably the place and the festival. The Shore is magical, I'll admit. Everywhere you look, there's something wonderful." He touched my arm and I turned toward him.

"It's true that plein air painters say their muse or source of our inspiration is nature – ever changing, always fascinating and surprising. What I'm talking about is different. To me, a muse is a goddess who has the power to inspire an artist, this artist." He pulled me into his arms. "I may seem distracted or absorbed, but I'm always aware of what is around me.

His finger traced a curl of my hair. "I look for the shape of things." His touch sent a ripple that went right through me.

"As an artist, I'm always aware of color and shading." His finger trailed down to my forehead, over my eyebrow and around to my cheek.

"This artist feels texture." His finger outlined my lips. "As if he is the tip of his brush, painting what you are."

He lightly touched his lips to mine. The electricity almost crackled in the dark. Then, he kissed me again, his lips pressing, urgent, searching for the innermost part of me. I wound my arms around his neck and—

A bright light blinded me.

"Oh, I'm sorry, Miss Abigail." Dawkins was holding an industrial-sized flashlight on my face. "I didn't know it was you. I saw some movement over here and wanted to investigate."

Seth released his hold on me and I stepped back.

"Could you shine that thing somewhere else?" I said, squinting and trying to block the intense beam with my hand.

"Oh, I'm terribly sorry." He swung the beam and aimed it directly in Seth's face.

"Hey!" Seth jumped away.

"I beg your pardon." He redirected his spotlight to

the ground. "I am so sorry for the intrusion. I hope you can understand, Miss Abigail."

"No, I don't."

"I have a perfectly good rationale for my actions. With everything going on and a murderer at large, I've taken to patrolling the grounds before I go to bed, to make sure that all is well."

"Murder?" Seth acted as if he'd never heard the word before.

"Why, yes —"

"Dawkins," I interrupted. "As you can see, I am perfectly fine. This would be a good time for you to say good night." I tried to paste a pleasant expression on my face though I really wanted to jam that flashlight down his throat.

Dawkins looked at me, a little surprised. He swung his gaze around to Seth who was standing well away from us. "Why, yes. Yes, of course. I see." He breathed in a slow, deep breath and let it out slowly. "Good night," he announced.

He walked back toward the big house, following the light playing across the grass. Without turning around, he said in a voice just louder than the breeze. "I only wanted to make sure you were all right."

I felt a twinge of regret. I wasn't used to a guardian angel, especially one who wore a vest and a watch chain.

"Who was that?" Seth sounded like he wasn't sure what had just happened.

I sighed. "It's a long story, too long for telling tonight."

"If you say so." He looked at his watch with a

radiant dial. "It's getting late for me. Got to get up early and get back to work."

We walked up to his truck. He gave me a peck on the forehead and got in. As he drove down the drive, there was a rustling in the bushes nearby. My skin went cold. Dawkins had planted fear in my mind.

A bundle of black fur streaked through the headlight beam toward me. My best guy was there to walk me home.

CHAPTER TWENTY

A piece of sterling silver is part of the family tradition of the House. It is your responsibility care for it, enhance it and keep it safe so it can be passed down from generation to generation.

—"The Butler's Guide to Fine Silver" Mr. Hollister, 1898

My phone rang before I had my first cup of coffee. It was never good news at that hour of the morning. My hand clenched the case when I saw the caller ID.

"Abby, it's Chief Lucan." I was still trying to get my other eye open. "Abby, are you there? Don't tell me I woke you? You're going to sleep the day away, girl."

"What time is it?" I muttered.

"Ten after eight. Come on, Abby. Wake up and listen to me."

There was a note of concern in his voice that woke me up all the way. "What's going on? Has something happened?"

"I wanted to make sure you're okay and..." he paused. "And to suggest you stay away from the Plein Air Festival until things settle down."

I sat straight up in bed. Simon was so startled, he almost rolled off the edge. "Why?" I remembered the events at dinner the night before and the paramedics rushing one of the most popular artists to the hospital. "It's Larry, isn't it?"

There was a long sigh at the other end of the call. "I'm afraid so. He succumbed about an hour ago."

"What? Why?" I was having trouble catching my breath.

"They suspect…" He rushed on. "Now, there's nothing for sure yet, mind you." He signed again. "You'll find out anyway. They suspect it was poison."

I gasped. Simon, concerned, sat next to me and licked my face. "How? Why?"

"All good questions," said the Chief.

"Chief, there's a killer on the loose, isn't there? Your friend Detective Ingram was right."

"Ah, there you go jumping to conclusions. Let's just say the police are investigating. In the meantime, you might want to steer clear of the festival. Stay home. Work on your silver things. It's a good excuse to stay out of the heat." His attempt to put a light-hearted tone in his voice failed.

"Chief, I'm not sure I can do that. Over the past few days, I've made some friends who will be devastated by this news. I feel like I need to —"

"You don't need to do anything." He groaned. "Why do I even try? Why can't I ever persuade you to stay out of harm's way?" I started to protest, but he ignored me. "Okay, okay. Just watch yourself." He cut the connection.

I sat in the tangle of sheets and dog. The thought of Larry, such a vibrant, creative person… What a loss to the people who loved him and called him a friend. It was a loss to the art world, as well. So many pictures he'd never paint. I thought of George and his offhand comment last night about the one true way of increasing the value of an artist's body of work: death. A cold feeling ran over my bare arms and I rubbed them frantically. Simon thought it was a new game and bounced around the bed. It was funny until...Ooof! He landed on me.

"You're getting too big to play puppy games."

He was content with a good scratch all the way down his back. I jumped out of bed and hoped the shower would steam out the thoughts unsettling my mind. What a way to wake up.

It was a miracle that I found a parking place close to the Avalon where the Information Center was operating. I stepped into the room with hesitation, not knowing what I'd find. There were loud, happy people bustling here and there, all on important missions, though I couldn't think what they could be. There were no tears or hushed speculations. They didn't know Larry was dead. Well, they weren't going to hear it from me. I smiled and nodded at people, not trusting myself to open my mouth. It took a few minutes before I reached the map that showed where the painters were working, all limited to the city limits of Easton. I made some notes in my phone about Filly and Claudia. Daphney's name was on the board, too. She was working right down the street. A bubbly volunteer headed my way was the last thing I needed. I smiled and scooted back out the door.

It only took a few minutes to walk to Daphney's location. Nestled in the shade of some very tall trees on the edge of a park, two easels were set up near each other, but facing in opposite directions. Standing in front of her painting, Daphney listened to another woman, pointing from the canvas to the toy store in an old brick building across the street, the subject of the painting. An almost life-sized pirate in a red jacket and blue captain's hat stood at attention by the store's front door. The older woman was none other than brusque, business-minded Margaret, having a creative conversation with Daphney. Was that because Larry wasn't around or did Margaret have a nurturing quality she kept well-hidden? I suspected that was the case since Daphney responded to what Margaret was saying by dabbing her brush here and there on the picture.

Oh, Margaret. You're such an old phony. You're all bark. Underneath, you're an old softie. Margaret, your secret is safe with me. I don't want to be the one to blow your cover and incur your wrath.

Margaret said something and they laughed together. I hoped she would be there for Daphney when the tears came. She would need all the support she could get, now that she was alone: no mentor, Larry; no boyfriend, David.

I slipped away before they noticed me.

I checked my phone and found that Filly was working only two blocks away. I couldn't see her from the street, so I wandered through an open iron gate, around a stone planter and down an old brick walkway. Around to the left, I spotted Filly in a secluded spot, picking up a sweating plastic bottle of water.

"Oh, you found me. You must be part bloodhound,"

she said, sounding a little wilted.

"What are you doing in such a remote spot?" I failed to hide my concern.

Filly picked up on it. Her hand holding the water bottle stopped in midair. "What's happened? What's wrong?"

I tried to cover. "Nothing, I just wanted to see how you were doing."

She wasn't buying my nonchalant attitude. "No, Missy. That dog don't hunt." She screwed the top back on the bottle. "Tell me what's happened. Tell me right now."

I sighed and walked closer to her. There was no need to announce the news to the entire neighborhood. "It's Larry. He didn't make it. I'm sorry."

She stared at me, trying to absorb the information. Then, she threw her hands up in the air and let them flop down against her body. "I knew it. I knew it," she kept saying as she paced around her easel, wanting to go somewhere, to do something, but not knowing what.

"That detective must have suspected something was screwy right from the start or why else would he be hanging around us so much?" She had a point. "I mean, we're fascinating, but really? He's been sticking too close. That night on Bruff's Island, he went down where I found Walt caught up in the old tree limbs in the water. The detective was walking around... He went to the pond... Walt's easel... Something is very wrong." She raised her index finger in my face. "You mark my words."

Afraid that the elderly bundle of energy would

make herself sick, I made a suggestion. "Maybe it would be better to move your easel and work in a more public place." I looked around. "Why are you working back here anyway?"

She pointed to a set of brick steps leading up to a small patio where some white wrought iron chairs were waiting for people to come for a nice chat.

"It's charming, but it might be prudent for you to set up somewhere else. Maybe the —"

She planted her feet. "I'm not going anywhere. Nobody dictates to me. I paint what I want to paint and where I want to paint."

"But —"

"This isn't my first rodeo." She walked over to her easel where her red leather tote was hanging. She reached into a side pocket, and what she pulled out made me jump back and hold up my hands.

"Whoa! I was just concerned about your safety and —"

The shiny silver pistol glinted in the sun. She looked at it with pride. "This little beauty goes with me everywhere. I can take care of myself." She looked at me and shook her head. "Oh, for heaven's sakes, put your hands down. I'm not going to shoot you."

Slowly, I lowered them. "Do you know how to use that thing?" The thought of a gun in the hands of an ordinary citizen made me very nervous, especially after what happened to me last fall.

"Of course. My daddy taught me when I was knee high. I'm a lifetime member of the NRA. I have several at home, but this is my favorite travel companion. She's a Smith & Wesson Lady Smith .38 double action with five rounds." She hefted it and I took a step backward. "Light, less than a pound, but deadly, if you need it."

My face must have gone pale because she added, "Or I can use it just as a deterrent, if that makes you feel better." She took it by the barrel to show me the grip. "I really like the rosewood handle. Makes it classy, just right for a lady."

I watched as she tucked it back into her tote. "You just keep it in your purse?" Images of all kinds of possible accidents flew threw my head.

"Oh, this isn't just any ole purse." She picked it up and showed me the hidden compartment. "It has a concealed gun carry sac." She tucked away her secret weapon. "Nobody would ever know it's there."

"I sure didn't. You've had that tote with you every time I've seen you." She nodded. "And the gun's been inside?"

She nodded again. "All the time. I don't go anywhere without it. Even have a classy number for evening. Looks like one of those expensive Coco Chanel bags."

"But, is it legal?"

"Sure is. Want to see my concealed-carry permit?" She didn't wait for my answer before she reached inside the main section of the bag and pulled out her wallet. After thumbing through some cards, she turned her wallet around to show me the permit encased in plastic. "There you go."

I looked and looked again. "But, Filly. That was issued in Georgia."

"That's right. That's where I live. I took all the training, filled out all the paperwork, had the background check and they said I was good to go anywhere with my little gun."

"In Georgia," I said gently. "Isn't that permit limited to Georgia?" I had read just enough about the gun law controversy to know that Filly might run into a problem in Maryland.

She snapped her wallet closed and put it away. "The authorities in Georgia are satisfied and now, I'm taking care of myself."

"But —"

"But, nothing. I'd rather be tried by twelve on a jury, than carried by six to the cemetery."

With that pronouncement, she picked up a brush and started mixing a new color on her palette. "I'll see you later at Banning's."

Dismissed, I walked back toward my car.

On my way, I noticed an artist with earbuds firmly in place while she was working at her easel doing a street scene. A small crowd was peering over her shoulder as she painted. I hoped for Claudia's sake that the onlookers understood the signal, Don't talk to me. Time was getting short. The submission deadline for the competition was Friday at noon, and it was already Wednesday afternoon. The pressure was on. The artists had little more than a day and half to deal with their work… and an investigation into two murders.

CHAPTER TWENTY-ONE

Enhance the contrast of an ornate pattern that adorns a silver piece. Polish the high spots to a mirror shine. Use a very soft brush to clean the nooks and crannies but a little tarnish in the lowest spots will help display the pattern to the best advantage.

—"The Butler's Guide to Fine Silver" Mr. Hollister, 1898

Heavy footsteps followed me down the sidewalk as I cut through the empty park. Almost without thinking, I quickened my steps. Someone was hot on my trail. When a hand touched my arm, I whirled around and raised my fists. I wasn't sure what that would accomplish, but I had to do something.

"Whoa, easy there, tiger." Detective Ingram took a giant step back.

I dropped my arms, gasping for air.

"Abby?" He gripped my arms to hold me steady. "Easy, it's okay. I'm sorry if I scared you."

It was hard to catch my breath in the heavy, humid air. He guided me to a park bench close-by and pulled me down to sit.

"I'm sorry. I..."

He sat down next to me and watched me closely.

"Take your time. It's okay. Everyone's on edge." He looked off at the trees in the park and pursed his lips. "I'm sorry, I thought you knew I was trying to catch up to talk to you."

Feeling better, I waved off his apology. "Really, it's okay."

"The Chief said he told you what happened and to stay home. I see that worked."

"Well, I..." I could feel myself getting red. Better to change the subject. "Have you got more news?"

"I can tell you what I haven't been told."

"What you haven't been told?" I repeated.

"No one has told me to back off. The sheriff wants the Walt Stanton investigation linked to Larry's death. Final results aren't in from Baltimore's medical examiner's office yet. The boss wants answers before the winners are announced on Friday night at the Collectors' Preview Party. Everybody is planning to leave this weekend."

"What about the Quick Draw and Quick Draw for Kids?"

"You mean the excuse to close streets and create traffic problems all over town?"

"Detective, that's a jaded way of looking at things. We should promote the arts—"

"All this artsy stuff can't get in my way." He got up, stuck his hands in his pant pockets and started to pace in front of the bench. "I have a job to do."

"And you and your officers are out here working the case, hot on his trail. It should only be a matter of time, I suppose."

"What if I was hot on her trail?" He watched me for a reaction.

"That's possible. Who?"

"Margaret."

"Margaret?" I repeated slowly, mulling over the possibility. The scene of the tough, no-nonsense artist working with Daphney popped into my mind. I shook my head. "No, no, I can't see that."

"She's the prime suspect. She's got motive and plenty of opportunity. Nobody would suspect her. She is always right where you'd expect her to be, which is the same place the killer would be." He looked at what I suspected was a skeptical look on my face. "What have you seen?"

I shrugged. "Nothing to support the idea that she's your prime suspect."

"Abby?"

"Okay. She's always talking about money... art for money. Everybody's heard her talk about it. It does seem to be her prime motivation for painting."

"The big prize of $10,000 can buy a lot of paint," he said and started pacing again. "And pay the rent for a while."

"Keep in mind that it's not just the money for winning first prize that's at stake here. The artists submit two paintings for the competition and can sell an additional eight at the Collectors' Preview Party." I didn't want to make his case that the killer was an artist, but it was starting to make sense if I looked at the money angle. "Somebody said a prize-winning artist could pull in between $20,000 and $30,000." Ingram's eyebrows shot up. "Others can make, what...$10,000 - $20,000, maybe?"

"That's not very much for a yearly income, but it's a pretty good payday for a week's work in my book," he declared. "Now, can you see why Margaret is a good suspect?"

I shrugged. "I guess she could be. Still, I don't think she's the one."

"If she isn't, it's back to square one." He was pacing again. "Funny thing that the festival chairman left out that little detail of how much money is involved."

"No, no, I don't think he was trying to ..." Ingram wasn't listening to me.

He scratched his chin then rubbed his face that was sprouting stubble. "You're a better source of information than the officials."

"I have other sources."

He sat down on the bench. "I guess you do. If the motive is money, who else is a prime suspect? Any of the artists?"

I raised my finger. "Any of the better artists. Out of the fifty-eight competing artists – no, make that fifty-six now, some are better than others. All of them are good painters, I'm sure. Some are sentimental favorites, like Walt was."

"And accomplished professionals, like Larry." He was following my line of thinking.

"Find the favorites, find the killer." He slapped his hands down on his thighs and got up. "It's as good an approach as any. I'll still be following up on some other ideas. I'll have someone run a quick analysis. It will be interesting to see who pops up on the list. Thank you, Miss Abby. See you around." He walked out of the park with a new purpose.

Margaret? Could the woman I'd seen working with Daphney really kill someone? Did my eyes… and my gut deceive me? What about George, the collector who suggested that Larry should die at the crab feast to raise the prices for his artwork? And what about the metal detector man? He wasn't around when Larry was poisoned, but he could have been responsible for Walt's death.

Before I knew it, I was up and retracing my steps back to the park where I'd seen them working. A debate started to rage in my head. According to Agatha Christie, the greatest murder mystery writer, poison was the murder weapon of a woman. Larry's death pointed to a woman. Or was it such common knowledge that a sneaky man might be trying to throw the police off his trail? I was getting a headache and it wasn't from the heat.

I turned into the park again. Margaret had packed up her easel and moved on to some other location, but Daphney was taking a break on a bench. She was swabbing her sweaty face and taking long drinks from her water bottle.

"It seems I've caught you at a good time," I said, sitting down.

"Yes, I feel like I'm melting in this heat." Her voice was breathy.

"I hope you're not overdoing it."

"No, I'm pacing myself with lots of water and time

under these wonderful trees. I hate wearing a hat, but it does help. Margaret told me some of her tricks to stay cool, like the wet cloth across the back of the neck. That's really helped."

"I came by earlier and saw the two of you in deep conversation. I didn't say hello. Didn't want to disturb you."

"Thank you," she said, all smiles. "Margaret has been terrific, telling me ways to beat the heat and making suggestions about my painting. It's almost done."

"She seems like a tough bird. I was a little surprised to see her working with you."

Daphney laughed. "It's all a façade. Somebody called her crusty. She's not like that at all, once you get to know her. Larry smoothed my way with her several months back. You know, she's from New England – a small town in Massachusetts. I guess it's her tough Yankee stock you're seeing. Underneath, she has a heart of gold."

Suddenly, I felt so sorry for this sensitive young woman. Soon, she would learn that she'd lost Larry, her mentor and maybe more. I couldn't imagine the hurt she would feel. She wouldn't learn the truth from me.

"Well, you'd better get back to work."

She laughed. "Yes, ma'am. You're as bad as Margaret and Larry. I kid them, but I really appreciate all their support and advice. I'm very lucky. Have you heard anything about —?"

"See you soon." I walked away quickly, hoping to hide the ache I felt for her.

CHAPTER TWENTY-TWO

White cotton gloves must be worn when handling sterling silver pieces. The hands may be washed clean, but it is the unseen oils of the skin that do the damage.

—"The Butler's Guide to Fine Silver" Mr. Hollister, 1898

Back at Fair Winds, I made a short detour to the kitchen to see if there was any coffee. It was the middle of the afternoon. Lunch was over and no dinner-in-the-dining-room was planned since Lorraine was still out of town. Simon was asleep somewhere with his three big, furry buddies. The house was quiet and empty… and eerie.

I looked around slowly. For the first time in the main house, I felt uneasy, like the little hairs on my skin were standing up. With all the talk about murder, I wasn't surprised. Could Margaret be the killer? My thoughts wandered while I made some fresh coffee.

Margaret? She is a crusty old bird, no question about that.

I'd heard about the reputation of tough Yankees from New England. I had no firsthand experience.

Growing up on the West Coast, we had a different crop of eccentric personalities and cultures.

But a murderer? It didn't seem possible.

Then, I remembered with a shiver. After some horrendous crime was uncovered, reporters would interview neighbors of the murderer or predator. They would say, "Oh, he was so quiet. Such a nice man."

What we see isn't always the truth.

I poured a mug of coffee, turned to go to my office and jerked in surprise. Hot liquid slopped on me, the floor… and on Dawkins's shoes.

My head almost exploded in anger. "You. Must. Stop. Doing. That."

"I'm sorry, Miss Abigail. I thought you heard me come in." He dropped his eyes. It was the first time I'd seen him look contrite.

"Dawkins, there is nothing about you that makes noise. Your shoes don't squeak. You-You…" I searched for the right word. "You shimmer into a room like Jeeves, the English butler. You float from place to place like a ghost."

"Why, thank you, Miss Abigail. However, in the future, I shall endeavor to make noise when you're in the vicinity," he said in his usual calm tone, with a touch of apology.

We both reached for the paper towels at the same time. "I'll clean it up," I said. "It's my coffee."

"I could say it's my job. Perhaps we could do it together?" He suggested.

I stared at him as he tore off the paper towels. Could there be a normal human being underneath that facade somewhere?

While wiping up the puddles and stray droplets of coffee from the counter, cabinet doors, floor and our shoes, I felt a little guilty. If he could apologize, so could I.

"I'm sorry about this, too. I guess I'm a little jumpy after everything that's happened." I stood up. "Oh! You don't know. Larry, the artist—"

"...was poisoned," we said in unison.

"Yes, I heard," he continued. "There is quite the gossip grapevine here on the Shore and, when there's sensational news like that, it blossoms."

I had forgotten how effective a news network was in a small town. "What do your sources tell you about what happened at the crab feast?"

He paused in his cleanup process. "After what happened to the artist on Bruff's Island, there's no question in their minds that this was intentional. Nobody believes that the restaurant served bad crabs. Of course, it could be that they're looking for a bit of excitement. Things have been quiet lately. There hasn't been a good scandal or shocking event in weeks."

"What do you think, Dawkins?"

While he considered my question, we finished the cleanup and tossed away the sodden paper towels. I poured coffee for both of us and settled against the counter waiting for him to state his opinion.

After a sip, he said, "I think the poisoning of Larry Chambers was a malicious, premeditated act. In the case of Walt, the circumstances are unclear." I started to respond, but he motioned for me to wait. "Since you asked, I'm forced to solidify my thoughts. If, and I do say if, the first artist died at the hands of another person, there is someone posing as a sensitive, creative type who is capable of cold-blooded murder. I hate sounding melodramatic. In any case, I believe that prudence is our watchword. It might be prudent, Miss Abigail, for you to stay away from the plein air activities ..." I started to object. "While the police do their job or, at least, until Miss Lorraine returns so she can accompany you."

"Dawkins, I really think that you're overreacting." I countered. "I promise to be careful, stay with people, groups of people in public places." I remembered finding Filly in a deserted spot, tucked away from everything. Maybe it wasn't so outlandish for her to carry her little pistol.

Dawkins raised his eyebrows and looked at me doubtfully. "And your evening walks with a strange man?"

I shot back, "Seth isn't a strange man. I..." My tone of defiance trailed off. I didn't want to admit that Dawkins might have a point. Better to concede quickly and move on. "I'll avoid a possibly dangerous situation."

He beamed, but not in triumph. His face was bathed in relief. He cared, I realized with surprise. He really cared. I could be gracious. "I'm sorry about last night, you know, when I was walking with Seth in the dark. It must have alarmed you."

"You were doing more than walking, Miss Abigail." He sighed. "You're right, it was unnerving. I'm glad you were all right and that I won't have to worry about a repeat of that adventure in the future." He took a last drink of his coffee. "Now, I must get back to my duties. With Miss Lorraine in Baltimore, I have a wonderful opportunity to do some organizing that is sorely needed."

"Good luck with that. Maybe I should turn you loose in my office."

"A fate worse than death," he said as he pushed through the kitchen door.

Good, I thought with a smile. We're back to our old selves again.

CHAPTER TWENTY-THREE

When sadness strikes the House, mourning jewelry is often fashioned from sterling silver and woven hair that is irreplaceable. Take the responsibility of cleaning these pieces yourself.

—"The Butler's Guide to Fine Silver" Mr. Hollister, 1898

Later that afternoon, I walked along the brick sidewalk to Banning's in Easton. Few of the black wrought iron tables and chairs outside were occupied. The news of Larry's death must be common knowledge by now. I pushed open the heavy beveled glass door and walked into quiet room filled with people. A low rumble of conversation contrasted with the exuberant atmosphere I'd found earlier in the week. A few artists and volunteers I'd met over the past few days acknowledged my arrival by a silent salute with a beer mug, a weak smile or a quick wave of the hand.

Seth was sitting at a corner of the bar and pointed to the empty chair next to him. As I slid into place, I said in a low voice, "Everybody knows now, I guess."

He nodded slowly as if his head was too heavy for his neck. "It's a damn shame. A waste of a talented man."

"I'm sorry you lost your friend." Such a simple thing to say. It almost sounded insincere, but I meant it. In the brief time I'd known Larry, he impressed me as a genuine human being, who had nothing to prove to anyone and really cared about what you said and did.

"Who would do something like this, Abby?" There was so much pain in his voice.

"I wish I had the answer. The detective is working on some ideas. I hope it helps to know that the word is that he's a good man. He knows what he's doing, but it takes time. I know it's hard. You have to be patient while he investigates what happened to both Larry and Walt."

"Walt?" Seth's voice went right up the scale. "I didn't know there was anything to investigate."

I laid my hand on his arm to calm him. The warm of the sun was still radiating off his bare skin. "They want to be thorough, that's all."

Another pretty bartender came over to take my order. "Hi, sorry for the wait," she said as she wiped the rich wood of the bar. "They're keeping me a little busy today. Drowning their sorrows, I guess. What can I get for you?" she asked with a smile.

Paul zoomed up next to me. "She'll have a craft beer." He put his arm around my shoulders and squeezed. "You're one of us now. We're adopting you, right, Seth?" Scented waves of malt rolled off of Paul. I'd have a lot of catching up to do to reach his level of inebriation.

Paul pulled away and addressed the whole bar. "Hey, everybody. We lost a friend today. Larry was our friend and we're all gonna miss him." Paul's words were slurring a little, but no one seemed to mind. "I'm Irish. I know how these things are done." He raised his beer glass. Everyone else followed. "To Larry, a real talent. He knew how to paint. He knew how to be a friend and support each one of us, right?" There was a murmur in response. "To a good painter and a helluva guy." Paul raised his glass to his lips and drained it.

"Here, Here!" "To Larry!" People clinked, chugged their beers and banged their empty glasses on the bar. The bartender ran around refilling them. The crowd was ready for another round.

Paul wasn't done. "Our friend stood out, because he was his own man… did what he wanted, lived life his way, even dressed his own way. Early on, people called him Cowboy 'cause of his boots and big hat."

"Don't forget those big belt buckles," somebody yelled out.

Paul laughed and raised his beer. "How could I forget?"

The spirit ran around the room like a virus. People started calling out other little characteristics and idiosyncrasies of their friend. They shared tidbits that started "I remember when…"

When the exchange lost steam, Paul stood up, leaning heavily against the bar. "In tribute, we should sing one of those old cowboy songs."

The room fell silent. The man had gone too far, right over the cliff.

"Come on, people. It's for Larry." Paul raised his glass in the silence and stared singing in a tenor voice.

"Oh, give me a home where the buffalo roam, where the deer and the antelope play…"

One by one, the artists joined in. I did, too. Somehow it felt right...and good. By the time we got to the chorus, people were swinging their glasses in rhythm with the song.

"Home, home on the range…"

The front door swung open and a woman started to walk into the bar. Hearing the singing, seeing the gaiety, she froze in place. As the artists noticed her, their voices dropped out of the sing-along. By the time the lyrics reached the part about a discouraging word, Paul was doing a solo.

The words faded away as he followed everyone's stare. Rebecca.

What is she doing here? I thought.

As if hearing my question, Rebecca answered in a halting voice. "T-t-they took him —" Her voice broke, then she took a ragged breath and continued. "I can't do anything until… I don't want to sit in a stranger's house all alone.

"Oh, my dear." Filly's tone was full of compassion.

Rebecca stepped toward her. "Filly…I'd rather be with you, his friends… and mine." Tears ran down her face.

We all sat dumbstruck. Thank goodness for Filly, who slid off her bar chair and put her arms around Larry's widow. We all got up and gathered around her. Where the words of the cowboy song had bounced off the walls moments ago, now there was only the muted sounds of shuffling and murmured words as we offered our condolences in turn.

As the crowd around her thinned out, I expressed my sympathies, too. When she recognized me, her fingers clamped around my wrist.

"You, you were there when it happened. You saw everything. Did you —" Her eyes pleaded.

Anthony swooped in. "Come along, Rebecca. Why don't you sit down right over here?" He guided her to a table in the corner, away from the bar. She held on to my arm and dragged me along.

When she settled into a chair, she whispered, "Have you talked to the police? Have you told them what happened? You have to help them, Abby. You have to help them find who did this and make them pay."

At first, I was surprised by her urgency. Then, I thought, What do you expect? The woman just lost her husband to murder.

Anthony delivered a glass of red wine to Rebecca and a mug of beer for me. He stepped away with a look of relief that I could sit with the grieving widow for a few minutes and allow those who knew her well to get their bearings.

Rebecca tasted her wine and grimaced. She put the glass down. "I can't believe he's gone. The authorities believe he was poisoned. How is that possible?" Without thinking, without caring, she took another sip. It was something to do. "My brother is coming from California on Saturday. He can't get away before that. It works out, because they won't release the body —" Her lower lip started to quiver. She took out a tissue and dabbed her eyes.

I didn't know what to say. I thought of Lorraine and what she would do right now. I sat quietly and waited. Rebecca continued. "It's nice seeing you and Seth together." A feeble smile crossed her lips. "You two remind me of us, in the beginning. After graduation, Larry worked in management and hated every minute of it. All he ever wanted to do was paint. I couldn't understand it, really. I don't have a creative corpuscle in my body. I was so impressed with what he could do with a brush and a little paint. When he was able to quit his job, we moved to Phoenix. I was thrilled."

"It must have been hard for you to give up your law practice where you were," I said.

"No, it worked out for me, too. I joined a firm there as a partner, doing exactly what I wanted to do. I was fed up with prosecuting criminals in the DA's office. Too much politics. I worked at the criminal defense table for a while. Didn't like that either. I'm on the civil side now and almost never go to court."

Her eyes wandered into an empty space. What she saw in her mind must have brought her pleasure. A genuine smile eased the strain on her face. "I remember we used to go to wander the mesas outside of town, beyond all the housing and commercial buildings. He'd find the most beautiful spots – wide open sky, grasses, piñyon trees. And the rocks. He said they captured the sun's rays and held them prisoner for all time. That's why you could see the whole spectrum of color. When he found the right spot, he'd set up his easel and paint, while I sat on a blanket happily reading. It was… was…" Her lip quivered.

She reached into her purse for a tissue and touched it to the corner of her right eye. After another sip of wine, she took up the story again. "It was wonderful, until he started going to festivals like this one. At first, he stayed close to home. There is a thriving art community in Arizona and New Mexico. It was fun to travel with him to Colorado. As he developed a reputation, the invitations from festivals farther away started coming in.

She looked into her wine, on the edge of tears. "I didn't know he'd be gone so much. I missed him so much when he was away on weekends. Now, he'll never come home." Her control cracked and she sobbed.

Anthony came over, whispered something to her and she stood up. "I'll take her to our home. I think she'll be more comfortable there and Janet will keep her company." He guided Rebecca out of the bar.

I watched them leave. My heart was heavy as I reached for my glass. Only a crumpled tissue and a half-empty wine glass sat at Rebecca's place. I guess it was the air current I created when I got up and took my glass that moved the tissue. It rose in the air and drifted over the edge of the table. It floated gently to the floor. I started to reach for it.

"That's okay, ma'am. I'll get that." The server scooped up the tissue and put it in a water glass on her tray and took it away.

As I turned, Daphney walked in, her face red from crying. Her eyes darted around the barroom. Overwhelmed by all the people, she staggered backward and grabbed the doorframe for support. She shook her head in tiny movements, turned and fled the scene.

I almost followed her, but a thought stopped me. How much should someone intrude on a person's grief? Instead of going outside, I resumed my seat next to Seth.

CHAPTER TWENTY-FOUR

Art can ignite an emotion or a passion even though we do not understand why. I may not know why, but I know what I like. That is why it is such an important part of my life.

—Anthony Bruno, Chairman of the Plein Air-Easton Art Festival

George had slipped into the pub while I was sitting with Rebecca. Now that both the Anthony and Rebecca were gone, Margaret took aim at the pompous collector and fired. "George, you got your wish – your collection of Paintings by Lawrence is now worth a fortune."

George looked stricken. His mouth worked trying to come up with something to say, gave up, threw some money on the bar for his drink and walked out.

"Margaret, that was harsh," said Paul, through his drunken beer haze. "You shouldn't be so hard on the guy."

"He's right, Margaret," added Seth. "Whether someone is alive or dead isn't the only thing that determines the value of an artist's work."

"He's right," chimed in Filly. "People care about the subject matter."

"That should guarantee we sell everything we paint

here," Paul declared.

"But—" I started to make a point when Seth jumped in again.

"People buy postcards when they travel, right? People come to the Eastern Shore because they like the water vistas, the boats..."

"The gardens," Margaret added.

"The quaint street scenes," somebody else threw in.

"If they have the financial resources, they buy nicer postcards... meaning our paintings," Seth tied it all up with a ribbon.

I still wasn't convinced. "There must be more to it than that. If people just wanted representations of the area, they'd buy photographs."

"And they do," said Filly.

"But they're not as sexy as buying an oil painting or watercolor," declared Seth.

As I tried to process this shallow interpretation of why people buy art, Margaret waded into the conversation again. "Don't forget the other major reason why people buy one painting instead of another." She looked around the bar at the artists for the answer. "Come on, you all know this." Exasperated, she pronounced, "Color, of course. You mean to tell me you've never had someone ask you if you could paint the same scene again, but this time emphasize the – oh, I don't know – the orange tones in the sunset instead of the purples? One woman said she'd buy a painting if I'd make some of the flowers yellow instead of having so many pink ones." She cackled. "Those people don't get it."

Somebody in the bar called out, "Did you do it?"

"Not on your life." I heard her murmur as she picked up her glass, "Somebody else who doesn't get it."

The recorded music playing overhead sounded loud in the quiet bar. I suspected none of the artists wanted to admit to making changes to sell a painting.

"Here's another guideline for good sales," Margaret continued. "Don't paint something that is predominantly brown. They hate brown. Stick with warm colors… or blues. Red agitates some people and nobody wants to live with a painting that riles them up. If we want to sell and make a living, we have to keep these things in mind."

"How do you know all this, Margaret?" I asked, feeling a little overwhelmed by all she was saying.

"Experience, dear girl, experience. Also, I read the results of surveys taken by interior design associations and what not. Look them up on the internet."

Filly couldn't let it go. "Margaret, you have to admit that we paint because we're creative. We're driven, because of the challenge and the satisfaction we get when something comes out the way we want it."

"That's true," conceded Margaret, "I enjoy painting as much as you do, except I believe you have to keep your eye on the prize, so to speak. Sales and money are how we keep score."

"Oh, Margaret," sighed Filly.

"I said you're right, Filly. Creativity and art are important and the money we can charge shows how important." She downed the last of her drink and gathered up her things. "Speaking of sales, I have some work to do. I want to try my hand at another nocturne.

I'm becoming rather fond of painting at night and early in the morning, just after the sun comes up. It's so much cooler. I'm going to set up in the garden down the way tomorrow morning to see if I can get one more canvas done. I can usually knock off flowers pretty easily.

"I painted there today. You'll find lots of flowers in bloom."

Margaret gave Filly a little nod and said, "Good night, all." She didn't wait for anyone to respond.

Filly picked up her tote from where it was hanging off the back of her bar chair and started digging through it. I almost giggled at the thought of everyone seeing they had a gun-toting grandma in their midst. The look on the older woman's face erased my happy feeling.

"What's wrong, Filly?" I asked.

She continued to push things around in her tote. "I can't understand it. I put it in here when I finished painting this afternoon. I always put it in the same place. I…"

"What?" I prompted. "What did you lose?"

"My frog. I can't find it. I was going to paint this evening, too. I can't paint without it. I need it to help me focus or I'll be stumbling around all night and never get anything done." She pulled a few things out and put them on the bar. She pawed through them, making a mess. "It's not here." There was a hint of desperation in her voice. Quickly, she piled everything back in her tote. "Maybe it fell out in the car. I have to find it." She, too, did not wait for anyone's goodnights as she raced out the door.

Almost immediately, a woman slid into the vacant

space on the other side of Seth. "Did I overhear that you're an artist?" She smoothed down her blonde hair. The pert pixie haircut looked out of place on the 50-something woman in the yellow sundress.

"Yes, we all are," answered Seth.

"Most of us," I added quickly to join the conversation.

"Oh, you're an artist!" She only had eyes for Seth. "How wonderful."

"Wonderful, why?" His words were flat to show that he wasn't interested in her or her answer.

She missed the signals and shifted her body a little closer to him. "Well, I always thought being an artist was so romantic."

I wish I had Margaret's earbuds, I thought. The one she uses to block out distractions like this idiot.

"You know," she continued. "One minute you have this blank piece of white paper. You take a brush – you know, some of those brushes artists use are the funniest shapes. I mean, isn't a brush, a brush? Well, anyway, you mix some paints together and there you are. You have a painting. I bet you're very good," she cooed.

Seth turned slowly to the silly woman and fired away. "You're right, it's exciting to get an idea in your mind for a painting, but getting it down on the canvas is hard work. It takes training, study and experience to learn how to paint…to learn what works and what doesn't. It's a hard slog."

I put my hand on his arm to calm him. It didn't work. He pushed back his chair and stood up. His powerful body towered over the woman. He continued in a voice as rough as sandpaper. "You think it's romantic being an artist? You think it is easy sitting outside all day, every day baking in this heat?" His voice became strident. "You think it doesn't hurt when a buyer passes on one of your paintings, because it has too much green in it for her living room?" He chugged the last of his beer and slammed the glass on the bar. "If being an artist is so damn romantic and easy, why don't you try it?" He stormed out of the bar.

CHAPTER TWENTY-FIVE

Be mindful of the silver items on every writing desk, especially the letter opener. Its dull blade opens envelopes cleanly while preventing painful paper cuts. It is used often, therefore keep it well polished.

—"The Butler's Guide to Fine Silver" Mr. Hollister, 1898

I almost went after Seth, but something deep inside stopped me. He's not my responsibility. He just needs some time to cool down. It's only natural that he's on edge what with the brutal murder of his friend and then the food poisoning at the crab feast.

It was satisfying to see the shocked look plastered on her face. Quietly, her girlfriend suggested they leave. No one stopped them.

As I glanced up to see them go out the door, I saw Detective Ingram leaning against the wall in the corner, watching. Others around the bar noticed him, too.

"What are you doing here," Paul blurted out. "Why aren't you out catching Larry's killer?"

I gasped. What Paul said was valid, but to hear it put so bluntly was unsettling.

The detective didn't miss a beat. "You are absolutely

right…" He paused for a moment. "Paul, isn't it? Paul Galloway?"

Paul pulled back a little as if he smelled a trap. "Yeah, that's right." Even though the man was drunk, he still had some wits about him, the self-preservation kind. "What's it to you?"

"Well, Paul, I was just agreeing with you," Detective Ingram said as he walked up to the bar where we were sitting. "I should be working to catch the killer of your friend." His casual tone put me on the alert. "I want you to know, Paul,I… I want you all to know that I'm doing just that. You see, the person I'm searching for might be sitting in this room right now." He paused for effect. "Or might have been with you earlier this evening."

Paul lashed out. "What? You think it's one of us?"

Ingram raised his shoulders with a puzzled look on his face. "Could be."

Suddenly, the music playing in the background sounded very loud again in the silence. The detective waited for his words to sink in, then said in his official police voice that issued orders. "Tomorrow is the last full day of painting. I don't care what your plans are, no one leaves town. No one." He pushed open the heavy front door as is it was made of paper and left.

"Sounds like a bad western," somebody murmured.

Another artist, a man I hadn't met, jumped up. "I don't have time for this foolishness. I came to paint and I have to be up early!"

Following his lead, people dug out their wallets to pay their bills. Many paid in cash and, not waiting for change, scrambled for the door.

I wasn't going to sit at the bar alone, no matter how welcoming Banning's was. My mind was roiling with so many different thoughts: Who killed Larry and Walt? Was this the work of one person… or more? Was someone trying to improve the odds of winning the prize money and getting the bonus of selling the other nine canvases? Or was something else at work, something dark that we had no idea existed?

This was supposed to be a celebration of creativity and art. Seeing Rebecca's heartbreak was enough to shred my nerves. And where did Seth go? Should I try to find him? Or should I run back to Fair Winds and lock the door of my little cottage with Simon safe inside?

Outside, the street was wreathed in the growing darkness of evening. Pools of light from the street lamps dotted the walk. Up ahead, someone was leaning on a car. I tensed. All the talk of sudden death had frayed my nerves. I slowed my pace to give myself options, just in case. There was no reason for alarm. It was Seth, leaning against my car.

I took a deep breath in relief and quickened my step. "There you are. I wondered where you went in such a hurry."

"I'm sorry about that." He pulled himself off the car and stood out of the way while I put my things inside on the seat. "It was bad enough that bimbo was coming on to me, but her comments were inane. To think that an artist slaps some paint down and it's suddenly a picture. Talk about not having a clue." He shook his head in disbelief.

"You can relax. She got your message. Right after

you walked out the door, she and her friend left like two little puppies with their tails between their legs." I leaned back against the car and looked up at the night sky. "What a beautiful night. It's so clear you can see the stars."

He stood next to me and scanned the heavens. "You're right. I spend so much time looking at what's right in front of me that, I forget to look up. Usually the light pollution of a town wipes out the stars."

"Not here," I laughed. "So many things on the Shore seem to break the rules. That's probably why I'm falling in love with the area. You travel a lot. Do you ever feel that way about a place? Somewhere you want to set up your easel and stay?"

He crossed his arms. "Funny you should say that. I've been thinking about making a change. We need to talk."

"About what?" I felt sorry the words had slipped out of my mouth. A serious discussion was not what I wanted right now. "The week isn't over yet. We still have lots of time to talk."

I stepped away from the car, hoping to postpone the conversation, but he charged ahead. "All this talk about death – sudden death – and how limited our time can be... and the debate about money versus art... well, it's put things in perspective and got me thinking. I've been lucky to go out on my own and support myself through my art."

"Not everyone gets that opportunity," I said, hoping to point out how lucky he was.

He didn't take it the way I meant it. "I worked very

hard to get myself into this position," He took a step back and crossed his arms, not in anger but self-defense.

Oops, there's another touchy subject I have to dodge tonight.

"But," he went on. "It's very clear to me what's important. It's about the art. I don't just enjoy painting. It's a central part of my being, as vital as breathing, almost. I have to do whatever is necessary to enrich my art."

I nodded. "You should do what you have to do."

He pushed himself off the car and faced me. "I'm so glad you feel that way, Abby. Then it's safe to admit the truth to you."

A sudden shiver went down my back. Truth... about Walt and Larry? I glanced down the street. We were alone. I dragged my attention back to what he was saying.

"... feared to tell you the truth." He took a deep breath while I held mine. "My work has been treading water. It's been uninspired for months."

I exhaled in relief. "Is that all?" The shocked look on his face was proof that I'd just said the wrong thing. "I mean, I mean..." I cast around for something to say. "I mean, it's not an insurmountable problem, not like losing your life." Way to go, Abby. That was a ridiculous thing to say.

"In a way, it's just as important." He ran his hands through his black hair. "I'm not putting this very well. I'm better with paint than words. What I mean is that this year, my work reached a plateau and I haven't been able to go beyond it. Not until now." He grabbed my shoulders in a burst of enthusiasm. "Suddenly, my work has taken a huge leap forward. It's like a veil has been pulled from my eyes. I'm seeing things in a new way and, more importantly, getting those visions down on the canvas."

I looked at him with real delight. "That's wonderful! I'm so happy for you. You're so fortunate to spend your time doing what you love. And to have a breakthrough with your work… that's the best. I'm glad you shared that with me."

His face clouded. "Don't you understand, Abby? Don't you know what's made the difference?"

I felt like I was walking on slippery ground again. "No," I said slowly. "I'm afraid I don't."

He gave me a little enthusiastic shake. "It's you. You have made the difference. I told you at Fair Winds, you are my muse. You."

I was shocked. I wasn't a muse or even someone who could make a difference in an artist's life. The thought was more than I could manage. I tried to come up with something to say that would do no harm.

"Well, that's quite a compliment, Seth. I really don't think I've done anything. It's you and what you have inside."

"That's right, Abby. You do understand."

Oops, that was the wrong thing to say. Instead of cooling off his passion, I fanned the flames. I had no chance to backpedal. He was so excited, his words tumbled out.

"It does come from inside. So, you agree that I have to do what's right for my heart and my art."

"Well, I guess…"

"What's right is you. You have to come with me," he announced.

"Come with you? Where?"

He flung his arm out as he said, "Anywhere the winds take us. I want to paint the world. I know I can do that now..." Ever so gently, he put his hand back on my arm and said in a tender voice, "I can do it if you're by my side. Seth and his muse, Abby."

There it was, all tied up in a neat package. To be crucial part of someone's life was amazing. This was a special moment like the one when we kissed by the river. The moment my life could change.

He pushed a curly strand of my hair off my face. His touch was electrifying. "Abby, please say yes. It means, you mean so much to me."

I was tempted, oh so tempted.

Then, I remembered what had destroyed that moment at Fair Winds. It was the beam of light Dawkins shined in my face. The beam of reality.

I laid my hand on his cheek ever so lightly. "Seth, I don't know what to say." I really didn't. "This is such a surprise."

"It surprised me too," he said, almost out of breath.

"It's such a big step for me. Will you give me a little time to think about it?"

"It's a big step for me, too. You need to know that I'm ready to take it. In fact," he laughed a little. "I guess I've already taken that step, asking you to come with me. I hope you will, Abby. I need you with me. That's the way I want it." He kissed me on the forehead. "But, I understand. I don't mean to rush you. I have to leave this weekend, so I'm ready for the next festival coming up. Will you have an answer for me by then?"

I nodded. "I will, I promise."

"And I hope your answer is yes." He kissed me again. "Sleep tight."

I watched him walk down the brick walk, his feet barely touching the ground.

Unlike Seth, I felt an odd mixture of emotions. Was I ready to dedicate my life to someone else? Did I want the responsibility of being his muse? What did that mean? I looked up as a light breeze caressed the leaves over my head. It was hard making the leap from corporate city life to the Eastern Shore. Did I really want to leave this place?

These questions and more rattled around in my head as I turned into the long driveway of Fair Winds. I wish Lorraine was home and waiting for me in the library.

CHAPTER TWENTY-SIX

A piece of antique silver is a bit of history held in one's hands. It is a work of art crafted by an experienced silversmith. From its use over time, tiny scratches appear that create the valued patina that can be buffed to perfection with a soft chamois.

—"The Butler's Guide to Fine Silver" Mr. Hollister, 1898

When I parked the car I saw a shaft of light playing across the grass. Dawkins was making his security inspection again. As I walked toward him, I was surrounded by four dogs – Lorraine's three Chesapeake Bay retrievers and Simon – giving me an exuberant welcome home. I got slobbery licks on my hand and legs and nudges by the very strong Chessies that almost knocked me over. The big dogs overwhelmed Simon so he couldn't get close to me. When I saw him pouting on the periphery, I bullied my way through the crowd to give him a thorough rub around his neck and ears. His tail wagged so hard from happiness, I thought it was going to come off.

Dawkins cleared his throat and clapped his hands twice. "Sit!" All four dogs plopped down right where they were and looked to their pack leader, the tall, thin man in a neatly ironed white broadcloth dress shirt open at the collar and a dark blue sports jacket. It was the casual uniform he'd wear only when Lorraine was away from Fair Winds. Appearances and regimen were important to this man, though I had no idea why.

"Good. Now, stay." He turned to me. "Now, Miss Abigail, it is not my place to tell you what to do with Simon. He is your dog. I would just like to remind you that it was a scant two months ago that we rushed him to the vet in St. Michaels when he was in so much pain, he couldn't sit, could barely walk. I believe the diagnosis was happy tail."

I sighed. "Who would have thought that a dog could sprain his tail because he wagged it so much from happiness?. You're right, Dawkins. We don't want to go through that again. Simon, calm down, boy. Everything's okay."

Both Dawkins and I looked to the other end and swish, swish. Simon's tail was hard at work. "You always have good ideas, Dawkins. What's a girl to do?"

"In this case, I suggest we walk." He started down the path and the dogs scampered after him, sniffing in the bushes, racing one another over the grass so worn out by the heat.

I followed along. "How was your day, Dawkins?"

He looked at me in surprise. "Miss Abigail, it seems to me that we should be talking about your day. Did something happen that's caused consternation?"

Only Dawkins would use the word consternation during an evening stroll. It annoyed me a little bit that he was right. How does he do that?

"Miss Abigail?"

I blew out a deep breath. "Yes, you're right." Oh, how I hated to admit it. "I was talking to Seth a little while ago —"

"The artist who was here at Fair Winds." It was a statement, not a question.

"Yes, that's the one." I was glad the sun had set and it was hard to see in the dark. My cheeks felt warm and I knew I was blushing. That was the last thing I wanted Dawkins to see. Trying to sound casual and relaxed, I said, "We were talking about art and the artist's muse."

"Ah, the elusive muse. Every artist, in fact everyone in the arts, desires to have the muse to provide inspiration and brilliance. Whether it's painting, sculpture, music, poetry, everyone feels a desperate need for the muse. Did he say you are his muse?"

I stopped dead in place while he and the dogs continued on. "How did you know?" I demanded.

Dawkins continued to walk along with the dogs, swinging his flashlight in a wide arc. I scrambled to catch up.

"It makes complete sense," he explained. "An artist is inspired by whatever is around him. It might be a song, a colorful sunset, a leaf wafting on a breeze. It wouldn't be the first time a pretty girl inspired a painter."

Was that a compliment or just an observation? Better move right along.

"Perhaps," he continued, "he believes he is in love with you."

I stopped walking again and, this time, so did he.

"He wants me to go away with him." Even to my

ears, my voice sounded like a piece of taffy stretched to its limit. I didn't know if I should laugh, cry or run the other way. And I'm standing here in the dark talking with Dawkins. The world has tilted.

"Of course he does. It's the logical thing for an artist to do." He started walking again as if I'd said nothing more earth-shattering than I had to wash my hair. I had to wash my hair.

I stood, rooted to the ground. Of course, was the last thing I expected him to say. "I wouldn't have thought it was the most logical thing to do."

"That's because you have an analytical mind. It's the way you have to think if you write software or research silver. If you can't see it or touch it, it doesn't exist, right?"

I wanted to disagree, but he was right. I didn't want to reveal any more of myself. I quickly said, "We're talking about Seth."

He shined his light into a thicket of bushes. The dogs noticed, but continued to meander ahead of us. No threat there. We followed them.

Dawkins chose to reveal something about himself. "I don't particularly care for the work of Pablo Picasso. There was more to the man than paint and charcoal. He was astute about art and the people who made it. I think one of his sayings applies here." Dawkins stopped and squinted into the distance. "He said, 'Everything you can imagine is real.' Isn't that what an artist does, takes something from his mind and makes it real on a piece of paper or canvas?"

I agreed and he went on. "That's what is happening

with Seth. He believes his work has improved exponentially. He is spending time with you. Therefore, you must be the reason for the inspired work he's doing."

I was having trouble processing that idea.

"Don't work too hard with that," he added. "Mr. Picasso also said, 'The chief enemy of creativity is good sense.' Artists, like their art, aren't logical, or even rational sometimes."

"Dawkins, you are right about that. It's all too much for this tired brain. I'm going to bed. Good night."

I called Simon and we went to the cottage. There was comfort in closing the door on the world.

CHAPTER TWENTY-SEVEN

The keen interest in antique silver during this century has led to alteration. Carefully examine pieces for distorted or inappropriate hallmarks, solder to attach a new part or an uneven surface. These are all signs of piece that may not be what it appears.

—"The Butler's Guide to Fine Silver" Mr. Hollister, 1898

I hoped for a good night's sleep. A light rain broke the heat wave shortly after I crawled into bed. I was sure Dawkins had seen the shower coming and made it back to the big house before he got wet. That was something he would do. The soft pitter-pat of the raindrops should have lulled me to sleep. They didn't. I tossed and turned. In the early morning hours, I was thrashing around so much that Simon went downstairs to sleep.

Questions kept poking at me. Questions about the deaths of Walt and Larry. Questions about Seth. I had to admit that I was attracted to him. I was tempted by his offer.

After all, the time to do something crazy is while I'm young, right?

Maybe not, another part of me spoke up. I decided

I didn't have enough information. Part of what was keeping me awake was the realization that I'd known the man less than a week.

This isn't like me. I don't do things like this.

I punched the pillows for the umpteenth time that night. I wanted—no, needed—to talk to Lorraine, but I didn't want to call and bother her while she was dealing with her elderly aunt. Instead I silently wailed, Lorraine, come home.

When I saw the first rays of the sun through the narrow opening in the curtains, I admitted defeat. Maybe that helped relax my mind so a new idea could float to the surface. There was one artist who had known Seth since he started on the plein air circuit, someone who would not hide her true feelings behind obscure references. As Gran would say, she was someone who would shoot straight from the hip.

I needed to talk to Margaret. I'd overheard her telling someone at Banning's last night that she was going to do a quick painting in the garden behind the historic society building. I bet she would be there early this morning. If I can get to her before she puts those earbuds in. I threw back the sheets and jumped out of bed. If I hurried, I could get through our morning regimen and make it to the garden in Easton in time.

Later, turning out of Fair Winds, I was surprised by how many cars and pickup trucks were headed up the road in the direction of the largest town in the county. I had to laugh. Large by the standards here on the Shore, a town of about 10,000 people. That would be small anywhere else in country, I imagined. When I saw an opening in the steady stream of vehicles, I made the left turn. In the other direction, trucks, from semis to box trucks, were headed down to St. Michaels. It was going to be a busy weekend and they were making deliveries. I hoped the lawyers and clerks wouldn't head to the courthouse before I found a parking space.

As I rounded the corner at the entrance to the garden, I noticed the birds. No, it was the absence of birds. On my way from the parking space to the garden, the birds were singing at the top of their little lungs. It was like a cheerful battle of the songs. In the garden, it was as if someone had turned off the music. Only a light breeze made the leaves tremble.

The heavy, ornate wrought-iron gates by the entrance were open. I followed the walkway of old bricks as it meandered down to the garden. The flowers were in full bloom and the bees were hard at work.

This must be the way Margaret likes it: no crowds, no distractions, quiet, cool.

I saw an artist at an easel set up down toward the far end of the garden. It had to be Margaret. Her signature hat hung down her back, close at hand for the time when the hot sun climbed above the trees. She was hunched over the little table that held her paints and brushes, probably opening a new tube or contemplating a particular color combination. I moved forward, trying to be as unobtrusive as possible. She was not the type of person to hail from a distance, "Hey, Margaret!" A funny thought crossed my mind. That kind of greeting would probably get someone a paintbrush stuck in an eye.

As I got a little closer, I remembered the volunteer's warning not to surprise an artist who was working. I cleared my throat. No response. I tried a weak cough, then another, a little louder. Still no response.

"Margaret?" I said softly. "Good morning."

I was close enough now to see that she had one of her earbuds nestled in an ear. That's probably why she didn't hear me.

"Good morning, Margaret. It's Abby," I announced. "I'm sorry if I'm disturbing you. I only need—" One of the earbuds was dangling. She wasn't hunched over her paints. She was slumped. Her right hand, holding a paintbrush, hung by her side. Had she fallen asleep?

"Margaret?" Fear, urgency, a plea were all tied up together.

I touched her shoulder and her body toppled sideways. "Margaret!" I grabbed her before she crashed into her easel. The weight of her body was too much for me. Somehow, I guided her body slowly to the ground.

Her face was ashen.

"Margaret? Margaret!"

Her green eyes stared, but didn't see me. Even in the growing heat, her skin was cold to the touch. I took my hand away from her back. It was drenched in blood.

It felt like hours that I stared at my hand, red drops falling from my fingertips.

Get help. I have to get help!

I held my left hand away from my body as if it didn't belong to me. I pulled my phone out of my pocket. It took three tries for me to touch 9-1-1 correctly. When I heard it ringing, I told myself, Calm. Keep calm.

When the dispatcher came on the line and asked the nature of my emergency, I screamed, "Help! She's dead. There's blood." I looked at my hand and felt like I was going to pass out.

I guess the dispatcher talked me through things and got the details she needed. I don't remember that part. The next thing I knew, paramedics were running toward me with a back board and pieces of equipment. Someone lifted me to a standing position, walked me over to a wooden bench near a bush with bright pink flowers.

I don't know how long it was before the police officer sitting with me, gently asking me questions, got up and someone else sat down. I didn't think I'd ever be glad to see Detective Ingram's face, but, at that moment, I was.

He asked me to repeat what had happened. "I need to hear it for myself," he explained.

After I'd gone through it twice, he motioned one of his officers over and said something I couldn't hear. Then, he said, "Abby, I want you to do something for me. I want you to take a look at—" I started shaking my head slowly. "Abby, listen to me. I want you to walk over to the easel and look at the canvas for me."

"No."

"Abby, you won't see her. I just want you to look at a couple of things. I'd bring them to you, but I don't think you want to sit here waiting for the crime scene guys to finish."

I shook my head hard. "No, that's the last thing I want to do. I want to go home."

"Let's do this now so you can. I'll be with you the whole time," he promised.

Slowly, I got to my feet and he put his arm around my shoulders. It was reassuring and helped keep me stable.

A crime scene technician came over and handed him a plastic bag with something inside. "Here you go, detective. We're finished with this."

Ingram thanked him and held the bag up so I could see what was inside. "Do you recognize this, Abby?" The world reeled and he held on to me. "Okay?" I nodded. "You know what it is?" I nodded again. "And?"

"It's a frog," I managed to say. "A frog on a necklace."

"That's good." He was nodding, waving his right hand in tight circles to urge me to continue. "It's a frog necklace. Do you know who it belongs to?"

I nodded again. I didn't want to say her name.

"Abby, you have to tell me."

Desperation was in my voice. "She said she lost it yesterday. Maybe she lost it here and it doesn't have anything to do with…"

"We found it on the grass next to Margaret's easel. If it had been there when she set up, she probably would have picked it up."

Hope evaporated.

Tears flooded my eyes and streamed down my face. "I-It's Filly's frog, her creative talisman." Through the blur, I saw him frown. "It belongs to Filomena, the artist?"

I searched my pockets for a tissue to wipe my tears.

How ironic, I thought as I remembered the opening night party on Bruff's Island. I'd sat down next to Filly and given her a tissue, since she had shredded hers to bits. Now, when I need one... I tried to sniff back my tears and wipe my face with the sleeve of my sweatshirt.

The full impact of finding Filly's frog necklace at the murder scene hit me. Filly was their prime suspect. How could such a funny, confident woman commit such a crime? How could I have been so wrong about someone? But, she does carry a gun, I remembered.

Identifying the frog had used up the last bit of strength I had. I forced myself to stand up straight and take in deep breaths of air so I wouldn't topple over in a faint. Ingram misconstrued my movement.

"Good, you're feeling better." He took my arm and led me over to the place where Margaret had set up her equipment. It took every bit of willpower I had not to pull away from him and run, run anywhere far away from this garden. He never noticed. "There's something else I want you to see. It's right over here."

Come on, Abby. You can do this. Remember, Claudia said it was all about courage.

I went over to where he stood.

"Just keep your eyes on the easel. Look at the easel," he coached.

It really wasn't a painting, not yet. A tall shape in dark brown and two blocks of bright fuchsia marked the beginning of her picture of flowering bush by a tree. "She must have just started working. From what little I know about painting, she was blocking in the different elements. What's that—" I peered closer then looked at the live scene suggested by the shapes on the canvas and back again. A long, crooked line of glistening red paint was on the right side. "What is that? It's not in the scene."

Detective Ingram looked at it, too. "What do you think it is?"

"I don't know. It's not part of the scene she was painting. See?" I pointed. There wasn't any dramatic line like that in the garden.

"Don't artists add things to their pictures that aren't there in real life?" He asked.

"Sure, but that line is so, I don't know, out of place. It's such a bold stroke. I can't imagine what she was going to put there."

"Abby, I want to talk to the technician. Are you all right here alone for a minute?"

I nodded and he stepped away. I curled my left hand into a fist, something Gran taught me to do when I had to, what she called, keep a grip on myself. She had given me all kinds of little tricks like that to get through the rough times when I was a kid. I had flashbacks for years about the car accident that killed my mother. I didn't relax until the detective came back.

We stood and watched the technician examine the red swath on the picture. He used a cotton swab to take a sample. I couldn't see what he did with it, but a few moments later, he came over to us.

"You were right, detective. It's blood," he announced.

I had to take a deep breath to stay calm. Ingram's arm went around my waist and gave me the support I needed.

"Let's sit down," he suggested.

"No, not yet. I want to look at that mark again. It looks like it started at the bottom edge, goes up and then…"

"Making something like an oval shape," he said. There was a note of curiosity in his voice. "I wonder…"

"Do you think the killer…?"

"Maybe. Someone wanted to ruin her last painting,"

"Or was it a message?" I asked. "When I found her, she was holding a paintbrush."

He called the technician over again and mumbled something to him. "Abby, he's going to check the brush. I want you to turn around with me and look the other way."

We turned toward the other side of the garden and he stood next to me for support. I noticed that the old bricks in the wall that surrounded the garden had so much more character than the modern, monochrome red bricks made today. What a story they could tell. What an odd thought. It gave me an idea.

"Detective, do you think Margaret knew her killer? Do you think she was trying to tell us the identity?"

The technician returned, holding a paintbrush. "You were right again. I think this was in her hand when she…" He shifted his eyes to me and rushed on in a lower voice. "I can't be certain yet what happened."

"But, you can give me a hypothesis," finished Ingram.

"Yes, sir. From the amount of blood on the ground, I don't think she died immediately. I think she bled out.

It will have to be confirmed…" Ingram nodded his head impatiently. "Well, it seems the blood ran down her arm and over the brush to the ground. Somehow, she held on to the brush and, after the initial shock of the attack, she could have made the marks you see on the canvas."

"Painted them in her own blood?" He asked.

"Yes, sir. Of course—"

"I know, I know. It has to be confirmed by the lab. I want my own pictures of those marks." He handed the technician his phone. "Thank you." While we waited for the photos, Ingram led me back to the bench. "You could be right, Abby. She may have tried to identify her attacker."

When his phone was returned, he brought up the mark that filled the screen. "Any ideas?"

"I'm sorry, no. It looks like an oval shape, but wait…" I looked closer. "See how the loop doesn't go all the way to the bottom? Like the letter "P"?"

"Or maybe she started in the other direction and didn't have time to finish it." He let out a deep sigh. "I don't know. Let's get you home."

The garden, once a place of tranquility and beauty, was crowded with experts – people who gathered forensic evidence, those who made observations and gathered clues, and supervisors watching them. They were all there, trampling on the lush green grass, brushing against flowering bushes sending petals to the ground, making an unseemly racket with orders and requests. Margaret would have hated it.

Of course!

I held out a hand and Ingram stopped next to me.

I was touched by his concern.

"Are you dizzy? Are you going to be sick?"

"No, I'm fine. Well, considering." I looked around to be sure no one else was listening. I guess I didn't want to look any sillier than I had with my swooning and crying earlier. "You wanted my observations. Here's one: I remember that Margaret had her earbuds in place. Or at least one of them was still in an ear."

"Why is that important?" He looked confused.

"It was her signal that she didn't want to be disturbed. She liked to use them when a crowd gathered around to watch her paint. She told me, 'They're too distracting and there's great power in being able to block them out!' Maybe she was having a fight with someone and ended the conversation by putting her earbuds in place."

"It's an interesting idea," he said. "But…who?"

CHAPTER TWENTY-EIGHT

A proper hallmark clearly identifies a piece as containing the required silver content for sterling.

—"The Butler's Guide to Fine Silver" Mr. Hollister, 1898

Once outside the garden wall, Detective Ingram pulled a uniformed officer aside, whispered some instructions to him. Moments later, we were on our way to Ingram's car. He'd promised to have someone drive my car back to Fair Winds when I handed over the key.

"What was that all about, with that officer?" I asked. He was silent for a moment, at war with himself about whether he should tell me. "I think I —"

He blurted out, "You really want to know?"

Now, I wasn't so sure. I'd had enough gory details. He took my hesitation as an affirmative answer.

"I sent the officer to bring Filly in for questioning." He saw my stricken expression. "Come on, Abby, it's the most obvious answer."

I looked straight ahead, feeling like I would explode in frustration. How could I be wrong about Filly? She was always so sensitive to the feelings and needs of everybody else. Above all, she seemed to know exactly who she was and what made her tick. She might lecture someone to smithereens, but kill a person? No. Unless…

I turned to Ingram. "If Filly was in the garden this morning – and I'm not saying she was – maybe there was an argument. You know how irritating Margaret could be. Her opinions were pretty much set in stone."

The detective nodded. "Anything's possible."

I ran with this new line of thinking. "And if Margaret made Filly so angry that the older woman lashed out… well, stabbing isn't her style. She would have —" What are you doing? I can't tell a police officer that Filly is packing a concealed weapon!

"She would have… what?" he asked.

Think fast! "She would have gotten in a parting shot and walked away." Well, I wasn't exactly lying.

"She does have a mouth on her, one you wouldn't expect from an old lady."

If he only knew what was lurking in Filly's tote.

As we neared Ingram's unmarked car parked at the curb, we heard someone running down the sidewalk.

"Get in the car, Abby," he ordered. "Now."

When I saw Jack, the local reporter, racing toward us, I scurried into the car. Through the closed windows, I heard the exchange.

"Detective, the cycle of violence continues," said Jack, almost breathless. "Tell me what—"

"I'm not ready to make a statement yet," Ingram said emphatically.

"Detective, I have to know. The powers that be —"

"This power is going to arrest you if you don't step

away from the vehicle."

Jack looked at his proximity to the detective's car and took a giant step away. "There, now... wait!" he cried as Ingram got into the car. The reporter caught a glimpse of me. "Abby! Are they arresting you? Detective, is she the killer?"

Ingram drove away, leaving Jack yelling on the sidewalk.

"The least you could have done was tell him I'm not under arrest." I was not pleased that the blabbermouth reporter had his own theory. "What if he prints or posts on their website that I'm the killer?"

A little smile crept over his mouth. "Hmm, a little misdirection might be helpful right now."

"At my expense?" I folded my arms and stared out the windshield. "Thank you very much."

As he turned down Route 33, he said, "Don't feel bad. I have a problem, too. I feel like I'm starting this investigation all over again. I was sure that Margaret --" He heaved a sigh. "It just shows ,you have to follow the evidence and not jump to conclusions."

"Like pulling Filly in for questioning?"

"Think of it as a kind gesture to return her frog."

I turned my head away and watched the scenery as it passed by. Did he really expect me to buy that? I peered into the side mirror. "Where's the officer bringing my car? Think he'll have trouble driving a stick shift?" A sheepish look appeared on the gentle detective's face. "What? Now, you tell me. I should have sent her to pick up Filly and had the male officer bring your car."

"Why?" I shifted around toward him, even against

the constraint of the seatbelt. "That car is very important to me. If anything —"

"I forgot. Officer Sweeny likes to spend her off-hours working on cars and going to racetracks around, even in Delaware and Pennsylvania."

"So, she knows what a Saab 9-3 turbo can do." It was more of a statement than a question.

"Probably. It will be fine. Nothing's going to happen."

I looked behind us and saw a flash of teal blue streak through the light and barrel towards us. "Nothing – but a ticket, maybe."

Ingram looked in the mirror and shook his head a little. "At least we know where she is and what she's doing."

I checked to see that Officer Sweeny had given up the idea of passing and settled behind us, doing the speed limit. That's better. She must have recognized Ingram's car… and just in time. I settled back in my seat, satisfied that at least something was under control.

Ingram didn't notice the fields of ripening corn or the turkey vultures cleaning up some road-kill on the shoulder. His thoughts finally spilled over into conversation.

"I was sure it was Margaret. She was the obvious suspect. I even approved overtime for a plainclothes officer to keep her under surveillance today. She'd already left the host family's home this morning, so he went to the Information Center to find out where she was working. It didn't open until 8. By that time, she was probably already dead."

His brutally honest words suggested that he'd forgotten I was in the car and was thinking out loud. His fist hit the steering wheel. "She'd still be alive if I'd closed the festival. I should have followed my instincts."

His comment stung. I was the one who told him about the map so he could track the artists at any given time. I was the one who made a case for letting the festival go forward, though I felt sure that Anthony would have been all over the sheriff and pulled strings with the higher-ups if Ingram had tried to shut down the festival.

"What were you going to do?" I said in what started as a weak voice that grew stronger as I made my argument. "Hold hostage fifty some-odd artists and their families in Easton while you investigated Walt's death?"

"Thanks for that. If I had, Larry might still be alive, too. I don't want discuss it. It's done."

I folded my arms and willed the car to go faster, to get to Fair Winds.

Once we arrived, I asked Ingram to drop me at the front door. I released the seatbelt. I wasn't going to let him blame me for anyone's death. My anger, frustration and a tinge of guilt sent me flying out of the car as soon as it stopped.

Officer Sweeney pulled up behind us. In a flash, I was at the driver's door of my car. "Okay, put it in neutral and set the brake." The officer paused, reluctant to get out of my high performance car. "Out!"

I got into the driver's seat and silently apologized to my little car. I drove it around the side of house and tucked it into its usual parking space. Not feeling like talking to anyone, I slipped down the path to the cottage. Heavy breathing warned me of Simon's approach. I turned to fend off his normal greeting.

"No jumping! Do not jump!"

I held out my hands to protect against the compact body of black fur speeding toward me. One minute he was running flat out in delight at my arrival, then his brain made the connection of No Jump. His long legs stuck out, trying to stop. Too late. He barreled into me and down I went. At least he didn't jump, I thought and started to laugh. My face was wet with his wet, slobbery kisses.

"Okay, okay! That's enough. I was only gone for a few hours." Only it felt like a year. "I'm glad you missed me." He was not listening. Now, that I was down on his level, he was happy to romp all over me. I could feel the wetness from his muddy paws seeping through my shirt. There was no telling where he'd been. In self-defense, I muttered the cookies.

He stopped in an instant, only his tail wagging madly, while he panted for breath.

"Go to the cottage." And he was off like a shot to the door.

I got up, brushed off my clothes. No, the only thing to do was to change clothes. I was more than ready to start this day over.

CHAPTER TWENTY-NINE

The master butter knife has a sharp pointed end with a dull blade. It is used only to serve a pat of butter from the main butter dish to a diner's plate. It is never used to spread butter on bread to prevent contamination of all the butter in the dish.

—"The Butler's Guide to Fine Silver" Mr. Hollister, 1898

I put on a clean top and shorts and made myself some coffee. Somehow, the hot mug of java wasn't satisfying. I wanted to sit down and recuperate from the harrowing, shocking events of the morning, but I couldn't seem to settle. Again, Simon stalked my footsteps as I prowled the cottage.

Something danced at the edge of my brain. Something that happened this morning. It was... No, gone again.

"This is ridiculous. Simon, let's practice that new game I taught you. Lorraine will be so impressed when she gets home." He sat with his ears up and his tail wagging, looking too cute for words.

I got some dog cookies from the jar in the kitchen. "Stay!" I ordered and went to the living room when I looked back and caught him shifting his position closer to the doorway. "Do I know you or what?" I scratched him behind one ear since my other hand held the goodies he loved so much. "At least you've learned to sit on command. That's a start. Now, back you go." With a little attitude, he went to sit under the kitchen table again.

I reviewed the rules of the new game. "Stay, until I tell you to Go Find. No peeking! Now, stay."

He did, while I ran up the stairs and hid a cookie in my bedroom. "Go Find," I called down the stairs and moved out of the way. I didn't want a repeat of what happened outside.

Simon darted up the stairs, paused for a split-second on the landing and dashed into the bedroom with his nose a half-inch above the sky-blue carpeting. He made a beeline for the bed and poked his nose under the bed skirt.

"No, Cold, Cold." I'd adapted the old children's game of Hot and Cold, a form of Hide and Seek, desperate to keep this active puppy engaged. "Cold, I said." Simon backed away. When we first started to play this game, putting a cookie under the bed seemed like a good idea. Now that he was in another growth spurt, he might get under there and not be able to get out. We didn't need that hassle. "Good boy!" He continued his sniffs around the room.

Between his improving sense of smell and my prompts, he found the cookie sitting behind a leg of the dresser. Happy with his triumph, he crunched his way through his prize in a moment and sat at my feet, ready to play again.

We played Go Find throughout the cottage and I was hiding the fourth cookie when guilt struck. The vet had warned me not to feed him too many cookies or he'd get fat.

"Last one, boy." I made this turn extra hard. The cookie sat behind one of the pillows on the sofa for all of four minutes, a long search for my wonder dog. After devouring the treat, he sat at my feet for another round and didn't understand that the game was over.

"You can't always have things the way you want, buddy. Go find your bone." As if he understood, he took off and was back in a no time, prancing around with his bone in his mouth.

You can't always have things the way you want them.

There was one person at the festival who knew what he wanted: Seth… and he wanted me. He wasn't content to let things develop naturally. Ever a man of action, he'd declared that I was his muse. He was clear about the positive effect I had on his art. As his muse, my place was with him.

Can I do that? Is there any way that I…

I dropped down on the sofa, almost overwhelmed by the thought. Simon banged his bone against my leg. Automatically, I grabbed the bone and held it while he gnawed on it happily.

Seth, a murderer? What an outrageous thought.

Only, it wouldn't go away. He had said the night before that he felt he had to do whatever was necessary to enrich his art. Was it necessary for him to murder three artists?

I racked my brain. Was Seth painting close to the pond where Walt was working that first night? Seth could have walked right up to Walt. They were friends. If he hit the man over the head with a rock, Seth was strong enough to drag him to the water's edge and hurl him into the water. He'd had a falling-out with Larry at some other festival, something about wanting to paint from the same place. No, Seth wouldn't discount art or turn the plein air experience into something that was all about the money. Seth had made his money by the time he was 38, so he could take off the corporate coat and tie and paint. But he had that in common with Larry, though he was older. The notion of painting for the joy of it ... and making money along the way went against Margaret's view of the world. Seth hated how she boiled it all down to dollars and cents.

A chill ran over my skin. Simon pulled his bone away, lay down with it under his chin and watched me.

"And you don't like him." Simon wagged his tail in response.

Maybe the detective is right, though I didn't want to admit it. Maybe the killer is an artist who has gone crazy.

Then, I remembered the feel of his lips on mine. The sound of his voice as he asked me to run away with him, to be his companion on an artistic journey.

"No," I said aloud. "I hope I'm a better judge of people than that. It can't be..." I hope it isn't, I whispered in the privacy of my mind. What about Filly? She was probably sitting in an interrogation room right now. Am I such a lousy judge of people?

All of a sudden, the room was too small. It felt like the walls were moving in. My imagination was on a rampage. No wonder after the events of the morning. I jumped up.

"Come on, Simon. We're going for a walk."

Outside, I looked up toward the main house and got the best surprise ever. Lorraine's car was parked by the kitchen door. She was home.

CHAPTER THIRTY

The ice cream fork, a newly-designed piece of silver flatware, combines tines to cut, spear and lift a firm bite and a wide, shallow bowl for enjoying the softer part of a serving.

—"The Butler's Guide to Fine Silver" Mr. Hollister, 1898

I found Lorraine in the kitchen, along with everyone else making a fuss to welcome her home. There were quick exchanges of news, of questions asked and answered. This woman meant so much to us all. She'd only been gone a few days and it felt like weeks. Everything felt lighter, seemed brighter now that she was home. That's when it hit me how much I'd struggled to navigate everything happening at Plein Air. Knowing I had someone to help me make sense of it all lifted a heavy weight from my shoulders.

"Abby? Hello?" I realized with a start that the cook, Mrs. Clark, was talking to me. "I asked, are you going to join Miss Lorraine for lunch or not?"

"Oh, I'm sorry. Yes, of course. Who am I to miss one of your special meals?"

"And it will be special," she agreed, with a broad

grin. "It will be a special lunch for the traveler come home." She shooed us out of the kitchen with a promise of something good to eat in thirty minutes.

Lorraine started up the back stairs to her bedroom. "I have just enough time to jump in the shower before we eat. When I'm away, I never feel clean, really clean until I come home and take a hot shower in my own water. Call me weird! Maybe I am." She laughed and it was wonderful to hear. "I'll be down in a few minutes and then, I want to hear about everything that's happened." She disappeared around the corner.

I want to tell you about the murders, but I'm afraid you want to know about Seth.

While I waited, I browsed through the paper, careful to ignore any stories about the strange happenings at Plein Air. I noticed Jack had a by-line on one article. Maybe now he would stop pushing so hard and act like a responsible journalist, not a sensationalist.

It wasn't long before I heard Lorraine come down the stairs and go into the library. When I walked in, she was going through the mail and seemed happy to have an excuse to leave it piled on the desk.

She sat in her favorite chair by the fireplace now decorated with a spray of fresh flowers from the garden. "Ah, that feels so good. I've missed our chats in this room. Tell me, have you chained yourself to your desk while I've been gone?"

I felt a stab of guilt, but was honest. "No, I followed your advice. I've taken advantage of some of the art festival activities. It's so special to be able to peer over the shoulder of an artist working at an easel. It's a thrill to think that the painting taking shape in front of your eyes might be the one to win the First Prize."

She leaned back against the soft cushion. "Yes, it is a rare opportunity. Usually, artists barricade themselves in a studio or want to be left alone when they paint. I'm glad you've gone." She cleared her throat and wouldn't meet my gaze as she asked, "Have you visited with any of the artists we met at last Saturday's party?"

I knew she was fishing for information about Seth. I felt a little self-conscious as well and thought I'd sidestep the question for now since there was more to it than spending a little time with someone. "Yes, I've seen several of them at work in this wilting heat. Oh, I went to the town of Oxford for the first time, too."

"Oxford is such an old-fashioned town. I have a booklet about it somewhere here." Lorraine bounced up from her chair and went to one particular bookcase. "This is where I keep things about local history." She ran her finger along the spines then, pulled out one slim publication to check the title. "Yes, here it is." Thumbing through booklet, she sat down again.

"You must have a reference for everything here," I said, with admiration.

"Not at all, but I do have things about the Shore," Lorraine said. "Oxford has a long history that dates back to 1669 when it was officially designated a town. Later Robert Morris turned it into a thriving port with large ships bringing things from England and sailing off with tobacco grown on the Shore's plantations."

"Plantations?" That surprised me.

"Oh yes, we're south of the Mason-Dixon Line."

Lorraine continued, "Would you like to hear one of my favorite stories about Oxford? It's about a woman."

I nodded and she was off.

"Her name was Mary Stewart—Miss Mary Stewart, appointed the postmistress for Oxford in ... Wait, let me check it." She flipped through the booklet. "Here it is. It was 1877. She didn't retire until 1940!" Lorraine did a quick count using her fingers. "That's 63 years."

I clapped my hands in delight and laughed. "Imagine the stories she could tell!"

"I'm sure nothing happened in Oxford without her knowing about it. People went to the post office to pick up their mail and share the latest news and gossip. It's still that way in Oxford and St. Michaels."

Lorraine grew quiet and focused her attention on turning the pages of the booklet. Finally, she blurted out, "How was it with Seth in Oxford?"

I stifled a laugh. She was so transparent. "The breakfast picnic was wonderful," I answered slowly. "He loved Mrs. Clark's biscuits. Simon had a good time and I learned a little bit about painting. That's all that happened in Oxford."

That's all that happened in Oxford, I thought. What you want to know about happened in

Easton and right here at Fair Winds.

"It's a long story —" I started to say.

I was grateful when Mrs. Clark appeared in the doorway and interrupted me. "Well, I hope it can wait." She looked at Lorraine and smiled with pride and pleasure. "Luncheon is served on the terrace."

It wasn't much later when Lorraine and I leaned

back in the wicker chairs on the terrace overlooking the Miles River, completely satisfied by Mrs. Clark's delicious lunch. There were only tiny bits left of her signature chicken salad with pecans and celery, stuffed in heirloom tomatoes grown right here at Fair Winds. Crumbs of her freshly baked sourdough bread and sweet butter were on our plates. I refilled our glasses with the cook's famous iced tea flavored with fresh mint.

"Ah, that was good," sighed Lorraine. "Dorothy was right. There's no place like home."

"Do you want to talk about your trip?" I wanted to be supportive and maybe my question was a delay tactic. She was so relaxed. Why ruin it with talk about death and complications in my life?

"Thanks, but not really. Alzheimer's is a terrible disease. I wish they'd hurry up and find a cure for the people who have it and a vaccination for those who don't. My aunt settled in as well as can be expected. Thanks for asking." She sat up in her chair. "Tell me everything that's been going on here."

I filled her in about the open case involving Walt's death. As gently as I could, I told her about the night Larry was stricken at the dinner and the cause of death.

"I heard about it on the Baltimore news station, but nothing was said about poison. They just said there was an ongoing investigation." She looked sad. "He seemed like such a lovely man. His wife must be devastated. Oh, to lose such a talented artist, that's another crime."

Mrs. Clark bustled through the French doors carrying a tray. "Oh, good. I see I timed things just right. You've had a few minutes to rest after eating the main course. Now, you're ready for some nice Italian ice." She placed two parfait glasses on the table and gathered up all the used dishes. "I've added a crispy cookie dipped in Belgian chocolate for each one of you. Chocolate puts the final touch to a meal, I always say." Lost in her own culinary world, she looked up at the sky for inspiration. "Yes, chocolate is like an exclamation point to a good meal." She chuckled, pleased with herself.

I didn't have the heart to tell her that I really had no taste for chocolate. I could take it or leave it. She'd worked so hard. Why ruin her day?

"Thank you, Mrs. Clark. It looks delicious," Lorraine exclaimed.

I joined in. "Yes, it looks ..." I stumbled around for an appropriate word since my mind was cluttered with thoughts of murder. "Refreshing. Yes, it looks refreshing. Thank you."

She went back to the kitchen with a big smile on her face.

When she was safely gone, Lorraine leaned toward me. "I don't think I can eat another bite."

"That lunch was very filling. We can save the cookie for later, but..." I paused, hesitant to go on. "Have some of the ice. You're going to need something sweet to balance the next part of my story."

Her eyes narrowed and she moved her head at angle that radiated suspicion. "Ab-by..." She strung out my name like Gran used to do when she suspected I'd done something naughty. "Spit it out. What have you done?"

I held my hands up in self-defense. "It wasn't my

fault." The story about that morning, finding Margaret and the interrogation that followed, all tumbled out. Lorraine's shock and concern deepened with each development. At the end, she was sitting on the edge of her chair, her hand holding on to mine.

"Oh, Abby. How awful for you. Are you—?"

"I'm fine now," I wanted to reassure her. "It was a shock, no question. Now that I'm here… and you're home, I'm fine."

She frowned a little while inspecting my face.

"What, what's wrong?" I picked up my napkin. "Do I have something on my face? A crumb?" I wiped my mouth. She continued to look closely. "Didn't I get it?"

She shook her head. "You can't hide from me. There's something else, isn't there? Something you're not telling me."

I started to lie. "No, I've told you…" I couldn't look her in the eye. "All right. It's nothing really. I'm sure I'm overreacting, because of what happened this morning." I gave up. "Detective Ingram said that if he had followed his instincts and closed down the festival while he investigated Walt's death, Larry and now Margaret would probably still be alive."

"That could be," she said calmly. "We'll never know. It was his call and he made it."

"Yes, but I lobbied hard for him to let the festival go on. I told him about the map that showed where the artists were working. If I—"

Lorraine cut me off. "If you hadn't told him about it, Anthony would have. The only way he'd let anyone close down the festival would have been with an act of Congress."

"Well, Ingram is right. I insisted. I didn't want the festival ruined and—"

"Wait, did that detective say it was your fault?" She didn't give me a moment to respond. She threw down her napkin on the table, got up and started pacing around the terrace. "Who does this guy think he is? He has no right blaming you. It's his job to find the killer, not yours."

"I know, but—"

"No buts. It's not your job. It's. Not. Your. Fault. Do you hear me?"

I answered, meek as a mouse. "Yes, ma'am."

"Oh, some of these self-important law enforcement officers make me so mad. They don't have a compassionate bone in their bodies. They should be more like our police chief here in St. Michaels." She made a sound, sort of like a growl, as she sat down. I thought it was prudent to sit back, keep my head down and wait.

Finally, she ate a few bites of the dessert ice and seemed to cool down. "Okay, you keep defending this paragon of a detective. If he thinks you're so smart, why don't you tell me who is on this killing rampage of plein air artists?"

I took the question seriously and reviewed the basic elements of the artists' deaths, one by one. "The bottom line is that each situation must be linked to the others, unless we have a homicidal manic running around."

Lorraine leaned back in her chair and focused on a

single fluffy cloud in the brilliant blue sky. "You know what they say on all those TV cop shows, look at the spouse."

"Normally, that's a good idea, except Walt's wife died from cancer months ago and Margaret isn't—I mean, wasn't married."

"What about Larry and... what was her name?"

"Rebecca. No, I think you're reaching. You saw them together at the party last Saturday night. They seemed very happy together, very much in love. If you had seen her last night at the pub." I shook my head. "She was distraught, barely holding it together."

"Yes, I guess you're right," she admitted.

My mind wandered. There was something, something lurking beyond my attention, where I couldn't grasp it.

"Abby? Abby?"

"Huh? Oh, sorry. I just..."

"You were on another planet. What were you thinking?"

"I don't know. We were talking about last night at the pub and..." I shook my head. "It's like I saw something... or heard something." I shrugged. "Whatever it was, it's gone now."

The way she looked at me showed that she wasn't entirely comfortable with my reaction. She asked, "Do you think you're getting a little too close to this?"

"No, it's not like the other time. I'm on the periphery. Just reporting on what you missed. Oh, I remember what I was going to tell you. After Larry was poisoned, the detective was convinced that Margaret was behind the deaths. He was so sure." I took a bite of the cookie, the chocolate melting in the heat. "Now, all bets are off. Margaret didn't stab herself. I don't know who he suspects now."

"It must be very complicated and difficult," Lorraine said.

"Ingram thinks that all the deaths are linked. He thinks the motive was the almighty dollar, that someone is wiping out the competition so he… or she has a clear shot at the $10,000 prize money and enhanced sales." I pulled my chair closer to Lorraine. "You know, I've had the craziest thought that Seth might be involved somehow."

There was a sudden chill in the air. "Oh?"

"Um, yes. Maybe I'm trying to force a solution. As Gran would say, seeing gremlins where there's nothing."

"And she would probably be right. Why don't you give it a rest? Let the authorities do their job, even though this detective seems to have the compassion of a toad."

"No, he seems—"

She held up her hand like a traffic cop. "You don't have to defend him to me." Slowly, she got up from her chair. "If you leave it alone for a while, things may become clearer." She stood and smoothed down her skirt. "And why don't you steer clear of that man." She wouldn't let me say anything in his defense. "I'm tired. I'm going to take a little nap. I have several meetings tomorrow and we have an invitation to attend the Collectors' Preview Party tomorrow night. I hope all this sadness won't make it a morbid event. If it is, I might make an appearance and leave."

"You'll have to stay long enough to find out who wins the prizes. That alone should liven up the evening," I suggested.

"You're right about that. It may all be resolved by then. We'll have to wait and see."

CHAPTER THIRTY-ONE

The unique handle design used on a porringer facilitates the process of feeding a child or an invalid.

—"The Butler's Guide to Fine Silver" Mr. Hollister, 1898

Lorraine stood up and started to reach for her glass of water. Her face scrunched up as if in pain. Her breath came in short gasps. She tried to put the glass back on the table, missed and it shattered on the patio stone.

I was helpless. I could only watch as she grabbed a wad of tissues to block a thunderous sneeze. It even woke the dogs.

"Confounded allergies," she grumbled. "A few days in the city and I have to get acclimated to the air here all over again."

I commiserated. "I guess it's part of the price you pay for living in the country. It took me weeks and a mound of allergy medicine before I could live comfortably here on the Shore."

"You'd think after all these years..." She took another wad of tissues out of another pocket and blew her nose. "That's better."

I stared at the clump of tissues she'd put on the table.

Her voice finally penetrated my brain. "Abby? Abby, are you all right? You're staring at my tissues."

"Oh, sorry…" My words trailed off. Something was still sitting at the edge of my mind, like a word on the tip of the tongue. I couldn't quite grasp it. "You reminded me of something… something important."

"Important?"

I nodded.

"But, you can't remember what it was?"

"No, I can't." My flat answer sounded lame.

"Let's see what we can do to nudge that sharp mind of yours. Does it have anything to do with a sneeze?"

"No, I don't think so."

As if on cue, Lorraine sneezed again. This time it was a small one, so it didn't shake the rafters. "Oh, I hate this." She madly wiped her nose again. "At this rate, I'll have to get more tissues."

"That's it!" I cried. "It was the tissue."

"Hold that thought. I'll be back in a minute." She took a step and the broken glass crunched under her foot. She moaned. "Don't get up until this is cleaned up. And keep the dogs away."

She was back in a minute, the tissue box in one hand and a broom in the other.

She led the dogs on to the grass and tossed cookies in all directions, away from the terrace. "That should keep them busy for a few minutes. Now…" She swept up the big pieces and sat down again with a tissue at her watering eye. "We'd better make this quick, before I completely sell-destruct."

"I'm not sure it's anything at all." Maybe I was trying to make something out of nothing.

"Try me," Lorraine said.

"Okay, when Rebecca came into Banning's, we sat at a table and talked for a few minutes. She broke down and cried."

"That's understandable. Her husband had been poisoned and died." Lorraine pulled another tissue from the box.

"Yes, that's true." I wanted to look at this logically. "When someone is crying and wipes her eyes, the tissue should be wet, right?"

Lorraine looked at me in surprise. "That's the natural progression."

"Rebecca cried, wiped her tears with a tissue and left it on the table when she left the pub with Anthony," I continued.

"Go on."

"You know, there can be a lot of air currents moving around in a restaurant with servers moving around, patrons going to and from the tables."

Lorraine added, "Don't forget that some air conditioning systems blow so much cold air, it feels like a gale in Alaska"

"That's right. Those air currents moved the tissue off the table and it fell to the floor."

"Okay," she said tentatively. "I'm not sure…"

"The tissue was light enough for the air currents to move it along the tabletop and over the edge. A used tissue would have just sat there, wouldn't it?"

We both looked at the pile of Lorraine's wet tissues sitting in a sodden clump on the table. They weren't going anywhere.

"I know what you're thinking," I was eager to make my point. "Rebecca left only one tissue on the table. It must have been dry. When was the last time you saw a used, wet tissue float around?"

She picked up the wad of wet tissues and looked at them in her hand. "Well, I guess it all depends on the water content, if it was wadded up..." The little gasps started again. She lunged for more tissues and caught another monster sneeze. One of her Chessies, Moses, started to howl. "Okay, that's it." She vigorously wiped her nose, grabbed the tissue box and got up. "I'd better go upstairs before I sneeze my brains out all over the table. To be honest, your idea sounds a little farfetched to me. If you think it's a valid theory, you need to tell that detective friend of yours. I'll see you later, I hope." She went inside with the dogs trailing behind. They had missed her as much as I had and weren't going to let her out of their sight.

I sat there alone in the growing heat, turning the idea over in my mind. With my eyes closed, I tried to conjure up in my mind's eye what had happened that night at Banning's. I remembered our conversation, but it was more important to focus on her actions. While we talked, she fought to control her emotions until it all became too much and the tears flowed. The tissue came out and she wiped her eyes. Wait! There was something....

I squeezed my eyes tight, as if that would help. It

did. There were tiny smudges of black mascara on the tissue. It had touched her eyes. Was that a sign that the tissue was wet? The scene played out in my mind. Rebecca sat at the table, sobbing… at least it sounded like she was sobbing. Anthony came over and led Rebecca from the table and out the door. I could see the tissue sitting on the table. As I got up, the tissue went air-borne, slowly floated over the edge and down to the floor. I remembered leaning over to pick it up, but the server was there first, doing a great job.

It had to be dry.

Rebecca faked her tears.

Lorraine said I should tell the detective. I collapsed back in my chair and cringed. Ingram will think I'm cracking under the stress of finding Margaret this morning. The memory of finding her body slumped over sent a shiver through me. He's probably too busy investigating that incident to talk to me. Was I being honest with myself? What if Ingram laughs at me? Maybe I should do a little experiment before I talk to him.

At that moment, Simon appeared at the French doors and whined.

I got up and opened the door so he could come outside. "Nice of you to remember I exist." We walked back to the cottage together.

In my tiny kitchen, I gathered all the pieces needed for the experiment: a box of tissues and a glass of water. I put everything on the table and kept up a running commentary, more for me than Simon, though his eyes followed me every time I moved.

I pulled out a clean tissue from the box. "Okay, this will represent the crying towel. A woman is sad, starts to cry, wipes her tears..." I sprinkled a few drops of water from the glass on the tissue. "...and leaves it on the table." I got up and moved around. "The air currents should move the tissue." Only they didn't. I got a section of the newspaper and fanned the tabletop gently. It had no effect on the tissue. I fanned harder. Nothing. I got a magazine and created quite a windstorm. A dry corner of the tissue waved in the breeze. It sat as if glued in place.

"Maybe I'm not making a valid assumption." I pulled out a new tissue, scrunched it up and put it on the table. It only took a little moving around to cause the tissue to skitter across the table. Then, I dampened the scrunched-up tissue and put it on the table. It fluttered in the breeze I manufactured, but it didn't more.

"I don't know. What do you think?" Simon cocked his head to the side, looking very cute, though clueless. "You don't have to be smart about this. You're good company and so cute." His tail wagged against a cabinet door, making a thumping sound. "Easy there, big fellow. Remember your tail." In response, he stretched out on the floor.

I put two tiny drops of water on a fresh tissue and waved the newspaper around. The wet one moved a little, but the dry one went flying over the edge. Simon saw it and sprang at the flying white plaything.

"No, Simon!" I screamed as I scrambled around the side of the table.

I was so distracted by my little experiment, I forgot

Simon loved tissues. He even checked the trash baskets in case I tossed one away. If he found one, he would bat it around, tear it into tiny pieces and eat them joyfully. Not a good thing for a puppy's tummy.

He grabbed the flying tissue in his jaws and the race was on.

I chased him through the living room, up the stairs and around the bedroom, shouting Drop it. I thought I'd cornered him. He flew over the top of the bed and he dashed into the bathroom. I blocked the doorway. He went down flat on his front paws, ready to spring when he had the chance. I waited. He waited. I took a stance ready to lunge. He dropped the soppy tissue on the tile and panted. I moved forward in slow motion to grab it. He grabbed it first and bounded through a small opening between my legs. He thundered down the stairs with me in hot, frustrated pursuit. It took a jarring dive to head him off, grab him and wrestle away the sodden piece of paper. I deposited it in the kitchen trash basket that had a lid and went back in the living room to reprimand him. He was panting so hard that his mouth was pulled in a smile, so proud of himself. I couldn't stop laughing.

Back in the kitchen, it took both of us several minutes to recover from our little race. Simon stretched out on the cool floor and was soon sound asleep. Ever so quietly, I repeated my experiment with fresh tissues. Guess I shouldn't have been surprised that I always the same result: sodden, damp, or dry, crumpled or flat—the dry one flew; the wet one did not. I caught myself staring at the wet tissues and came to a decision. I had to tell Ingram. I half expected Simon to bark in agreement, but no. He was stretched out on the cool floor, sound asleep.

A call to the sheriff's office confirmed Ingram was there and on the phone. I decided to leave Simon where he was and tiptoed out the door. The run up to Easton shouldn't take long.

CHAPTER THIRTY-TWO

A silver piece may have a gold wash in a particular area like the bowl of a berry spoon or a sauce ladle. Certain foods can tarnish or damage silver. The wash protects the silver because gold does not react to these foods.

—"The Butler's Guide to Fine Silver" Mr. Hollister, 1898

I walked into the county sheriff's department's building and bumped into Detective Ingram, who was on his way out.

"Good, they told me you were coming. You got here just in time. Walk with me. I want to check something at —" He stopped and looked like someone caught with his hand in the cookie jar. "Look, I'm sorry. Maybe it would be better if we talked later."

What made him so self-conscious, all of a sudden? "This is important."

He paused to consider then started walking. "All right, come with me. I have to check out something at the garden where… you know, where Margaret died. It might be unpleasant for you to go back there. I shouldn't ask you to do this. I'm sorry, but I'm running out of time.

It's up to you." He started to walk out the front door.

"Wait! Detective Ingram, I'm coming with you." Gallantly, he stepped aside and held the door for me. As I passed him, I said, "I think I have something that you'll find very interesting."

My comment caught him off-guard and he had to hurry to catch up with me on the sidewalk. "What do you mean?"

"Tell me first why we're going back to the garden. I need to know so I can do this."

We took several steps in silence as I suspected he considered what to so. "Okay, I can't remember if there's more than one entrance to the garden. It's tucked away so almost no one but the locals would know it was there. If there's only one entrance, you might have passed someone on the street who…" He didn't finish the sentence, but his idea was clear.

"You think I passed the murderer on my way to the garden?" I had to admit, it was a valid thought, but still unnerving.

"Well, it is possible."

I got hold of my emotions and asked, "When did Margaret die?"

He rubbed the back of his neck as we walked. "Well, that's the thing. The forensics team gave me a window. A small window, it's true. Since the blood was still wet on the canvas and hadn't congealed in the brush, it's possible that you missed the killer by minutes."

My skin started to feel cold even as we crossed the asphalt street, its heat almost burning my feet through my summer sandals.

"Are you all right, Abby? He stopped under a small tree in a small patch of shade. "Your face is pale."

I used the tree trunk to steady myself then marched down the sidewalk. Determination was driving me. This person, this killer couldn't, wouldn't get away with these terrible crimes. "I'm fine. Let's get this done."

"Now, I need to ask you to think back to this morning. You parked your car and..."

"I parked my car and walked down the sidewalk toward the entrance to the garden."

"Did you pass anyone? See anything out of the ordinary?"

I shook my head. "No, no, I didn't. I'm sorry. It was so early. None of the shops were open. I don't remember seeing anyone."

"Okay, that's what I have for now. Now, tell me what you drove all the way up from Fair Winds to tell me... what you couldn't say on the phone. Do you think we are in the midst of a killing spree with hot-and-cold-running psychopaths?"

"No, nothing that simple," I said with a shrug. I looked around the garden, the yellow police tape still in place. "Could we..." I pointed back in the direction we'd come.

"Oh, yes. Sure." He followed me back to the black wrought-iron gates at the entrance. One lone artist was working on a painting of the quaint street of shops. We sat down on a bench. "Is this better?"

"Yes, thank you." Now that I had his attention, I wasn't sure how to start.

"Well?" He said impatiently.

The words came out in a rush. "I want you to look at his wife." I took a breath and held it, unsure about how he would react.

"Look, I can understand wives kill husbands. It happens all the time. Wait! Whose wife are you talking about? Walt didn't —""

"Larry's wife, Rebecca."

That caught him by surprise. "Rebecca? She's devastated. She was right there at the table when he got sick. So were you. Did you see her give him anything, feed him a bite, put something on his plate? Did she hand him a pill? Anything like that?"

I thought for a moment. "No, in fact he gave her an ear of corn. But —"

"We're not sure about the poison yet. The medical examiner is still running tests. If she gave him the poison, it might not have been a kind that acts immediately." He rubbed his forehead. "Let me think." He seemed to focus his attention on the lone artist, but the way he was working his lips, he must have been going through the evidence and possibilities very carefully.

Finally, he let me in on what he was thinking. "A wife killing a husband is not that unusual, but Rebecca also killing Walt and Margaret... you have to admit that's a reach. They were all friends, right? Nothing more?"

"As far as I know, they were only friends who saw one another at these plein air festivals."

Ingram reached in his pocket and took out a bottle of aspirin. He shook out three, tossed them down his throat and gulped. I thought he was going to choke. Without missing a beat, he snapped the top back in place and dropped the bottle back in his pocket.

"This case is giving me a migraine." He sat quietly. I thought he was waiting for the aspirin to work, but I was at the center of his thoughts. "Chief Lucan told me to listen to whatever you had to say, no matter how looney tunes it sounded."

"Looney tunes?" I think I was offended. "Did he say that?"

"Well, not exactly. That's my word, not his." Rushing on, he spoke in a more official tone. "So tell me, why do you think Rebecca is the killer?"

"She didn't cry." I burst out. After taking a deep breath, I went on. "She was faking her tears. At least, I think she was."

I braced for a laugh or something, but he wanted to know why I thought she hadn't cried real tears. I repeated the story I'd told Lorraine about the night in Banning's. Ingram looked straight ahead as he listened, as if he didn't want to be distracted by my face or gestures.

He let me talk without interruption. Feeling more confident, I told him about my tissue test and my conclusion. "It wasn't a scientific test, I'll grant you that. The bottom line is, I don't think a tearful tissue can float on air currents."

When I finished, he sat perfectly still for a long moment, then slowly turned to look at me, almost in disbelief. "Guilty, based on the evidence of a tissue." He shook his head swung slowly back and forth. "I've got to admit that's a new one. Abby, I need something more."

"You hauled Filly in for questioning just because her necklace – the necklace she lost was at the scene and nothing came of that."

"The necklace she said she lost," he corrected. "We have to check everything."

"Fine, just bring Rebecca in. Talk to her. Ask her the tough questions." I leaned closer. "Make her cry. See if she actually produces tears."

He leaned away from me. "Whoa, that's harsh. You really dislike this woman."

I felt defiant and stood up. "Yes, I do. If she killed three innocent people, all talented artists, she is lower than low. Interrogate her. See what happens. If she cries, check to make sure the tissue she uses to wipe away the tears is wet. Will you do that?"

I towered over him as he sat on the bench and waited. I wanted an answer, his commitment that he would follow through.

He halfheartedly raised his arms in resignation. "All right, all right. I'll talk to her. I'm just not sure that you're going to be happy with the outcome. You must think she's a pretty good actress."

"I think she is. I really do."

CHAPTER THIRTY-THREE

It is essential to use great care when cleaning a piece with a gold wash. The layer of gold may be extremely thin. Intense polishing could wear it away.

—"The Butler's Guide to Fine Silver" Mr. Hollister, 1898

For the first time in almost a week, I spent a quiet evening at the cottage with Simon. It wasn't relaxing. I tried to settle down with a good mystery that had sat on my nightstand for months. My mind couldn't stay with the story. It kept wandering back to the real mystery I was living in. I found I was pacing the cottage again. Simon got so tired and bored with following me around that he stretched out on the sofa and let his eyes follow me as I made the circuit. Nothing seemed to help.

I tried following Gran's example. Whenever something was bothering her to the point that she couldn't settle down, she'd scrub the kitchen floor. If that didn't do the trick, she'd scour the bathtub. Then, she'd fill the sparkling clean tub with a hot bubble bath, relax with a glass of wine and let go of whatever it was. A search of the cabinets turned up a bottle of cleaner and a clean sponge. The kitchen floor held no interest for me so I opted for the bathtub. This time, Simon pulled himself from his cozy spot and settled himself on the bed so he could watch what I was doing. I went through the motions of cleaning, but all that activity didn't calm the thoughts tumbling around in my mind. The one benefit was a very clean tub. Too bad I was too tired to run a bath. After going through our nightly ritual, I crawled into bed and had a toss-and-turn night.

The next morning, I awoke to the swirling sound of wind in the trees. A quick peek through the curtains revealed a quick summer rainstorm racing through. It wasn't uncommon, though it usually happened in the late afternoon.

I started to go back to bed, but Simon had other ideas. He was eager to start his day, so I had to follow him down the steps and wait by the door while he went outside. The rain tapered off to a light drizzle with droplets still clinging to blades of grass. They looked like molten silver daubed by an artist's brush here and there to reflect the leaden sky. All the talk about art at the plein air art festival had made me aware of subtle colors in nature. If I were painting this scene, I'd have shades of silver as well as green on my palette…the same way Larry had used shades of silver in his painting after the storm the day of the party. He'd captured the atmosphere of Bruff's Island though the colors were muted by the cloudy sky.

Suddenly, I felt sad, as if the rain reminded me how fleeting happiness was, how unpredictable life was. I wondered if Larry had had a premonition that he was painting one of his last canvases.

I tried to shake off the depressing feeling, then decided, just this once, not to fight it. I fed Simon and dragged myself back upstairs. It felt comforting to crawl back into bed and curl up. I must have drifted off because the ringtone of my phone shocked me awake.

"Oh, I woke you, didn't I?" The Chief sounded apologetic, but only for a moment. "Why are you still in bed? Are you sick? It's almost ten o'clock on a workday or don't you work on Fridays at Fair Winds?"

Just what I needed, a wisecracking police chief. I sat up quickly, so quickly that I felt dizzy. I took a deep breath and tried to sound wide awake. It didn't work.

"Tut, tut. Sleeping late after partying last night? You really should wait for the weekend, Abby. There's no telling you young people. You'll learn – the hard way – as you get older, I expect." He went on in a sarcastic tone. "Well, I guess you're too tired to care about an interesting find."

That news jerked me awake "Find? Did they find the murderer?" Why wasn't Ingram calling?

"Don't know about that. It isn't my case, remember? I'm talking about something that's more up your alley. Sterling silver."

The part of my brain devoted to work in silver clicked into gear. It felt good to be involved, maybe able to make a contribution to the situation surrounding Walt's murder. "Silver? Did you find something?"

"Not me. Your buddy with the metal detector I caught earlier this week. It seems he was out at dawn, when the storm blew through, thinking no one would notice him trespassing at the Bruff-Mansfield House again. I got the call and found him kneeling by a hole he'd dug in the grass. He was holding a spoon. Thought you might like to come down and see it, but if you're too tired…"

"No, no," I said, throwing back the covers. "I'm on my way. I'll be there in a few minutes."

It only took me forty minutes to take care of Simon, get dressed and roar down Route 33 to St. Michaels. The Chief was a patient man, but I wasn't surprised that he teased me when I walked into the St. Michaels Police Station.

He greeted me with, "At least you made it here before noon. That's good."

We went into his office and he told me the whole story. It seemed that my buddy, as he called the man with the metal detector, had gotten a strong reading earlier in the week and he'd gone back to investigate. "The man said that a good time to sneak onto someone's property is very early in the morning or at dusk. It's not that easy for someone to spot a trespasser in the weak light and, if they do, they're less likely to freak out and call the police the way they would at night. I'll have to keep that in mind."

"Where did he get this strong reading?"

"Right where you sent him." He had a serious expression on his face. He wasn't playing games. Suddenly, I wondered if he would charge me as an accessory to the crime. "You sent him to the Bruff-Mansfield House on Muskrat Park here in St. Michaels and that's where he found and dug up what appears to be an old silver spoon." He rubbed his chin. "This whole situation involves more than the law against trespassing. We're talking about disturbing archeological or historical artifacts. It's one thing to find the location of something. It's a whole different ballgame to dig it up." He looked down at some notes on his desk. "Now, I have to deal with the American Antiquities Act of 1906, the Archaeological Resources Protection Act—and those are just the federal laws. I don't know what all else Maryland says about this."

In a very respectful voice, I tried to defend myself. "Let me just say again that I didn't send him there and I certainly didn't tell him to search private property or dig up anything."

The Chief continued his no-nonsense look. Slowly, his eyes started to twinkle and his mouth pulled up into a big smile. "Gotcha! I know you didn't tell him, but now hear this: Don't make any suggestions to anyone that involves breaking the law. You never know when someone, like your buddy, will take you seriously."

"Okay, okay, lesson learned. Tell me what happened with him and he's not my buddy."

"Okay, earlier this week, he was poking around the Bruff-Mansfield House property and got this wild off-the-chart reading. Before he could investigate, a neighbor rolled out his recycling bin for pickup and started pulling weeds. Our guy melted away. He went back several times, but it seemed like there was always someone around. I guess he couldn't wait anymore. He went back early this morning to do some digging at the spot. A neighbor got suspicious and called 911. I rolled up and found him sitting by a freshly-dug hole with a small open box and a ratty piece of fabric, examining this."

He held up a spoon. In one small spot, tarnish and dirt had been rubbed away to reveal the glint of silver. He followed me to the sink in the small bathroom. I rinsed off the spoon and, using a soft rag, lightly rubbed the bowl.

"It needs to be tested, but I think this is coin silver, not sterling." I turned the spoon over and ever so carefully rubbed the area where the handle met the bowl. There appeared to be a mark there. "Do you have a magnifying glass?"

He walked back to his office saying, "Of course, I do. What kind of an investigator would I be without a Sherlock Holmes magnifying glass? We will not discuss the fact that fine print is getting smaller for me every day, too small even for reading glasses." He came back and handed me the glass.

"Yes, I think this is a silversmith's hallmark. I'd have to check, but I think it is a Bruff hallmark. It may or may not be the mark of Thomas Bruff, the first one in the American family line of silversmiths. I need my reference book. Wait!" My heart was beating faster. "May I use your computer? I can look it up online." I walked down the hall.

He hurried after me. "Of course. Why not? This is only a police station with all kinds of sensitive information and access to secure databases."

In the office, he worked his way around me, slid into his desk chair and woke up his computer. I guided him to the website that listed all kinds of silver hallmark information.

"In the search box, type 'Bruff'. That should bring up the marks of the whole family so we can scroll right through them all."

A list of four marks appeared, four of the nine. I didn't need the full list. The mark was at the top. I whispered, "He did it."

"Who did what?" the Chief wanted to know, always thinking about someone committing a crime.

"Mr. Jones, our metal detector man. He actually found one of the spoons made by the original Thomas Bruff. It's probably one of the spoons depicted in his portrait at Bruff House. It doesn't have an English hallmark."

"So, it's valuable?" He cringed when I nodded. "Great. That complicates things."

"Before you start being all judicial," I said, with hesitation. "Could we tell the man that he found his treasure?"

He paused for a moment, then, slapped his hands on his desk and pushed himself up. "Just for the record, I don't do the judicial part of law enforcement. I gather the facts and the alleged guilty parties. Then I turn the case over to the prosecutor."

As I followed him down the brightly painted yellow hallway, I said, "I stand corrected. It won't happen again."

He unlocked the room where the trespasser was waiting and we went in with the bright silver spoon to deliver the good news.

It was good to see the excitement on the man's

weather-beaten face. It told of many hours spent in the sun, wind and heat or cold, of a man committed to the search.

"I knew it was special," he said, dancing in his chair. "It was in the right place and it had the right look. You know, Miss, it's providential that I found it at this time and just down the street from the church."

What was a curious thing to say. "Why?"

"The spoon is really important in the Bible. The Lord told Moses to make golden spoons for the Tabernacle. Solomon was anointed King of Israel with oil poured from a spoon. Ya know, oil was too valuable back then to just pour it over the king's head. It's providence. It shows I'm supposed to continue my searches."

"Well, before you go rushing off looking for something else," the Chief cautioned, "we've got some complicated issues to work out, like ownership, trespassing and more."

I added, "And you need a licensed appraiser to confirm my identification, but I think it's right."

The man brushed all that aside. "I don't want to keep the spoon. If I can make some money from the find, that's good. For me, it's the thrill of the hunt and holding what I've been looking for so long."

His smile faded as the Chief took the spoon and slipped it into an evidence bag. "I guess you're going to have to find something else to hunt."

He shook his head with a smile. "No danger of me running out of things to look for. I have a long, long list. You see, I've gotta do a lot of research before I strap on my equipment and start looking. I've got to be sure

I know what I'm looking for, where I might find it and stuff like that. It's time-consuming. I've got things in various stages of the process. I'll just move on to the next one on my list."

"Which is?" the Chief asked.

The man smiled. "Oh, I can't tell you that. It'll be a surprise."

CHAPTER THIRTY-FOUR

Silver conducts heat at a high level. Use extreme care to avoid burns.

—"The Butler's Guide to Fine Silver" Mr. Hollister, 1898

There wasn't much for me to do until it was time to get ready for the Plein Air Collector's Preview Party, when the winners of the competition would be announced. Well, that's wasn't exactly true. There was plenty for me to do in my office. The To-Do list was so long, it was scary. I just didn't feel like doing it. It had been quite a week with the art competition, meeting so many creative people, three murders and, of course, Seth. It was enough to sap anyone's energy.

The clock on the dashboard showed it was a little after noontime. The competition was officially over. Artists were delivering their paintings to the Academy Art Museum in Easton. Probably, it would be the last chance to see my new artist friends, especially when buyers… oops, I mean, the collectors would be vying for their attention, ready to spend their money. Paintings would disappear from the walls of the show and, by the end of the weekend, so would the artists. It would be over. The families and collectors would leave. The volunteers would spend the coming months spinning stories about the events of the art festival: the police interrogation after Walt's body was found floating in the tangled branches of a toppled old tree; where they were when Larry began to gasp for breath; how they didn't care for Margaret's brusque attitude. The need to tell stories – all part of human nature.

Those things weren't the true heart of the competition and festival. It was the art and the artists. Soon, they would move on to the next plein air competition or go back to their studios. I was a little surprised to realize that I'd miss them – their quirky personalities and the experience of watching them create a work of art. Based on the sales of their work, many would be leaving with their expenses covered and a few extra dollars in their pockets, some with thousands more than they had a week ago.

It was wrenching to think that three artists would be leaving in coffins. How could a creative person destroy another artistic individual? They spend their lives making, not destroying.

It didn't feel right for Detective Ingram to consider that one or more of them were guilty. They didn't deserve that. What they deserved were some answers. Who had done these terrible things? I thought of Rebecca, but couldn't quite figure out why she would harm three people.

I felt motivated now more than ever to figure out why things had gone so terribly wrong during this art festival. I thought of Claudia who'd learned the key to survival was putting one foot in front of the other every day, so important in her art and her life. The sweet nature of Filly, the Southern, gun-toting mama came to mind. She must have convinced Ingram that someone had stolen her necklace from her purse. Still, could her natural innocence and enthusiasm be an act? Seth was a complex personality to say the least, so committed to art. And all the others – they too deserved some answers so they could put this experience behind them. If it turned out that it was one of them who caused it all, that person deserved to be in the hands of the police, whoever it was.

Last chance to see my new friends. Last chance to find some answers. I touched the accelerator and the Saab sprang forward toward Easton.

There were always more cars and pedestrians on Friday in all three nearby tourist destinations on the Shore: Easton, Oxford and St. Michaels. It seemed extra busy that afternoon. A lot of people came for the weekend to see the results of all the painting done during the week. Some came to participate in the Quick Draw art competition on Saturday for anyone with some art supplies and $10. On Sunday, they turned things over to the kids with Quick Draw – The Next Generation. It seemed like the whole world had descended on the little town of Easton for fun with art. I was driving down yet another residential street when someone pulled out of a space. It meant I'd have to parallel park, but I was desperate. I walked around the corner to find I was only a block from my destination: The Academy Art Museum, the scene of the final judging and Collector's Party.

The white building with several additions that had

been added over the decades had a tower at the main entrance with a crowning cupola that added to a feeling of permanence and respect for the arts. As I hurried along the white picket fence toward the entrance, a voice calling my name stopped me.

"Abby, Abby!"

I searched the groups of people streaming toward the museum. An alto voice that sounded vaguely familiar rang out again and a hand waved above the heads of everyone else. My golf car chauffeur, Sara-V joined me on the sidewalk.

"I thought that was you." She looked crisp and cool in her black and white striped linen top and white capris. Large Mabe pearl earrings hung silently from her ear lobes. "I see you've survived all the events of this past week."

"Yes, it's been an interesting few days," I agreed, without leaking any details.

"It wasn't what I expected when I signed up as a volunteer, that's for sure," Sara-V stated.

Remembering my earlier thoughts, I said, "You'll have something to tell your grandchildren."

She gave me a strange look. "I'm not sure I want to contaminate their world with tales of meanness and murder. They're children for such a short period of time nowadays." Quickly, she changed the subject. "Are you going inside?"

For the first time, I noticed that there were men at the entrance checking IDs to prevent buyers from getting a sneak peek. "Oh, I thought I…"

"Come on, you can go in with me." Sara-V planted

her hand on my elbow and guided me through the clusters of people.

Inside, I felt instant relief from the heat. It's funny I didn't always notice how hot it was outside... until I went into an air-conditioned building. A wall of heat was always there to hit me in the face when it was time to leave. A short line had formed at a line of tables. Both artists and volunteers were scurrying around, handling paintings for the competition and sale.

Filly was across the room, her face more serious than I'd ever seen it. What did I expect? This sale was what she'd been working toward all week while dealing with all the questions from the police. I looked over just in time to see Claudia disappear into another room looking stressed as well. There were other artists I recognized, but those were the only two I knew.

Sara-V interrupted my thoughts. "Oh, they need me. Wait right here and I'll be back in a minute."

Rolling up on my toes, I tried to spot Seth. Instead, I was the one who was spotted. A shrill voice froze my blood.

"Well, if it isn't the great detective." Sarcasm dripped from every syllable Rebecca uttered. "Dear Miss Abby, sticking her nose in where it's not wanted."

She sidled up next to me. Her face was drawn, her eye makeup in shambles. She had the look of a weeping widow though her manner was more of a raving harpy.

Continuing her attack, she attracted the attention of others close-by. "I hope you're satisfied. It's not enough that I've lost my husband. You turned the police dogs loose on me, calling me a murderer."

One of the volunteers gasped when she heard the accusation. Hearing the reaction, Rebecca gave me a satisfied, cruel smile. "You're heartless and jealous. They had me at their station for most of the morning. You know what they got? Nothing. Because there is nothing."

Rebecca straightened up, took a deep breath and brought her hands together at her waist. She took her time inspecting me from head to toe. Her anger burned off, she assumed a cool demeanor. The venom oozed from every word. "I pity you. You don't know what it's like to love an artist, to be close to the creation and loved by the creator. My husband is the dearest part of me. His love makes it worth getting up in the morning."

Why is she talking about Larry in the present tense, as if he's still alive? Has she lost her sanity?

Rebecca walked around me and shook her head, her eyes never leaving my face. "You think you have something special with Seth?" She tossed her head back, opened her mouth wide. "Ha! He doesn't have half the talent that Larry has. He doesn't have the heart that Larry has. Larry is special, one-of-a-kind. To live with him is the closest I can come to perfection. I know that every waking day."

People stopped what they were doing and stared, not at her—at me. Was the whole world closing ranks against me? I haven't done anything wrong. I don't deserve this. This madwoman scene was over the top. That's what it was, a scene with an actress at center stage.

Her voice quavered. Her eyes glistened. Then,

very real tears welled up in her eyes. As she spoke the next words, they overflowed and rolled down her face. "I love him. I will never do anything to hurt him."

That was too much. "Stop it, Rebecca. He's dead." I blurted out the words before I realized what I was saying. I braced for an explosion.

As quickly as her tears came, they stopped. She wiped her cheeks with the back of her hand and huffed, a sound of disgust. "What do you take me for? Of course, I know he's dead. He will always live in my heart." She scanned the horrified onlookers around us. "And he'll live in their memories, as well."

She took a few steps over to a part of the room I hadn't seen yet. It was draped in black velvet with Larry's name printed in gold on a sign handing there. She glared at me and then, her whole attitude changed again. She planted her hands on her hips, her chin rose slightly and she looked down her nose at me with an expression of triumph. "See?, see what they've done to honor my husband? Larry..." She began again to make a declaration. "Laurence Chambers, an artist extraordinaire, will live on through his art. At least some people recognize his talent and his place in the art world." She lowered her voice so only I could hear it. "There's nothing you can do to change that," she sneered. "He will always live in my heart. The two of us will always be together, never apart, never." She turned on her heel and people parted to make a path for her as she flounced out of the room and the building.

In her wake, there was silence. My eyes drifted around the room. Harsh stares of accusation, looks of disgust and glances of embarrassment smothered me. I wanted to sink through the floor. My only avenue of escape was to follow the footsteps of the wronged wife. I willed my feet to move slowly and deliberating toward the front door, hoping no one would feel compelled to stop me, challenge me. As I neared the door, I hoped crazed Rebecca wasn't waiting to jump me.

I shouldn't have worried. Her work was done here. As I stepped from the building, I could hear a growing din of voices behind me. Was there anyone in those rooms who would stand up for me? I rounded the corner of the street where I'd parked and picked up my pace. I wanted escape, to leave Rebecca, the festival and all the people who'd witnessed my humiliation far behind.

I was running by the time I got to my car. I threw myself into the seat, slammed the door and hit the lock. Perspiration was wet on my face. The awful scene started to play out again in my mind. The poisoned words, the indictment she'd laid at my feet echoed in my head. There was the creepy way she kept referring to Larry as if he was still alive.

It wasn't my fault. I only told Ingram about the dry tissue.

With a stab of guilt, I visualized the very real tears rolling down Rebecca's face moments ago. Was I wrong? Had my past experiences with complex, confusing situations in St. Michaels made me overconfident, arrogant even? I didn't know what I was doing. Just because I'd made some lucky guesses in the past, didn't make me a competent investigator. Now, more than ever, I wanted to retreat to my silver and the safety and security of Fair Winds. I made a U-turn so I wouldn't have to pass the museum and got the hell out of town.

CHAPTER THIRTY-FIVE

The famous silver sailing trophy known as "The America's Cup" was crafted by the silversmiths at R. & S. Garrard in London. The company was named the Crown Jeweller by Queen Victoria.

—"The Butler's Guide to Fine Silver" Mr. Hollister, 1898

At Fair Winds, I parked in my spot by the kitchen door, turned off the ignition and sat. I wasn't thinking any real thoughts, only feeling the wallops of accusation and indignation hurled at me by Rebecca. It was hot, too hot. I couldn't sit there for the rest of the day. What was I supposed to do now? Oh yes, the Collector's Preview Party. I should tell Lorraine that I wouldn't be going. Her car was parked in its usual space. She must be home. I'd tell her. Only then could I retreat to my little cottage and lock the door against the world.

I went in the main house to find her. There was no one on the main floor. Was she upstairs? Slowly, I climbed the front stairs. It felt uncomfortable. When I stayed in the main house, I moved between the two floors without any problem. This was different. What if she was napping? Was I invading her privacy by going upstairs unannounced? I was turning around to go downstairs again when I heard someone clapping.

"Yes! That's the way!! Yay!" A woman's voice called out in sheer excitement.

Lorraine?

There was the drone of the television. It sounded like an announcer at a sporting event. Along with the roar of… engines?

I walked up the last steps and almost tiptoed down the hallway. The door to her sitting room was partially open. I knocked softly on the door. "Lorraine?"

She didn't respond, probably couldn't hear me over the noise from the plasma set. "Lorraine?" I said, this time, more emphatically.

"Oh, Abby. Come in." Her eyes were shining with glee and, as they say, her grin went from ear to ear. Then, it all changed. Her eyes flew back to the screen as the announcer declared loudly so he could be heard over the cheers of the crowd. "And here is our winner, taking the checkered flag by one car length. What a race!"

Lorraine's face took on a pink tinge that was fast changing to red. "Ah, you caught me. Now, you know my dirty little secret."

"A car race?" I breathed.

She nodded slowly. "Yes, I'm a closet NASCAR fanatic."

"I-I don't know. I'm sorry, I'll just go…" I pointed back toward the hallway and started to move in that direction.

"Abby, don't leave." She muted the sound of the race coverage. "Come in and sit down. I won't make you watch it, don't worry." She paused the action on the screen. "I missed the race last Sunday and wanted to watch it before this Sunday's action."

"I had no idea." I was so surprised. It didn't go with her image, how she lived at Fair Winds or her style. I moved to a wing chair and lowered myself into it.

She leaned back and smiled, the blush fading away. "I've been watching for years. Follow the stories in the paper, too. We used to go to the races from time to time."

I sat and tried to take it all in.

She shut off the television. "I've seen enough. It was a great finish." She put down the remote control. "Abby, you really need to stop looking at me like that. A woman is entitled to a few secrets and this one is dear to my heart."

Her strange comment woke me from my daze. "Really?"

She smiled, not the exuberant kind from moments ago. This was a sweet smile of remembering. "As you know, my husband came from Philadelphia." She straightened up and looked stern. "From a very proper Main Line family. When we were dating, our time together was filled with parties at the estate home, country clubs and the Union Club with behavior expectations and strict dress codes. Imagine, no pants for ladies. If someone tried to walk in wearing jeans, the doorman would have fainted, I think. It was all very stuffy for two people who were deliriously in love.

"I remember the morning he told me we were going to steal away for the afternoon and to put a pair of casual slacks in the big tote he'd told me to bring for my visit at his parents' home. We stopped at a diner miles from their house where we changed into our ..." She made quotes in the air with her fingers. "Casual clothes." When we got back in his car, an MGB, he peeled out of the parking lot and raced down the road. I was completely confused, no idea who he'd become, no idea at all where we were going. Can you imagine my shock when he pulled into the line for the parking lot at the speedway?"

Lorraine laughed a little at the memory. "Poor man. Once we arrived, he was terrified how I would react. Up until that moment, he'd only know a prim and polite young woman. Ever so quietly, he asked if it was all right for us to go in. At that moment, I would have fallen in love with him... if I didn't love him so completely already.

"His passion was cars. The mechanics of the engine – the effort it took to get just a couple more miles of speed out of a car – intrigued him. I've often speculated that if he'd been born into another family, he might have gone into the racing world. Of course, that was out of the question." She sighed. "From the moment he was born, his father planned for him to join their investment firm."

"Maybe he couldn't be on the track, but there was nothing stopping him from enjoying the thrill from the stands... as long as his parents didn't find out. He introduced me to his secret passion. I embraced it wholeheartedly and we made it ours. Sometimes, he'd plan a business trip close to one of the big races, like Daytona. I'd fly down and we'd have a great weekend that was our little secret. As we established our financial independence, he started his car collection. We'd drive one of them whenever we went to a track here in Maryland or Delaware. He was driving the vintage red Mustang when…" Her voice quavered. "The night the drunk driver plowed into him head-on." A single tear trailed down her face.

It seemed that all I could do today was make widows cry. Since I really cared about Lorraine, I jumped up and grabbed the remote. "Shall we watch the festivities in the winner's circle? Don't they do something with milk?"

Surprised, but only for a moment, she settled back and we watched the end of the pre-recorded broadcast.

CHAPTER THIRTY-SIX

As the Crown Jeweller, R. & S. Garrard manufactures exquisite sterling silver pieces, including swords, for the Royal Family. Those pieces meet the same silver standard as the pieces in the silver closet over which you preside.

—"The Butler's Guide to Fine Silver" Mr. Hollister, 1898

After we watched the race recap and the celebration for the winners, Lorraine reset the equipment to record Sunday's race. "I prefer to watch the action live. You never know when someone's going to drop a comment about the winner and knowing who crosses the finish line first before watching the race seems to take the fun out of it for me. Only thing is, I never know what I'm going to be doing. It would be worse to miss the race entirely than watch a recording, knowing who won." She carefully went through the different screens and pressed some buttons on the remote control. "There. All set."

She turned off the TV and looked at me, curious. She sensed something was going on. It was time to tell her.

"Well?" She asked.

"Um, well… what?" I tried to come up with a viable excuse for not going to the party. Nothing was coming to mind.

"You must have had a reason for coming upstairs to find me. What was it?" Her face changed to concern. "Oh dear, has something happened?"

"Well, sort of." How was I going to tell her I'd gone to Easton, been accosted by a deranged widow and embarrassed myself in front of a mass of festival people? I gave up. The only way out of this predicament was to be honest, tell it simply and race off to the cottage. So, I did. I told her what happened.

Only she stopped me before I could escape from the room.

"What?! Is the woman insane?" Lorraine's voice was strained.

"Insane with grief, maybe."

"You're right, grief makes people do strange things. Believe me, I know," she said, having seen her fair share, especially lately.

I finished, "Anyway, that's why I'm not going to the Collector's Party tonight."

"Don't be ridiculous." She put her hands up. "Don't say a word, just listen. I know it must have been horrible to have that woman go after you in public like that. You didn't do anything wrong. When you told me about your theory of the dry tissue, we agreed you should talk with the detective. That was the right thing to do."

"When I talked to him, he didn't buy it right off, but he finally agreed to talk with her." I filled in the details for Lorraine. "From what she said, he went by her host-family's home this morning and escorted her to the sheriff's office for questioning. She said he grilled her all morning."

"Have you seen or talked to him since then?" she asked.

I shook my head. "After what happened at the museum, I came home to Fair Winds as fast as I could."

We were quiet for a moment. The phrase home to Fair Winds felt good to me as I said it. Hearing it brought a smile to Lorraine's face. Then, as if someone had flipped a switch, we were dealing with the situation again.

"Maybe you should call Ingram to see if he found out anything interesting?" Lorraine suggested.

I shook my head again. "It wouldn't do any good. If he learned something to incriminate her, she'd be in custody, wouldn't she? He let her go. There's nothing to my idea that she's hiding something."

Lorraine got up and walked to the window overlooking the garden her mother had helped her design years ago. She seemed lost in her own thoughts. Quietly, I rose from the chair, ready to make my escape. Her words slowed me down. "The garden is so beautiful at this time of year. I think Momma and I chose flowers that all bloomed at the same time. You know, you're supposed to select plantings so the garden will be in flower throughout the season. We just picked our favorites." She turned away from the window with a wistful look on her face. "Isn't it funny, even though there's sadness here at the festival – violence and murder – there is still beauty in the world. There are all the paintings that the artists created this week… and my lovely garden." She peered out the window again. "I wish somebody would come and paint it. That's one painting I'd buy. That way I'd have it in bloom year round."

A light tap on the door revealed that Dawkins had materialized. "Excuse me, Madam. About dinner this evening for you and Miss Abigail before the —"

"Oh, nothing for me, Dawkins. Thank you. I'm going to eat a light supper at the cottage." I turned to Lorraine to explain. "My tummy feels queasy from all the upset. I think I'll go to bed early."

Lorraine looked at her watch. "I think that's a good idea."

I felt so relieved. I'd talked myself out of an unpleasant situation.

Lorraine wasn't done. "Why don't you take a couple of antacids and lie down for a little while. You have plenty of time to rest and change before we have to leave for the museum where the doors open at six."

I shook my head around like a little kid. "Lorraine, I don't want to go to the party," I whined.

"Oh, but you have to. I suggest that there's going to be more excitement and fireworks tonight than just the announcement of awards and the presentation of a big check." She came over and put her arm around my shoulders. "Abby, you want to finish this, don't you? You want to see the police catch the person who killed Walt, Larry and Margaret, don't you?"

"Yes, but—"

"All right, then." She gave me a little squeeze and

slowly walked me to the door. "You run along and follow this doctor's orders. I'll see you dressed and downstairs at five. Dawkins will come up with something soothing for that tummy of yours. After a quick bite, we'll go to the party. You don't have to worry. I'll be with you." She flashed a big smile. "I'll even drive."

I thought I saw Dawkins roll his eyes. With a little shove, I was out the door and on my way to the cottage.

CHAPTER THIRTY-SEVEN

R. & S. Gerrard also oversees the care and maintenance of the Crown Jewels for the Royal Family.

—"The Butler's Guide to Fine Silver" Mr. Hollister, 1898

I had to admit that when I got into Lorraine's car, I felt fine. Maybe it was the antacids or the short rest – though I probably would have fallen asleep if Simon wasn't snuffling so loud having a puppy dream. Maybe it was the new apple-green print summer dress I'd bought at the beginning of the summer, but hadn't had a reason to wear, until now. It was light and gauzy, perfect for a humid evening.

We flew up Route 33 and were in Easton in no time. I made a silent vow that I wouldn't let Lorraine drive ever again right after she'd watched a NASCAR race. Though we were early, it was a long walk from the parking space to the party at the museum.

Along the way, a woman called out my name, "Abby, Abby!" This time, it was in a friendly tone. A young woman with a handsome man in tow was threading their way through the crowd moving along the sidewalk. It was Daphney.

While Lorraine and I stopped and waited for them to catch up, I tried to figure out who the man was. Earlier in the festival week, Daphney had talked about ending her relationship with the man she thought she could love for the rest of her life. Now, it was obvious that something had changed. The young woman who dashed up to us was beaming with happiness.

Breathlessly, she said, "Look!" She held out her left hand. On her ring finger was a sparkling round diamond surrounded by swirls of platinum that made the stone look as if it was suspended in air. A very unusual setting.

Lorraine said all the appropriate things while I stood there, confused. Tentatively, I said, "Daphney, congratulations. I thought… is this sudden? Um…"

She laughed and it sounded like tinkling bells. "Oh, Abby, it's all right! This is David, my David. He wouldn't accept my good-bye. He flew in this morning and was here when I arrived with my competition paintings. I was thunderstruck, that's the best way to describe how I felt when I saw him."

David jumped in. "She was so surprised. Before she could say anything, like Go Away, I dropped to one knee and brought out the ring I'd been working on with a designer for months. I wanted to propose a long time ago, but I wanted to have the ring when I did. That's the way my dad did it. I knew some regular old solitaire wouldn't do for Daphney, the artist, the most amazing woman I've ever met. It took so long to find the jeweler and to come up with the design and to create the setting…"

She picked up the story. "He proposed right by the front door where everybody was coming in with their work. When I said yes…" She almost squealed the word as she clapped her hands. "And he slipped this amazing ring on my finger, everyone applauded. It was so much fun."

David put his arm around his new fiancée. "She's the one who is amazing."

While Lorraine dealt with the love-struck pair, I did a quick calculation. Figuring the deadline for delivering finished canvases, I must have had my confrontation with Rebecca and fled the museum just before Daphney and David arrived. Thank goodness, he wasn't proposing while Rebecca was having her meltdown. At least they would have a nice memory of this afternoon.

The reminder of Rebecca and the faces of everyone who was there put me on edge again. Lorraine must have sensed the change in my demeanor, because she sent the lovers on ahead and put her arm through mine as we joined the line at the entrance.

The collectors, casual buyers and people like us, interested in the art, stood in line waiting for the doors to open. The way they were dressed added to the festive atmosphere: women in brightly colored sundresses and shawls,; men in summer sports jackets. The air seemed to crackle with excitement. Some people were moving around, anxious to get inside. When the doors opened, a spark of heightened anticipation flashed through the crowd, along with a gentle surge of bodies moving forward.

When we reached the volunteers acting as

gatekeepers, Lorraine handed in our tickets and we stepped across the threshold. This was the time the buyers went into action. One couple careened around us and rushed into a far room. Another couple split and raced around us. We stepped to the side, out of the mainstream, to get acclimated.

"Some of the buyers and collectors are very enthusiastic, I see," Lorraine said with an air of disapproval.

Not wanting to allow impolite people to ruin our evening, I tried to distract her. "You've been to this party before, right? How does it work?"

Still a little annoyed, Lorraine tried to get in the spirit of the evening. "Two competition paintings by each artist are hung alphabetically, one above another."

That explained why that couple had raced past us. Their favorite artist's name must start with a letter at the end of the alphabet.

"They'll announce the winners shortly and they'll sell paintings all evening. The festival people are very open about the sales. In fact, last year, they reported that a painting was sold every 45 seconds for a total of well over $300,000!"

I was stunned. "This sale is too rich for me."

Lorraine laughed and put her hand on my arm. "Oh no, no, no. It is true that some of the art by big names are more expensive, but the average price —"

"Is more within my budget." I finished for her.

"That's right. They want to keep it that way so many people can participate in this wonderful festival. Shall we look at some very good artwork painted en plein air?"

As we strolled, I confided to Lorraine, "I really don't know much about art. I mean, I took art appreciation in college, but…"

"You know what you like, right?"

I nodded.

"That's the first step."

We came up behind a couple looking at a landscape featuring a small body of water and a small grove of trees. The woman said, "I don't know, my first thought was, it's so orange."

We wandered away as I whispered to Lorraine, "I don't feel so bad now. I don't think I'd make a comment like that, at least not aloud."

Lorraine gave me one of her more tolerant looks. "Oh, I don't think she was being ignorant. The comment was a natural reaction. In fact, I read in the Washington paper about a curator who saw a painting for the first time – I think it was by Degas –and was surprised at how green it was. She went on to say that photographs, even those in color, don't do paintings justice. That's why we have to go to galleries, museums, and plein air festivals to see them in real life."

A waiter came up and invited us to visit the bar and hors d'oeuvre tables. A large man jostled his way through the crowd, with a drink in his hand. It was George, bulling his way around, as usual. Somehow, he didn't spill a drop.

""Ladies!" George's voice boomed over the crowd and everyone looked our way. "Isn't this a marvelous event?" He was truly in his element.

I couldn't stop myself. "George, have you bought up all the paintings?"

He winked at me. "Only the ones that are worthwhile." When he laughed, his left hand went to his impressive tummy, perhaps to stop it from jiggling. "It's good to see lots of people supporting the festival. That's the way it should be." He chuckled and shook his head. In a low voice, he continued, "I love to listen to people talking seriously about the art. They have no idea what they're talking about." He nudged my arm with his elbow. "It's fun to pretend, isn't it? It gives us a feeling that we belong, that we've arrived. Talking about art gives us a patina of sophistication. What's the buzz word today?" He took another sip. "Ah yes, community. It gives a sense of community. You have to admit this is better than Facebook or Twitter. If you'll excuse me, I must mingle. Enjoy!" He toasted us with his glass and moved on.

Fortified with adult beverages, we made our way around some frantic buyers. The quality of the work I'd seen on the easels in progress throughout the week was impressive. Seeing it gathered all in one place was more than a fine presentation of art. It was the essence of the Eastern Shore captured in paint and watercolors. We had to move along quickly. They were gathering people in one room to make the presentations.

Anthony, as festival chairman, stepped to the microphone. Was it only last Saturday, less than a week ago, that I'd first met him? He appeared to have aged ten years since then.

"Ladies and gentlemen, welcome to the tenth

anniversary of Plein Air-Easton." There was polite applause. "Every week of competition for our artists is exciting, stressful, frightening, exhilarating, challenging… oh, I could probably go right through the thesaurus. This year, we've all faced other emotions that I never thought we'd have at our art festival – sadness, loss, grief and, yes, fear." The atmosphere in the room filled with tension.

"As you all know, we've lost three fine artists and human beings this week: Margaret Reynolds, Walter Stanton and Lawrence Chambers. I invite you all to take time to view their work on the Memorial Wall we've created in their honor."

Anthony cleared his throat. It was clear he was struggling to maintain control of his emotions. "I wish I could say it was due to natural causes. It was not. I'm thankful to the police for allowing our festival to continue. I know they considered shutting it down."

I overheard someone behind me whisper, "If they had, at least one of the artists would still be alive."

"Maybe two," added his companion.

Their words made my stomach twist with guilt. I had helped persuade Detective Ingram to let the festival continue. There was no way to undo what had happened.

"A special thank you goes to Detective Ingram and his team." He directed the audience's attention to Detective Ingram standing at the left side of the stage. "Thank you, Detective, for letting us have our festival."

Ingram didn't acknowledge everyone's applause. He didn't seem to notice it at all. He stood tall and straight, his eyes cruising the room, examining faces, gauging reactions.

Of course, I thought. He still suspects the artists or someone close to the festival. I joined Ingram in observing the people.

A few volunteers with very serious expressions were dashing around on the periphery, probably taking care of last-minute details. Some faces I recognized from the Information Center and Banning's but I didn't know their names. In a sea of strangers, I saw one face, bright and beaming with excitement: Filly. I hadn't spoken to her since the confrontation with Rebecca. I wondered what she must think of me. Would she believe the accusations made by Rebecca, a woman she'd known for a long time?

Jack was in the thick of the crowd with his glasses sliding down his nose as he madly scribbled notes in his reporter's notebook. I groaned silently. If he had seen the crazy scene this afternoon, he would have had a field day. I didn't want to imagine what kind of headlines he'd run: Grieving Widow Accused of Murder... by Stranger; A Coverup by Real Killer. Just the thought made my head hurt.

A fidgety movement caught my eye. No wonder Paul was so thin. H, he was constantly moving. Tonight, was it because of nerves, excitement... or was it guilt? Deep down inside, I suspected that he really wanted to be the first artist to repeat a win this festival. Was this man, who seemed so nervous all the time, capable of murdering not one, but three people?

So often, the guilty person is the one you'd almost never suspect.

Wait. There was something else, something that pointed the finger in Paul's direction. It was Margaret's canvas, the one she was painting in the garden yesterday morning. A little shiver ran through me. The last time she'd touched her brush to the canvas, it was to paint something with her own blood. It was a shape, a shape that resembled a P. Ingram was quick to discount it. Maybe he was too quick. What if Margaret knew she was dying and wanted to tell us the name of her killer? What if it was Paul?

I shot a quick glance at Ingram. He was still checking out the faces in the room. I couldn't yell out or shove my way through the crowd. I looked back at Paul. His face was filled with anticipation. He wasn't going anywhere, not yet.

Seth slipped just inside the doorway to the room and leaned against the wall, looking bored. He crossed his arms across that strong chest and stood waiting. He wasn't thinking about murder. For him, it was all about the art. I wished I could share his obsession. Being passionate about something added electricity and meaning to life. Was art a strong enough motive for murder? For me, the answer was no. Art was not a trade-off for another person's life. I could enjoy art and being around artists, but I couldn't go to that extreme. A little part of me wanted to take the place in that creative world that Seth offered. I had to be honest with myself. I wasn't sure I could and that realization came with a little sadness.

I forced my eyes to move on. Daphney and David were standing close to each other, his arm wrapped around her. They were so certain about each other. Together, they had dispelled all worry and doubt. I envied their happiness and confidence.

Claudia stood nearby, alone in a room full of people. She wasn't focused on the stage. She seemed lost in her own thoughts and they were painful. She bit her lip as she took in a ragged deep breath. Once, she'd had a husband, a family that she believed was happy, solid and supportive. Clearly, the ache of abandonment and betrayal was still fresh though it had all happened years ago. What if she won? Who would celebrate with her beyond her acquaintances here at Plein Air? The hurt was so palpable that I wondered if jealousy had driven her to lash out at Larry.?

Wild applause drew my attention back to the stage. A different person was standing at the microphone, the man brought in to judge the competition. Two people were scurrying around a large ornate easel made of mahogany, suitable for the formal living room at Fair Winds. They stepped back and the winning painting was displayed for all to see and appreciate. The subject, a Victorian home surrounded by a garden, was enchanting. The winning artist was welcomed to the stage with hugs and applause. It was Daphney, the young artist who had such hopes for this festival. She had captured the charm, architectural detail and ambiance of an era. Similar to many homes trimmed in gingerbread, found on the streets of Easton, the winning painting harkened back to a time when the pace was slower, when people had time to tend gardens like the one along the home's white picket fence. While some people celebrated around the stage, congratulating all the artists who won prizes, the sale began in earnest.

"Come on, Abby." Lorraine blazed a path around knots of people chatting and pointing. "We need to move or we won't see the work in the last gallery room." She led me past buyers moving leisurely from one favorite artist to another and away from volunteers moving canvases from one room to another.

With everyone milling around, there was no way to have a private conversation about a potential purchase. Some people stood whispering, eyes darting around to identify anyone trying to listen in. It all looked very cloak-and-dagger. What choice did they have? If they went outside to discuss a possible purchase, by the time they got back with a decision to buy, the painting would be gone. It was a constantly changing show. As one painting was sold, another by the same artist went up in its place from what the festival insiders called the library.

As we walked into another room and looked around, I cringed a little.

Lorraine noticed. What is it?"

With a slight nod, I directed her attention to the older couple having an animated conversation with several other people by the far exhibit wall. It was Harriet, the busybody, with her white-haired and oh-so-patient husband Ben positioned right behind her, as usual. She was raving about a particular painting.

"Are you going to buy it?" someone asked.

Harriet frowned, "Oh, no, we certainly couldn't spend $1,900 on a painting when we don't have any more room on our walls at home. We downsized when we moved here, you know." She smiled broadly, "But we can come here to the Academy Art Museum and enjoy the work of so many artists. Are you a member? Oh, you really…" I walked away as Harriet was extolling the benefits of membership and all the good work done by the museum. I had to admit it was impressive, especially for such a small town. I reminded myself that the activities – classes, exhibitions, lectures, children's programs – drew people from all over Talbot County, probably from all over the Shore. I just didn't think I would have chosen Harriet as a spokesperson. I stopped myself. She probably was perfect. She would have those people signed up for membership before they left… either out of a desire to be part of an organization dedicated to the arts, or out of self-preservation. Well, it didn't matter as long as the organization survived and thrived.

Lorraine and I worked our way over to a wall of paintings we hadn't seen yet. We had to look quickly as a volunteer swooped in and took away one of them, sold. There were snippets of conversations floating all around me. One caught my attention.

A very overweight man said, "I drive by that place all the time and I never noticed…"

That was the comment Larry said I'd hear spoken by someone at this party. His words came back to me. "As artists, we find a place and paint it, focusing on some aspect of the scene. The magic is that we look at something differently and capture that new reality on canvas or paper. If we make one person realize something special about that place, we've done our job."

A wave of sadness passed over me, peppered with seeds of anger. Larry was not only an outstanding artist, he was an insightful person. Who could have snuffed out his life like that? He didn't deserve to die. He didn't deserve such pain. I flashed back to the night of the crab dinner when he sat across the table from me. I saw his face, the look of surprise that he was feeling ill. There was the shock and fear that he was in serious trouble. Then, his face, contorted with agony, as the poison ate away at his body and his life. No one noticed the uneasiness the memory brought, no one except Lorraine.

"Are you all right, Abby?" She asked, filled with concern.

I nodded and looked around as people chatted merrily about the artwork, pricing and what they planned for the rest of the weekend. Were they callous, uncaring? No, I admitted to myself. Human.

Lorraine and I had to keep moving. Usually, an art show hangs one set of paintings. You make one sweep and you've seen the work. Not here. The show was constantly changing as canvases were sold and removed, while new ones were hung in the vacant places.

"Hello, Abby." Sara-V appeared at my side wearing a little black dress. Her earrings had five dangling rows of tiny silver balls that rang like bells with her every move. "I'm glad to see you. I mean, I just wanted to say how sorry I was about what happened earlier today. If I had stayed with you —"

I put my hand on her arm. "Don't be silly. I don't believe anything could have stopped her. As a friend of mine said, grief makes a person do strange things."

She shrugged, not convinced. "I must admit that it was one of the strangest things I've ever seen."

It was easy to see that Sara-V cared deeply about her volunteer work and the festival itself. That kind of dedication shouldn't be tainted. "You had a job to do and you went when and where you were needed. That's the important thing." Slowly, a smile bloomed on her face. "I'm so impressed by what you and all the volunteers do. You are the true lifeblood of the festival."

Almost shyly, she responded, "Thank you for that, Abby. It does take a lot of work by a lot of people pulling together and..." She stopped because someone caught her attention and she gave a quick nod. "Speaking of work, I have to get back to it." Excitement crept into her voice. "I'm assigned to that woman over there. She is a big-time gallery owner from Baltimore. Please excuse me."

Lorraine returned to my side and whispered, "See? You're not without allies and friends here."

"I know. It's just—" I began, before a familiar voice that had ranted and raved in this building only hours earlier interrupted me.

"Oh, Abby, Abby!"

It was Rebecca.

CHAPTER THIRTY-EIGHT

A sterling silver vesta box, or match safe, is carried in the pocket. The tightly-closed container is designed to protect against a match lighting unexpectedly. Its silver exterior, exposed to frequent, casual use, requires constant attention.

—"The Butler's Guide to Fine Silver" Mr. Hollister, 1898

"Oh, Abby, I was so hoping that I'd see you tonight," said Rebecca, the sugary syrup of her voice almost drowning me. "I was afraid I'd scared you off." Rebecca stepped up and threw her arms around me.

Over her shoulder, I could see Lorraine's look of surprise – her eyes wide, her eyebrows pushed high. It must have mirrored my own. Of all the things I imagined might happen, this never entered my mind. As the pressure of the tight hug eased, I tried to compose myself.

"Rebecca! I —"

"Don't say a word until I apologize for my outrageous behavior. I'm so sorry, really, from the bottom of my heart. I don't know what got into me. It must be..." She began again. "It must be the shock of everything. I'm doing much better now, thank you." She moved around to my side and put her arm through mine and eyed Lorraine. "Tell me your friend's name again."

I renewed the introductions and Lorraine made all the appropriate comments. She was so good at knowing the right thing to say at the right time. That's another thing I could learn from her.

Rebecca was dominating the conversation. "...his paintings are on what they call the Memorial Wall. I didn't want to look. It seems so gruesome, but, maybe if you go with me—?"

Lorraine was quick in responding. "Of course we will." She took Rebecca's other arm and we started to move toward the room where the paintings by all three deceased artists hung.

The crowd of art lovers was boiling with the urgency of seeing the new paintings as they went up and selecting the ones that they just had to have, but people noticed and made room for us to pass. We must have made quite a picture as we supported the widow. Moving along at a funereal pace toward the Memorial Wall, Rebecca acknowledged murmured comments of condolence with a slight nod of her head or a weak smile. Who would have thought I'd be here like this with Rebecca, where she had tortured me in front of so many people?

I followed Lorraine's example and continued moving. We finally stopped in front of the display of her husband's paintings. Every one of them was marked with a red dot, Sold.

Rebecca sagged a little. Lorraine's grip tightened to support her. She said, "You're doing fine."

"Yes, yes. I think I am. It's just that—"

"Don't worry. Abby and I are here. Would you like to sit down?" asked Lorraine.

Her words of support seemed to give Rebecca a dose of strength. "No, I can do this." She pulled herself up tall, proud. Her face showed strength and determination. Carefully, she stepped away from us and our support. She moved closer to the wall to consider the paintings – the composition, the colors, and, moving closer, the brushstrokes.

"He was truly gifted. I'm glad people recognize his talent and are adding his work to their collections." She cocked her head to the side. "I may do a retrospective show in Phoenix." Turning back to us, she asked, "Don't you think that would be nice?"

Thank goodness, Lorraine made appropriate noises of approval. I thought it was bizarre that a widow would think about an art show before she'd even buried her husband. I could hear Lorraine's voice in my head: Abby, don't be harsh. Grief affects everyone differently. We shouldn't judge. She was right, of course. I hurried to catch up as Rebecca walked away from the memorial exhibit with Lorraine following behind.

When we entered the next room, Rebecca turned and put her arms around both of us. "Thank you so much for staying with me. You are such dear friends." She released us, but stayed close so no one else could hear her words. "Everyone has tried to be so kind, but they have no idea what to say or do. That makes it awkward for everybody. But, you two, you're wonderful. Thank you."

Claudia joined our little group and I had to admit, it was a relief to see her. Things were getting a little too chummy with Rebecca. Wearing a peasant blouse and a long print skirt that flowed with her every movement, she looked like the ultimate artistic personality. "Oh, Rebecca." Claudia gave the widow a peck on the cheek. "I know it must be hard, but I'm glad you're here. I hope tonight brings you some comfort."

Rebecca nodded silently and dabbed the corner of her eye. Her movements reminded me of that night in Banning's, the tissue that flew to the floor and my late night experiments.

I watched as Claudia asked, "Do you need a refill of your wine?"

"No, thank you. I—" As if someone had thrown a switch, her face hardened. "What's she so happy about?" I turned around and found she was staring at Daphney. Rebecca said with a sneer, "Look at her grinning. She must have sold a lot of paintings."

"Actually, she won the festival's Grand Prize." I could feel myself grinning.

Rebecca's head whipped around. "What? No, she's not the winner. She—"

Lorraine went on to say exactly the wrong thing. "That's not the only grand prize here at the festival. See the man standing next to her with his arm around her waist?"

Rebecca spun around. "What about him? I haven't seen him before. He doesn't look creative. He can't be an artist."

"He's her boyfriend, David. She broke up with him just before coming to the festival so she could focus on her work."

Rebecca's lips moved as she mumbled to herself, "That's why she's been so sad all week? I thought..." She paused for a moment, then asked, "If they broke up, why is he here?"

I picked up the story. "He gave her the room she thought she needed for her art. This morning, he hopped a plane from Houston to be with her to see her paintings hung here at the festival."

"Isn't it wonderful that he was here to see her win the Grand Prize?" Lorraine added.

Rebecca bristled. "How romantic," she said, dully.

Knowing she was capable of violent reactions, I tried to distract her from her own loss. "Over there, did you see —?"

But Lorraine continued. "That's not the best part. He proposed, got down on one knee and everything. He designed the ring himself. When I saw them outside, she said she never knew he was so artistic. She'll show it to you. I think they'll have a good life together, don't you?"

Rebecca's whole body jerked.

"Oh dear," Claudia said. "Rebecca, you've spilled wine on your blouse." She drew out a white handkerchief from a pocket. "Here, let me..."

But Rebecca had walked away.

"Ladies, why the long faces?" Anthony had walked up behind us. "I hope you didn't lose out on a painting you really wanted."

Lorraine jumped in to cover our confusion caused by Rebecca's sudden departure. "Oh no, all is well. Are you pleased with the turnout?"

"Yes, very. I think this will be our best year yet, if you forget about what happened." He sighed. "Life must go on. The sales are the lifeblood of this festival and, thank goodness, we're very healthy. I guess it's too much to ask that people take a little time during the week to understand the process – watch the artists at work, go to our lectures – instead of buying something that goes with their home décor. The people who watch a painting take shape learn about the creative process that went into that work they're going to put in their own home. Oh well, everybody is busy." He sighed and took a long drink of his wine.

Later, Lorraine and I were musing over one sweet painting of a child picking a flower in the garden.

"I don't know. I think I like it well enough to buy it. Or maybe it's this new obsession I have with the garden. If she was in my garden at Fair Winds, I'd —"

A bloodcurdling scream shattered the civilized atmosphere of the galleries.

CHAPTER THIRTY-NINE

Since the Renaissance, married couples have worn English silver gimmal rings to help ensure fidelity. If a spouse removes the ring to conduct a liaison, the intricate puzzle design made of three, five or seven bands comes apart and cannot be reassembled, thus revealing the indiscretion.

—"The Butler's Guide to Fine Silver" Mr. Hollister, 1898

More screams, angry words and the sounds of people scuffling around came from the next room. We rushed over to find what looked like a war zone. People, paralyzed by the violence, stood and watched.

In the middle of it all, Rebecca was attacking Daphney. Arms flailed around. Daphney tried to escape. Rebecca grabbed her and flung her away. Drinks spilled. People screamed. Rebecca yanked a fistful of her hair. Daphney yelled, in pain. David waded into the melee and Rebecca punched him in the face.

The women teetered and tumbled to the floor. Daphney tried to crawl away. Rebecca caught her ankle and tugged. They rolled around and crashed into the wall.

I held my breath as the framed paintings clattered on their wires. The combatants rolled away and the artwork settled.

Somehow, Daphney broke loose and staggered to her feet.

Rebecca let loose a string of words that belonged in a rap video, not an art gallery. With a roar, she jumped and slammed Daphney against the wall again.

That's when everything went into slow motion. Above the fighting women, a painting swayed. Its silver tones of a garden in a misty morning rain reminded me of Larry's first painting on Bruff's Island.

The framed canvas, glistening with wet paint, rocked, then fell.

A woman shrieked. "My painting! My beautiful painting!" It was on the floor.

The fighting women, driven by hatred and an instinct to survive, rolled over it. The still-wet image transferred itself to their bodies.

This has to stop! Before I realized what I was doing, I sprang forward, wrapped my arms around Rebecca. With her in a vice-like grip, I lunged backward, pulling her off Daphney and down on top of me. She was stunned by the fall.

Her ear was next to my lips as she hissed, "It was you. You —"

She surged against me to break my hold. She jabbed her elbows and wiggled and jerked with strength fueled by anger.

One voice cut through the noise. "Stop it!" A voice with a Southern accent. "Don't move, or I'll shoot."

Filly, sweet, petite Filly aimed her pistol right at Rebecca's face. "I swear I'll shoot." The words squeezed through her clenched teeth. "I swear I will."

Everybody held their breath. I felt the fight go out of Rebecca as her body sagged.

Then, Detective Ingram said, in a voice as soft as cashmere. "Filly, it's all right now. Hand me the gun. I'll take care of things."

We were frozen that way for what seemed like forever: Rebecca sprawled on top of me, Filly's silver gun glinting in the light.

"Filly?" Ingram repeated, without moving.

With a loud sigh, Filly lowered the pistol, looked at the detective and moved to deliver it into his hands.

As everyone started to breathe again, three men and a woman stepped up next to Ingram. He directed them to pull Rebecca off of me. I should have known that the detective wouldn't come alone.

Rebecca stood weakly in the grasp of two undercover police officers with her head hung low. Globs of wet paint glistened in her hair, her skin and clothing streaked as well from rolling through the garden scene.

Slowly, Rebecca raised her eyes and locked on me. "You have to understand. I couldn't let him leave me, not for that tart. I had to stop him. He had to stay with me forever."

"He wasn't going to leave. He loved you." I added in a voice so low she couldn't hear me. "Though I don't know why."

Rebecca's body tensed again. Instead of lashing out, she muttered, "I knew that. It was so obvious at the crab feast. By then, it was too late. The oleander in the pill I gave him that morning was killing him." She collapsed in heaving sobs. Her tears cut through tracks through shades of the silver gray paint on her face. I couldn't feel sorry for her. If she could poison her own husband, she must have destroyed all three creative artists. Finally, she's shedding real tears, but tears only for herself.

As he officers took Rebecca away and Filly was escorted to a quiet place where she could sit down, Ingram made a suggestion. "Mr. Chairman, perhaps you'd like to continue the sale?" Ingram suggested.

As if awoken from a bad dream, Anthony sprang into action. "All right, everybody. The action is over. Please continue to ..."

His voice faded as Ingram took my arm and led me from the room. In a quiet place, he scanned my face. "Are you hurt?"

I shook my head, my breath still coming in short pants.

"That was a crazy thing to do." His words bit into the air between us.

"I'm sorry, please don't be mad. I—"

He looked away. "I'm mad only because you got there first. When Filly drew that pistol..." He swung his head around to ask, "Did you know she was a gun-toting granny?"

Someone walked by with a painting and he waited until he was out of earshot. That gave me time to change the subject. "I should have known you'd have the party staked out."

"I was watching, hoping the killer would give herself away. Yes, I was watching Rebecca. I did the tissue test myself, but I needed more before I could make the arrest."

"She poisoned him at the crab feast? That doesn't make sense. She got sick, too. A lot of people did, but they didn't die."

"She used two different poisons. The medical examiner is looking at everything again. They found a strong laxative in some of the cans of Old Bay seasoning we collected from the tables at the crab feast, strong enough to make people sick, but not kill them. That's what caused all the cramping."

"What about Larry? Did he get a super dose or something?"

"No, he ingested a different poison. We're not sure how she administered it yet, but we'll figure it out."

I thought for a moment. Something the host family people said at Banning's ... "Check his medicines. She always set out his pills for him in the morning. Check the prescription for high blood pressure."

"Great minds." He chuckled softly. "I asked the ME the same question when he called. They're checking, but none of them appeared to be tampered with."

I thought about Rebecca – careful, focused, deliberate. "Maybe she only touched one pill."

Ingram smiled slowly. "I'll pass that along. They haven't released his body yet." He scratched his nose. "The only question is why." There was the sound of footsteps. "Maybe we'll find out now.

The officers, one on each side, had an iron grip

on Rebecca's arms. "We're taking her in now, sir. We cleaned her up a little. Didn't want to ruin the seat of the patrol car."

"Did you arrest her and read her her rights?" Ingram asked.

"Yes, sir."

"Good." He moved to stand in front of the killer widow. He stood there quietly, close enough to have her attention, but not to be intimidating. Everyone waited expectantly as he stood with his eyes cast down at the floor, thinking. Finally, he raised his head, cocked it to the side a little and considered Rebecca. Yesterday, she would have challenged him. Tonight, she was only a shell of herself. She stood silently, unable to meet his gaze.

Ingram looked away again and said, "This has been a difficult time for you, hasn't it, Rebecca?" In his usual style, his eyes focused on her again to take in her reaction to his question.

With head hung low, she nodded slightly.

"I'm sorry about that." No ulterior message, just a statement. He sighed and raised his eyebrows, creasing his forehead into furrows. "But, I'm afraid, you brought the trouble with you." No reaction from Rebecca. "Didn't you?"

She nodded again.

"Yes." He paced a little circle. "You came believing that your husband was having an affair with Daphney and he was going to leave you, isn't that right?"

Again, his eyes zoomed in on the broken woman and watched as fat tears rolled down her face unchecked and fell to the floor. I thought I'd feel triumphant at the moment when the killer was in custody, but I didn't. It was embarrassing to watch someone self-destruct. I wanted to leave, but I stayed rooted to the floor. Nothing should distract Ingram from doing his job and putting an end to this nightmare.

He looked down at his shoes and said softly, "No one could have your husband, only you, because…?"

The question hung in the air. Sounds of people partying again drifted into the silence. Ingram waited. I was almost afraid to breathe.

Finally, Rebecca raised her head. "Larry couldn't leave me, not the way dad did." Her head dropped down on her chest again.

"Your dad left you?" Ingram tried to keep the story moving.

She mumbled a response.

Ingram cocked his ear. "Sorry, didn't hear that."

She raised her head slowly, painfully, as if she didn't want to face the truth. "He left me with her."

"Your mother?"

She nodded.

Ingram shifted his weight to the other foot. "Your father left and bad things happened. I see."

"No, you don't," she snapped. "Being left alone to fend for myself, protect myself, wasn't the worst part."

That surprised me. Only a twitch of an eyebrow gave away Ingram's reaction.

Rebecca went on. "Everybody knew my father left. They didn't know why he didn't take me with him, even though my mother was a raging alcoholic and hung out with people just like her." She hunched up her shoulders and narrowed her eyes. "They tried to find out, always poking into our business, asking questions. The worst part was, everywhere I went, people looked at me. Always staring at me, pointing and whispering. All I saw was pity on their faces. I couldn't stand it." She held her head high. "I showed them. I got my degrees, even ended up prosecuting some of those lowlifes. When I married Larry, that was the best part. He loves me no matter what."

I glanced over at Ingram and suspected the same thought went through our minds: I wonder what he'd say if he knew you murdered him?

"If Larry left you for another woman, what did you think would happen?" he asked.

"People would look at me with pity. Again. Even if they didn't say anything, it would be in their eyes, the way they'd talk to me. I couldn't stand going through that again. He shouldn't have been on the road all the time, going to festivals. Leaving me home alone. I didn't want to be alone."

"You killed him, yes?" Ingram asked softly.

She paused a moment, then nodded. "Don't you see? I had to stop him." She raised her eyes and looked at Ingram with a silent plea in her eyes. "Larry wasn't going to betray me and put me through that again." She declared, "He protected me then. Now, he always will."

"He can't protect you, Rebecca. Larry's gone."

"No, he's not. He'll always be with me." Rebecca stood straight, defiant. "I was Larry's beloved wife. Now, I'll always be his beloved widow," she said with pride.

Ingram looked off to the side to avoid any feelings of intimidation. He still needed answers. "And you killed Margaret, too?"

"I had to or you would have suspected me right off. I know how police investigations work. If he was the only victim, you'd look hard at his life... and at me. If somebody else, another artist died, well..." She shrugged. "I didn't know who it was going to be. I was thinking about sweet, innocent Daphney," she said with a sneer. "But Margaret made me so mad, I decided it would be her!"

"And Walt?" The words were out of my mouth before I realized it.

Ingram turned and gave me a look of disapproval. I breathed the word sorry and shrunk back. He shook his head slightly and took a deep breath. "No, Abby, Rebecca didn't hurt Walt. He had a stroke. Probably stayed on his feet, staggered around from the pain. Went the wrong way. Fell in the water."

"But the drag marks?"

"Ah, yes, the drag marks. Walt made them. The stroke was on one side and he was dragging that foot. He drowned. Tragic. Nothing more. I was wrong to think it was murder."

Ingram cocked his head to the side and looked at Rebecca again. "You really didn't come here intent on killing Larry, did you?" She shook her head. "But, you were thinking about it." She sighed. "Walt's death set it up for you. You could keep Larry from leaving and shift suspicion to the artists. Why them?"

"Ha, you think they're so precious. It's always about the artists and their prized work. They're not better than you or me. Margaret was a money-grubbing lowlife. Everybody acts as if they're the only creative people in the world. Well, I'm creative, too."

Ingram completed her thought. "And this was your great creative achievement."

Rebecca raised her head high with pride. "And it almost worked." Slowly, the sadness took hold of her and the tears spilled out of her eyes.

CHAPTER FORTY

Use properly-lined wooden chests to store sterling silver flatware. The box helps protect the valued contents from particles in the air that are injurious to the pieces.

—"The Butler's Guide to Fine Silver" Mr. Hollister, 1898

In moments, the police took Rebecca away, Ingram left and I was standing alone. Not sure where to go, I wandered out to the main gallery area where Lorraine scooped me up and hustled me outside. We didn't need to talk. We needed to go back to Fair Winds, to go home. We were making our way down the street, passing by the gentle confusion of happy art buyers wrestling their new prized possessions into their cars, when someone called my name. It was Seth.

Lorraine whispered that she would meet me at the car and walked away. Part of me wanted to grab her arm and pin her to the spot. No, this was something I had to face. This is as good a time as any, I guessed.

We walked and made small talk about Rebecca. He was sorry to hear about Walt.

"Maybe it's for the best." He hurried on. "I know, I know. People always say that and it sounds lame. It was different with Walt. Painting was only his second love. His passion was his wife. He was a lost soul after she died."

When he put it that way, I couldn't argue.

"About two people wanting to be together..." I tensed. "Have you decided to come with me, Abby?"

We walked on silently for a few minutes. He touched my arm and we stopped. "Abby, I need to know. The festival is over. I didn't win the big prize, but I found something, someone far more precious. You are my muse, Abby. Come with me."

Part of me wanted to throw myself in his arms though I'd never go with him. I willed myself to relax. Above all, every word had to be chosen carefully.

"Seth, you're a very special person." Way to go, Miss Brilliance. Your carefully-chosen words are a cliché. And he knew it.

"Great, here it comes. The ultimate brush-off. I would have expected better from you, of all people."

"So did I," I admitted. "Let me try again."

He threw his hands out and let them fall against his sides. "Fine, whatever."

"You are a gifted artist. To be blunt, that may be the problem. Oh, it's not like I'm jealous of your talent. It's just that you're two different people – like an extrovert and an introvert, all in one body."

"What? You'd better explain that."

"Okay, let me see if I can." I moistened my lips. "One minute, you're an extrovert. You connect with people. You're kind, considerate and, thoughtful. You reach out and envelop me in your personality and I find that wonderful." He stepped toward me, reaching out to put his arms around me. I took a step backward and gently pushed his arms away. "Wait, I'm not done."

Confident, he smiled, lowered his arms and gave me space.

"Then, something happens, like a switch is thrown and you change. Suddenly, you fold in on yourself. Become an introvert.

"Become an introvert?" he said, surprised.

"Yes, that's right." I felt a little uncomfortable. Maybe I was too blunt. His reaction really surprised me. He smiled.

"That's good." He was nodding, more and more enthusiastically. "Yes, that's very good."

"That's good?"

"Yes, you've given me a high compliment," he said. You've described the personality of a real artist. The psychologists have studied the traits of creative people, like musicians and painters, and have found they are different from most people."

"Do you mean their ability to play an instrument or draw?"

"That's more of a talent than a trait. Either most people are either introverts – shy, a little withdrawn – or they're extroverts – life of the party, involved and caring about others. Creative people are contradictions. For example, artists are different: They are both introverts and extroverts. I guess it all depends on what we're doing."

"That would explain it." I started walking around, pacing in tight circles the way Detective Ingram did when he was thinking. "I guess I noticed it first last Sunday when I found you painting by the water. You told me you had to go to work."

Seth looked contrite. "I'm sorry. I didn't mean to be rude."

"You weren't," I said quickly. "It's just that you closed yourself off from me, suddenly and completely."

He touched my arm and I stopped pacing. "But I have to if I'm going to paint. Other people's moods affect me. If things are going on around me, they'll affect my work. Sometimes I can't even pick up a brush. Shutting out the world is part of what I have to do to be an artist. Plus..." He shrugged as if it all made perfect sense. "Well, I needed to start painting, didn't I?"

"Because of the schedule for the festival." It was more of a statement than a question.

"Yes. To be honest, Walt's death really upset me. When I feel like that, if I can disappear into my work, I can find my equilibrium again. I needed to do that."

I could feel my shoulders sag. It was useless. He didn't understand. The only thing to do was to be clear and avoid any misunderstanding. "That's the problem. I'm not sure who I'm going to see in the afternoon or tomorrow morning for coffee." I hesitated. "And when you're turned inward, there's no room for me."

There, I'd said it. I wasn't going to go into a relationship ever again where I would be valued one minute and a sacrificial lamb the next.

Without meaning to it, I had wounded him. It was written all over his face. In disbelief, his eyes stared hard... at nothing, as if searching for answer. His head sank down to his shoulders so he looked like a whipped puppy. I wanted to reach out to comfort him. My honesty had taken away my right to do that. I didn't move. I could only give him time.

Slowly, he raised his head and swallowed hard. His eyes were filled with longing, then the curtain came down on his emotions. He had clicked into his other self. Just as I described, he'd disconnected from me and probably everyone else. With one last deep breath, he turned and walked away. The wounded puppy was gone. He didn't drag his heels against the pavement. His footsteps were strong, natural… normal. Just like that, Seth had moved on.

Alone on the sidewalk, I realized that I was right about the man. I'd done the right thing. Somehow, it didn't feel right. I was the one who walked slowly away in the opposite direction, dragging my feet.

Why is it that when you do something right, sometimes it hurts? Not fair.

I came around the corner and found Lorraine leaning against the car, her arms crossed, waiting. When I stepped into the pool of light from the lamppost, she dropped her arms, took a step toward me and paused. I felt the wetness of a single tear trickle down my cheek. It must have glistened in the dim light. She came and wrapped her arms around me.

CHAPTER FORTY-ONE

If you hear a voice from deep inside that says, "You can't do this," pay it no mind. The more you paint and create, the harder it'll be for the voice to be heard.

—Larry Chambers, Artist

It was another hot, humid July morning. I stayed in bed until I couldn't stand being alone anymore. I really wasn't alone, though I wasn't sure that a snoring Simon qualified as company. We roared through our morning ritual after I took a hot shower. Maybe I was washing away all the sadness: the loss of talented artists, a loving marriage haunted by abandonment issues and, of course, thoughts of Seth.

I delayed as long as I could, knowing Lorraine liked to start her Saturday mornings late. To be honest, I wanted her company. I knew she'd understand without a lot of conversation.

I was surprised to find her in the breakfast room off the kitchen overlooking the river. "Oh, I thought you'd still be upstairs."

"No, it seems this was not to be a morning for a leisurely breakfast in bed. Dawkins was extremely efficient. No sooner did I put down my coffee cup, the tray was whisked away and I was on my own. I suspect he had another engagement."

"Did he say anything?"

"No," she said. "When I asked if everything was all right, his affirmative answer was clipped as if he was preoccupied."

Seeing a half-full mug by her newspaper, I said, "At least you have coffee. Think I'll pour some for myself."

Her next words stopped me cold. "Yes, I made it myself."

I didn't want to be impolite, and claiming that I really didn't need any more coffee would have been obvious. Frankly, Lorraine couldn't cook. She'd never learned. She didn't realize that making coffee is an art. You have to study and practice to learn the right techniques. She was watching me closely.

"Oh, good," I said and poured a half cup. Ah, what we do for friendship. "What's on your agenda today?" I asked as I slipped a spoonful of sugar into the brown liquid. She eyed me carefully, probably remembering that I normally drink my coffee black. "I feel like something sweet." I shrugged. "Are you going out?" I took a sip and almost gagged. Fortunately, she was thinking about my question and didn't notice.

"I promised I'd make an appearance at the Plein Air Quick Draw event this morning," she pouted. "One of the committee chairs thought it would be good for me to walk around and tell the volunteers what a good job they've done. Said it would boost morale and encourage people to volunteer again next year." Her eyes dropped to the table. "After everything that's happened, I'd rather stay home."

Out of habit, I went to take another sip and quickly put down the cup. I found her looking at me with a sparkle in her eye. Not a good sign. I stammered an excuse. "I really had a lot of coffee before I —"

She waved away my comment. "I don't care about the coffee. I've had an idea. You could do me a great favor."

Another warning sign. Don't misunderstand. I loved doing things for Lorraine. It's just that when she said something like that with a mischievous look in her eye, I knew it was time to run in the other direction. This time, I couldn't.

I sighed. "And what would that be?"

"Come with me to the festival." She didn't give me a chance to say no. "It will be more of a normal crowd today. Anyone who has $10 and the inclination to paint or draw for two hours can be part of Plein Air's Quick Draw."

"That doesn't sound like much time to paint a picture, especially for amateurs. What happens at the end of two hours?"

"Their work is judged by the same man who judged the professional competition and picked the grand prize winner last night. It must be thrilling for people who love art."

"I guess." Personally, I've had enough of art and artists for a while.

Lorraine must have read my mind. "You can keep

me company while I do my duty." She ignored the I'm-less-than-thrilled look on my face. "You could say good-bye to your artist friends who still might be here, the ones you didn't see last night."

She was right, of course. After Detective Ingram arrested Rebecca, Lorraine and I had made for the door. It would be nice to see funny Filly and insightful Claudia one more time.

"All right, I'll get my sun hat." That was one thing I'd learned from the artists who painted all day in the sun. A hat had helped keep me cool while standing around an easel talking.

In Easton, the town was crammed with traffic. Streets were closed to allow the Quick Draw artists to set up and work everywhere. Lorraine took a circuitous route and made her way to a parking place hidden away from everything. "I don't think Ken and Pat will mind," she said. I left plenty of room for their cars and they'll know it's me. That's why I brought my car."

When we made our way out to the main street, I was shocked at what I saw. The town was bulging with people, busily checking perspective, mixing paint, dabbing their brushes on the canvas as fast as they could. There were throngs of family, art lovers, supporters and gawkers. I had to admit I was surprised at the high quality of what I saw. Some of the amateur painters were very good.

"I would have thought you'd had enough of art for a while." Detective Ingram stood there in what he considered casual clothes, crisp khakis and a shirt with the sleeves rolled up.

"I'm surprised to see you, too. I would have thought you'd be anywhere else," I frowned. "Unless you're still working the case." It was more of a question than a statement.

He shook his head. "No, no, it's my day off, thanks to you. You were right about Rebecca. She was jealous of Larry's talent and his commitment to his work… and she wasn't going to lose him to the tart, as she put it. If Walt hadn't had a stroke, she'd have killed somebody else, I'm sure of it. She had an elaborate plan that called for one more murder to throw us off."

Suddenly, it made sense to me. "She must have overheard Margaret in Banning's, talking about painting in the garden early the next morning."

"Could be," Ingram agreed. "She could have crept into the garden through one of several gates and attacked Margaret. She probably never knew what hit her, poor woman." He put his hands in his pants pockets. "It almost worked. Caught by a dry tissue. Who would have thought it?"

Lorraine was eager to change the subject. "You must be a closet art lover, detective, to be out in this heat, even though you've caught the killer."

He let his eyes roam over the many canvases nearby. "You have to put something on the walls. It might as well be nice."

"They're going to sell their creations?" I was surprised.

"Oh yes," said Lorraine. "If nothing else, the sale price goes toward supplies and the entry fee."

"Plus you have bragging rights that you sold your

painting at Plein Air," added Ingram.

I watched as he and Lorraine chatted comfortably about the work they saw as we strolled along. She seemed to enjoy his company. Their ages were about right. She'd been alone for years. Maybe it was time she had a man in her life again. I wondered if he might be a good candidate.

Lost in my thoughts, I walked right into Lorraine when she stopped dead. About to apologize, I was struck silent when I saw her face. She was shocked and surprised. I followed her stare and my mouth fell open.

There, in the forest of easels, was someone applying his typical high level of concentration to his canvas. It was Dawkins!

I started to call out, but Lorraine shook her head. Instead, we maneuvered around so we could see his canvas without being seen. That's when we got our second surprise. His painting was very good. He had chosen to paint a quaint storefront with window boxes filled with tall and cascading blooms. It had a delicate charm that I wouldn't have guessed was in the man.

Lorraine drew me back into the crowd. "Let's leave him to his fun. We can say something later." She wiggled her eyebrows and smiled.

Dawkins, just wait until you get home.

We seemed to have lost Detective Ingram in the crowd. I was distracted by the excitement going on just ahead. Seth was seated at an easel, surrounded by children and adults alike. Two freshly painted pieces were set aside to dry. His brush flew over another canvas while he answered questions and bantered with the children. He was combining his focused, introvert artist with the charming side of his personality. I was so glad that he was having such a good time. A little part of me wanted to wade into the group and be part of it. No, it was best to leave him in the midst of the adoring crowd. It reminded me that the man would always be happiest when he had a brush in his hand. The attention and the needs of one woman, this woman, threw him off balance. I didn't want to do that to him… or me.

I had done the right thing.

CHAPTER FORTY-TWO

Artists must look past how something appears in real life, search for the true significance and put that on the canvas. For us, that is all that is important. It is truly the essence of life.

—Margaret Reynolds, Artist

Later that afternoon, I watched Lorraine and Dawkins trying to hang his painting in the breakfast room. It was hard work not to laugh at the two of them. It started back at the Quick Draw competition, when I watched from a safe spot as a volunteer announced to Dawkins that his painting had sold. His reaction – a mixture of happiness and pride – quickly turned to horror and embarrassment when he discovered that Lorraine was the buyer. She walked away with the canvas, triumphant. Back at Fair Winds, she had briskly removed one of her framed prints from the wall and proclaimed that it was the perfect spot for Dawkins's painting.

"Really, I think we should wait until it dries before we —" he pleaded.

"Nonsense! It baked in that heat today. The frame you picked is perfect. It can finish drying while it's hanging on the wall where we can all enjoy it."

Dawkins, normally calm, almost devoid of emotion, was agitated. Judging from his attitude and the subtle changes in his facial expressions, he was annoyed with himself for not keeping his hobby and his talent a secret. He was irritated that he hadn't anticipated our visit to the public event. It was obvious he was irritated because he'd gone to the event at all. Lorraine tried to tease, then cajole him out of his funk, but it wasn't working. It was time for a direct attack.

I decided to try. "Dawkins, you have to face the fact that you have artistic talent." He started to object, but I ignored him. "It's just like a person with a limp or a limp or bad eyesight. Accept it and move on. It's obvious that you love painting." He dropped his head so it was hard to see his eyes. "No use trying to hide it. Lorraine and I both saw you painting out there in the sun and heat. Dawkins, this will come as a shock to you, but we saw you were happy."

He gave me a look that made me feel like I was rooting around in his sock drawer. "I'm sorry, Dawkins. Admit it. It's the truth. And we made another discovery: you are a very good artist. Now, Lorraine wants to share in your talent. Your work should be on display for everyone to enjoy."

Lorraine clapped. "Well said, Abby. I couldn't have said it better myself."

He gave a great sigh of defeat. "Well, if you insist, ma'am. I suppose it's all right as long as the painting is hung in here, where only you and the staff can see it. It definitely does not belong in the other areas of the house with your fine art work." He turned his back to us as he made some adjustments to the hanger and nail.

Lorraine and I could barely keep from breaking out in laughter. The poor man was wound so tight he must be in constant pain. He looked over his shoulder and we slapped our serious expressions back in place just in time.

"There. I think that will be satisfactory."

Lorraine took on a serious note. "You'd best learn how to hang a picture more efficiently since I hope you'll be doing it more and more."

Dawkins looked confused.

In a lighter, almost playful tone, she explained. "I hope you'll be painting more often so we can add more canvases to the walls. I want you to look around Fair Winds. Maybe you'll find inspiration for your art right here. There's the river view, the fields and, of course, Momma's garden. What was I saying just the other day, Abby?"

"You said you wished someone would paint the flowers in bloom before the heat claimed them. Guess you'd better get to work, Dawkins."

The front door bell chimed. Dawkins had such a look of relief that I almost burst out laughing. "Perhaps, but first, the door." He sprinted out of the room and down the hall.

"Are you expecting someone?" Lorraine asked.

I shook my head.

In only a moment, Dawkins returned. "Would you accompany me to the front door, Miss Abigail? You have a visitor." He was gone before I could ask him who it was. The only thing I could do was follow.

There, in the foyer stood Seth, holding a canvas.

"I hope you don't mind. I went by your cottage. I saw your car so I took a chance that you might be here." His words were tumbling out of his mouth.

"Of course, that's fine. You're welcome." I wasn't doing much better.

"Will there be anything else, Miss Abigail?" asked Dawkins.

I didn't want him to leave, but I couldn't think of a reason to have him stay. "No, Dawkins. Thank you."

Alone. With Seth. What do I say? Gran's lessons about gracious living kicked in. "This is a surprise. Would you like to sit down?"

"No, thank you. I really can't stay. Have to get down the road to the next plein air festival. It's a busy schedule during the summer. I've already spent too much time here today, what with the Quick Draw, and all." He must have realized he was babbling and paused. "I came to give you this." Silently, he turned the canvas around.

It was the finished painting of the water view he painted in Oxford the day we had our picnic breakfast. "I held it back from the sale. It seemed right that you should have it."

He handed it to me. I started to protest, but Seth touched my lips with his finger. "I will carry you in my heart, always." He kissed the top of my head and opened the front door. He looked back for a moment then, headed back to his truck without another word.

I stood on the steps and watched as he went down the long driveway out of Fair Winds… and out of my life.

Slowly, I turned back to the house and found Lorraine standing in the doorway. Over her shoulder, I saw Dawkins waiting.

Lorraine frowned a little and her voice cracked as she asked, "Is he gone?"

"Yes," I said.

With eyes filled with concern, she looked at me closely. "Did you change your mind?"

I shook my head. "I took the painting as a memento of something very special that he brought into my life, but I don't think I'll hang it now, not until I'm ready."

I looked at this woman, my dearest friend. "You've given me a new life here on the Eastern Shore. I want to see it through for all it has to offer."

Never one for silent reflection, Simon dropped his favorite orange ball on my toe. He was tired of being ignored and wanted to play.

I motioned to Dawkins. "Would you take this, put it in a safe place for me?"

He hurried forward. "Of course, Miss Abigail. My pleasure."

I thanked him and asked Lorraine, "Would you care to join us in a game of Throw My Ball Until Your Arm Falls Off?"

She smiled and we walked around the house, arm-in-arm together with Simon prancing ahead to the grassy hill overlooking the Miles River, ever flowing, quiet in its grace.

ACKNOWLEDGEMENTS

A big thank you to Tom Haschen, Stephen Mangasarian and their wonderful staff. Yes, Banning's Tavern really exists in Easton, Maryland. If you liked the old TV show "Cheers," you'll love Banning's. They really do know your name, even after just one visit… and have awesome offerings of craft beer.

Thanks to Larry Albright of Albright's Gun Shop in Easton, Maryland for selecting Filly's perfect little revolver and suggesting the specially-designed purses for gun-toting ladies. He made sure I followed the law about concealed-carry permits. It's the details that count.

Thank you to Richard Robinson (www.nzpainter.com) for his guidance and expertise in understanding how to paint. He knows what it takes to translate an artistic vision to the canvas—and he shares it.

Thanks to many special women: Barbara, Sarah, and Gemma for the character development support. The incredible librarians of St. Michaels – Shauna who somehow always come up with the right reference books for the story and the right DVDs for relaxation; Betty who finds the music CDs for the "soundtrack" to my writing sessions and Shirley who always has a smile and an Atta Girl!

Fact woven into fiction enriches the story so I spent a lot of hours doing research in the Maryland Room of the Talbot County Free Library with Becky Riti, Maryland Room Librarian and her wonderful volunteer, Ann Norbury.

Plein Air Easton is an annual event that brings together talented artists and art lovers. We all appreciate the hard work done by the Avalon Foundation to make it possible.

In the story, Simon suffers from Happy Tail. This is not product of my imagination. My Cody was rushed to the vet last year with this painful condition, a result of being too happy and wagging his tail too much! Thanks to Dr. Michael Coughlan for treating Cody, but his instruction of keep him from wagging his tail was beyond my ability.

To all my experts, if there are any mistakes, the responsibility is mine.

And to Lyn Bevard – thank you for your wild enthusiasm, support and encouragement! Your additional raffle prizes were a big hit… and the chocolate cookies… what can I say?!! Every writer should have a reader like you in her corner.

As always, thank you to family and friends for their enthusiastic support and patience.

Sara-V Gordon is a special character in this story.
She was imagined by Eleanor Welsh, the winner of the Name the Character Raffle. Her granddaughter, Vivienne, a 10-year-old writer, helped create the volunteer.
Every dollar raised in the raffle will benefit the students of Chesapeake College through its scholarship fund.
Thanks to everyone who participated!

Made in the USA
Middletown, DE
19 June 2016